*Chromosome X*

# younger

*Chromosome Y*

Library of Congress Control Number: 2002109925
0-9700027-3-4 Younger

Printed in U.S.A.

*For Budd*

*With special thanks to Dr. Isidore Edelman whose patience and lucid explanations of genomics provided me with the knowledge I needed to write this book. Izzy was the director of the genome project at The Columbia College of Physicians & Surgeons, and later co-director of the Genome Center at Columbia.*

*Chapter 1*

*Chromosome 1*

My name is Constance Gueyer. I'm a virologist at Bailey Medical College in New York City, where I teach and do research. I think of myself as a young woman, even though I'm nearly 48, in part because I'm told I look ten years younger, but chiefly because I've been seeing a 37-year-old geneticist, Peter Tarker, who came to Bailey in September of 1994. My first encounter with him was shortly after his arrival, when he was scheduled to give a lecture on genetic factors in aging. I was intrigued with the subject and also wanted to check out the new professor. It surprised me to find the lecture room crowded to capacity, and assumed many other staff members were there for the same reason.

Peter was introduced by the chairman of the Department of Genetics, who spoke glowingly of his prior achievements. I found the resume interesting, but I was more riveted by the man. When Peter stood and went to the podium, I was struck by his physical appearance. He was a type I'd always found attractive – tall, rather lanky and boyish, with straight brown hair that flopped onto his forehead. He was casually dressed in khaki pants, an open necked white shirt, and blue pullover sweater. When he spoke, it was in a deep baritone, which I suspected would appeal to many women in the audience. However, I had a couple of questions to ask about his work, and thought this would be as good a time as ever to meet him, so when the lecture and question period were over, I went down to the stage to introduce myself. He was talking to a few members of the audience, and turned to me after shaking the hand of his last questioner. He met my eyes with an intensity that took me aback. He gave an almost imperceptible shake of his head, looked off to the side momentarily, and then met my eyes again, this time with a slight smile, as if to say "Something happened...." Something *had*, but I succeeded in keeping a  professional tone, and told him I was a virologist and had a lab on the floor above his.

He nodded. "You know, virology and genetics are closely connected. Maybe we can be helpful to each other."

Why not? I thought. Later that day he came to up to my lab for a brief visit. I showed him the lab and introduced him to Saki, my assistant, and Saki's two lab workers. When he came into my office, he sat down on the well-worn couch and said, "Okay, tell me what you're working on now."

I filled him in on my latest project, and we started talking about other topics, such as where he was living. I learned he had just rented a flat in Brooklyn, since Manhattan was too expensive, and that he came from Cincinnati. He had one son, age three, and had just been divorced.

"I'm divorced, too." I said. "I got mine five years ago."

It was clear from the beginning that we were attracted to each other, but it was equally obvious to me that he was a good deal younger. It didn't seem to matter to Peter, who slowly began courting me. We started seeing each other for lunch a couple of times a week, then added dinner about once a week. Maybe because we both had been burned, we were wary about making a new commitment.

I knew I was holding back. I allowed him to kiss me, and loved it, but didn't encourage further advances. We were well matched that way, too. Peter seemed equally reserved. Yet the mutual attraction was strong, and we both fought going too fast with it. I was afraid that I'd get rejected again if I seemed too needy, which was my pattern. He later confessed feeling the same way. Despite holding back, we came together more and more, and within a month it became routine to have lunch together and dinner two or more nights a week. By Christmas, it seemed natural that we would spend whatever free time we had together.

I had taken a few days by myself over the long Presidents' Day weekend visiting my old college roommate and her husband on Long Island. I had missed Peter, and had been eager to get home. Betty and I no longer had much in common, so, with relief, I made my farewells early Tuesday morning, stopped off to keep an appointment with my gynecologist, and then caught a taxi to my lab at Bailey. Not only had I missed Peter, but also I missed my work, and wanted to see what had transpired while I was away.

Saki was at work checking on our mice. Saki is a young Israeli, whose real name is Yitsak Samuels. He had been in my lab for nearly nine months as a post doc, and at the end of two years was planning to return to Israel, hoping to join the medical faculty at the Hadassah Medical School, part of The Hebrew University in Jerusalem. Saki had quickly proven himself an exceptional researcher, and in return I had put him in charge of my lab. Once, when in haste I nearly made a miscalculation that could have contaminated the entire laboratory with a virulent virus, Saki, who had been observing, rushed to my side and aborted my mistake before it occurred. He never referred to this lapse again, and I am certain he never spoke of it outside the laboratory. Needless to say, he taught me a lesson that has served me very well.

Saki peered over his glasses as I entered and greeted me with his usual warmth, "Hi, Connie, how was your weekend? Did you have fun with your friend?"

I unlocked the door to my office. "Well," I admitted, "I wasn't too sorry to leave. We don't connect much anymore. How was yours?" I hung my coat on the inside of the door, and put on the white lab coat hanging next to it.

"Uneventful. I took in a couple of movies." Seeing that I was going into the office he added, "When you have a chance, could you look at that last batch of mice we injected? They look a little sick, but I can't find anything specific wrong with them."

I had been analyzing a particularly virulent virus, called the Congo River virus, which had been discovered in that river's basin in the spring of 1992. A large portion of the rainforest had recently been cut down to provide pasture land for domestic cattle. Several epidemiologists from the United States and France, who had been investigating the disease, felt that this clearing might have caused the virus to escape. They reasoned that disturbing the habitat of native animals harboring the virus put these host animals in contact with the cattle. The infected cattle showed only mild symptoms of disease, but it was lethal to humans, who were infected when they ate the contaminated beef or drank the milk. Fevers up to 108 °F, dehydration, and shock caused death. Autopsies performed on some of the victims revealed that the hypothalamus was the target of the virus. This part of the brain regulates many basic bodily functions, such as blood pressure, temperature control, and appetite. By early 1993, a scientist from France found the virus to be an unusual variant of the polio virus, and that oral polio vaccine conferred immunity. The disease was contained in the Congo area, and an epidemic was averted.

By January 1994, a team of geneticists from France learned more about the virus. They found that it had twelve different domains, each containing several genes in its genome or complement of chromosomes. They also determined that the disease was lethal to mice in the same way as it was to humans, by infecting the hypothalamus. This made mice the perfect laboratory animals for my investigation.

During the past four months, I had been trying to analyze each of the twelve DNA domains by removing all but one from the virus, while keeping the outer portion of the virus intact. This outer shell gave the virus its ability to enter the brain of the mouse. I hoped to learn what portion of the infected hypothalamus was affected and what function was compromised. So far, I had found the area that controlled temperature. The mice injected with that particular segment exhibited strong fluctuations of temperature a few days later, but did not die. On autopsy, I could see changes in a specific region of the hypothalamus.

I had injected the mice Saki was referring to with another small viral segment a week after I'd injected the first group, and I was curious to see what he meant when he said, 'they looked a little sick.' We proceeded to the isolation room adjacent to my lab that housed the mice, and Saki pulled two cages down from one of the shelves, each cage containing five white Swiss mice. After studying them a few moments I decided they didn't look acutely ill, just sort of lethargic. But they shouldn't have. They were only a few months old – not even middle aged. The normal life span of a mouse is about two years. I noticed that their three week's supply of food pellets were nearly gone, showing that they still had good appetites.

"Do they have any other symptoms?" I asked.

"No, none that I can determine," Saki replied.

"Well, I guess I'd better see what's going on here."

I opened the cage, removed a mouse, and put it on the counter. I found the next step, killing it, always difficult. This time was no exception. As a child I had had gerbils as pets, and mice are their close relatives. I had developed a habit of mentally asking the forgiveness of the animal, something that American Indians did when they killed game. It eased my guilt also to know that medical research usually depends on our findings from laboratory animals. Even knowing that, I don't think I could ever sacrifice dogs or primates. I'm relieved that I've never had to experiment with them.

With my thumb and index finger behind the mouse's skull, I pulled sharply on the tail with my other hand, breaking the mouse's neck and killing it instantly. I repeated this with a second mouse, then put both dead animals on a dissecting board. After removing their brains and taking sections of other organs for microscopic examination, I put the tissues in a solution that would harden them enough to slice and stain, a procedure that would take a few days. Stripping off my gloves, I returned to my office.

My desk was piled high with papers, which I had left in disarray before leaving for the weekend. I worked to tidy things up for a while, and then glanced up at the clock. It was close to one, past our usual lunch time. I hadn't spoken to Peter since leaving on Friday, and whenever possible we had lunch together in the doctors' dining room. Although he had been invited for the weekend too, he'd declined, saying he had a lot of work to do. One of the nice things about our relationship was our ability to say "no" to each other without feeling awkward. Peter normally called me when he was ready to eat, usually around twelve thirty. Where was he? I decided to go downstairs to hurry him along. When I entered his lab I saw Julie, the young East Indian woman who is his chief lab worker, bent over a microscope, her long, shiny black hair hanging in a loose braid. Julie is a beauty, with smooth, light coffee-colored skin and dark eyes with thick lashes. Glancing at her, I felt the usual twinge of envy, and was glad she lived with one of the surgical interns.

"Julie, where's Peter?" I asked, noting my abruptness. One of my less likeable idiosyncrasies is that I'm frequently brusque when I want to know something.

Predictably Julie jumped, as though startled. She turned her head and smiled, "Hello Connie. Peter's in Cincinnati. Didn't he tell you?"

I felt a warm flush on the back of my neck, Peter's ex-wife, Marcia, and three year old son lived in Cincinnati. This news was unexpected. "When did he go?" I asked, a tight smile on my face.

"He got a call from Marcia on Saturday and left that afternoon. It had something to do with his son."

"Was he sick?"

"I don't think so," frowned Julie, "I gathered it had to do with sending him to school. He's apparently hyperactive, according to Marcia. I was sure he'd called you." Julie knew about our friendship, and probably had inferred more.

"I was out of town for the weekend and I didn't give him the phone number," I replied. He could, however, have left a message on my answering machine.

Julie noticed my discomfort and added, "He's due back sometime today. I'm afraid I don't know when."

"Thanks, Julie." my cheeks felt flushed, I turned and left. Back in my office and slumped at the desk, I chastised myself for my reaction. After all, Peter went home regularly to visit his son. His parents also lived in Cincinnati and he saw them at the same time. But in the past he'd always told me when he was leaving.

Peter got married four years ago, just after he discovered Marcia was pregnant, but the relationship foundered after a year. Marcia couldn't stand his long hours in the lab and had no interest in his research. They had stayed together because of the baby, but when he was offered the position at Bailey, Marcia had refused to come, and they agreed to divorce. Peter generally went back to see his son about once a month, and each time I worried that Marcia might change her mind and want him back. His continual assurances that he wasn't interested should have relieved me, but at that moment, the image of Peter, Marcia, and their son as a happy family was hard for me to shake off.

Julie had said the call had to do with sending three-year-old Petey to school because he was hyperactive. What was the big deal about that, even if he was hyperactive? Then I drew a deep breath and stopped....I was being ridiculous. There was absolutely no basis for these suspicions. Peter had told me many times that, except for Petey, he was glad to be out of the marriage.

I pushed the chair back, pleased to have regained my perspective, and realized I was still hungry and had work to do. I retrieved my coat from behind the door, and went to buy a tuna sandwich at the College Deli across the street. I ate it at my desk while working on my grant proposal to the NIH to continue work on the Congo virus. Grant proposals are long and boring, but the funding is necessary.

It was after six when I decided to quit. Saki had gone, and there was no one else in the lab, so I locked the door and walked down the four flights of stairs to the street. It was cold and clear outside, a typical February evening. I stood for a while gazing up at the sky. I could make out the big dipper and Orion, and without the interference of the city lights I would have been able to see a lot more.

I loved the night sky. When I was growing up in Seattle, my father had owned a telescope, and we all used to go out behind the house on clear summer nights to study the stars. For a while I thought seriously of becoming an astronomer, but biology came more easily to me than math and physics.

However, medical research has its rewards, particularly when a positive result is achieved. Breakthroughs can have a huge, immediate impact, and ultimately be of benefit to mankind. This is probably what drives most of us in the field, the hope that we'll achieve that breakthrough moment that makes all the drudgery worthwhile.

The cold was beginning to get to me and I hailed a cab to my apartment building, about a mile away. When I reached into my pocket for my keys, I found a prescription from the gynecologist. I had meant to have it filled at the pharmacy but forgot, probably because I wanted to. Although I'd received a clean bill of health from him, there was one unexpected codicil. The doctor called me into his office after the examination and told me everything was fine, but my estrogen index from the previous visit was quite low. He asked me if I was having any symptoms of menopause. Forty-eight is not an unusual age to start menopause, but I was having no symptoms. When I mentioned this he answered,

"Some women are lucky," he said, "but as the estrogen level sinks, more subtle changes, such as bone loss occur. I'm going to give you a prescription for hormone replacement. It will help you avoid osteoporosis and possibly heart problems in the future."

Oh well, it'll keep for a while, I told myself, putting the prescription on the desk in my study. All the same, I went into the bathroom and studied myself in the mirror: a few lines around the eyes, maybe some deepening of the creases near the nose...nothing worse. The rest? Short light brown hair, with the increasing strands of grey covered by a rinse, five foot six, 128 pounds. I decided I could still pass for forty.

"But who am I fooling?" I muttered. "My hormones are sabotaging me." At the same time I remembered the problem my sister Sylvia had had with estrogen-progesterone replacement when she began menopause. She started gaining weight and felt bloated, all apparently due to the progesterone. Her physician was reluctant to give her estrogen alone because of the added risk of uterine cancer, but her problem was solved when she began to hemorrhage from endometrial fibroids and had to have a hysterectomy. After that she was able to take estrogen only and had no adverse symptoms. My uterus was intact and I didn't want to follow in her wake. I certainly didn't want a hysterectomy, nor did I want to feel side effects of progesterone.

As I was musing over this, the phone rang, and I went into the bedroom to answer it. David, the elder of my two sons, was on the line.

"Hi, Mom. How's it going?" David can be very funny, and at the same time sensitive to my moods. When my marriage to his father became rocky he could feel my dilemma and stood by me.

"Have you landed any acting jobs yet?" I asked. Dave is 24, and spends most of his time standing in casting lines hoping to get a part in a play. When he isn't doing that he works for a catering service. I've seen him act in a few minor productions off Broadway, and he's good, but that's a mother's opinion. I worry that he's going to become discouraged if something big doesn't come along soon. Then again, Dave – unlike me – doesn't ever seem to be negative about his career.

"I haven't heard anything yet, but in a couple of weeks I think they'll be casting a new play written by a friend of mine. He said there might be a good part for me in it."

"Did he tell you what it was about?"

"No, he was rushing off somewhere, but he said I should make sure to try out for it. I'm going to call him and ask more about it."

"That sounds promising, Dave, be sure to let me know what happens."

"I will. Mom. The reason I called is that Josh and I were wondering if you wanted some company when you go to that meeting, or whatever it is, in France. We thought it would be great if the three of us could go hiking in Switzerland afterwards."

I was slated to go to a virology symposium at the Pasteur Institute in Paris for a week in August. I hesitated, I had been hoping to convince Peter to come with me, but he didn't think he could leave his work at that time. It would be good to spend some time with Dave and Josh. We used to take a week every summer to go hiking before Walter and I were divorced. It was the only time, other than meals, we got together as a family. The rest of the year Walter spent all his leisure time on the golf course (well, not quite all, but I wasn't aware of his other activities then). I think hiking had assumed a special importance to Dave and Josh because of that, and it didn't escape me that the Alps, rather than the mountain ranges of the USA, added greatly to the appeal.

"Can Josh get away?" I asked. Joshua is 22 years old and getting his Master's in computer science at Columbia. He has an apartment near the campus that he shares with two other students.

"Josh has vacation in August, Mom," Dave said.

My thoughts had wandered. Of course he did.

"Sounds good to me, Dave. Can you afford it?" I replied.

"Yeah, as long as we don't get too fancy. Dad said he'd pay our airfare." He said the last sentence a bit hesitantly, knowing I would be annoyed.

"Oh, you've already discussed this with him," I said, with a certain coolness.

"Relax, Mom. He asked us what our summer plans were and I told him we wanted to do some hiking in Europe, and we hoped you'd go too. By the way, Sarah's pregnant."

"She is?" I gasped. Sarah, Walter's 30 year old wife, was the cause of our divorce. This news wasn't unexpected, but there was something ironic about the timing, Sarah pregnant and me in menopause.

"Well, I guess that was inevitable," I said, trying to be nonchalant. "When is she due?"

"In April, I think, they didn't tell us right away." Dave hesitated, "I wouldn't get all bent out of shape over this, Mom. You have your own life now."

"You're right," I agreed. As usual, he was. "Listen, I think it sounds like a fine idea for August. Why don't you and Josh come for dinner Friday, and we'll talk more about it."

"Sure, Mom. I'll let Josh know."

We hung up and I sat unmoving by the phone, looking idly down at a vein on the back of my hand. The hands are the first part of the body to show age, and it looked to me as though my veins were becoming more prominent. After a while I got up, and walked slowly into the kitchen to make dinner.

While I was waiting for the pasta water to come to a boil, I started thinking about my marriage to Walter Evans. We had met at Bailey University when I was getting my doctorate in molecular biology and he was in his last year of law. He was class president, generally a BMOC and I was proud to be seen with him. After we got engaged, he supported me in getting my degree and continuing on as a post doctoral fellow in biochemistry and molecular biology. I thought he was being broad minded, but in retrospect I realized it was simply that he had no interest in my work. His own career came first, and as long as I didn't get in his way, it didn't matter what I did.

I know that whatever love I had felt for Walter was long dead, but when he left me for a much younger woman, I was devastated, my pride and my self-confidence destroyed. Now Sarah's pregnancy had triggered my feelings of vulnerability, and I again regressed to the insecure woman I had been when Walter walked out on me.

I put a handful of spaghetti into the boiling water and some frozen homemade tomato sauce in the microwave oven, set the timer, and thought of how I used to rush home to prepare Walter's dinner every night. He never helped. What a difference between Walter and Peter, who is an inventive cook, and, more importantly, cares a lot about my work. I began to smile as I thought of him, and then, with a jolt, realized he hadn't called yet. Was he still in Cincinnati? I pushed the pot off the burner, hoping the pasta wouldn't overcook, and went to the telephone.

His phone rang four times and then his recorded message came on. I hung up, feeling anxious and a bit annoyed. Then, once again, common sense took over. Julie had told me he was returning today, no mention of any time. It was only a few minutes after 9 PM when I picked up the phone again and left a message: "Hi Peter, hope everything's okay. Julie told me you went to Cincinnati. Call me when you get in."

"I am not worried," I told myself, I bit into a strand of the pasta to see if it was ready. Luckily it had not over cooked. I dished it out and topped it with the sauce and grated Parmesan cheese. I poured myself a glass of red wine and sat at the kitchen counter next to the telephone to eat. I had been hungry before making the call, now I wasn't, but I ate it all anyway, including a small mixed green salad. By 9: 30 I was ready for bed, and Peter still hadn't called. I tossed around for an hour or so, and tried yogic breathing to calm myself down. Finally, I fell asleep, and awakened the next morning to snow.

# *Chapter 2*

 *Chromosome 2*

I like to sleep with the window open even in the dead of winter. Now, as I awoke the room was icy cold and snow had accumulated on the window sill. It took real will power for me to spring out of bed, close the window, and jump back under the covers. I peered at the clock, it was only 6 AM, and I could lie there a little longer while the room warmed up. I could hear the pipes clanking in the radiators, a comforting sound that reminded me of my bedroom in Seattle.

My two sisters and I grew up in an old, three-story Victorian house that had belonged to my father's parents. Father's tastes were old-fashioned in everything but women. The dark, wood-paneled interior somehow resisted Mother's attempts to soften it with light draperies and upholstery. She was never permitted to touch the office that had been his father's, and from which my father continued the practice of medicine. It remained exactly as it had been during my grandfather's occupation, and was generally off-limits to us children. On the few occasions when I was invited into the inner sanctum, I remember being oppressed by the dim light and heavy furnishings. There was even a stained glass window in the waiting area, giving the room a church-like ambience. I used to think that any patient waiting there would feel he was about to receive last rites.

Andrew Gueyer, my father, fortunately did not fit into his funereal surroundings. He was tall and handsome, with greying, thick brown hair and a bushy moustache. He exuded self confidence, and had many patients, most of them women. Around his patients, he showed humor, optimism, and charm. Unfortunately, he rarely presented the same face to our family. Depending on his mood, there were many occasions when he seemed remote and preoccupied. At these times, my sisters, Anne and Sylvia, and I stayed out of his way. He was apparently not interested in our small problems, so we took them to Mother.

It was clear to me early in life that Mother, a small pretty woman with fading blond hair, was the real victim of Father's darker moods. It was impossible for her to please him when he was in the throes of one of them. Unlike us, however, she kept trying. As I grew older, I had trouble accepting her deferential manner. I thought her behavior was demeaning and wanted to shake her and say, "For God's sake, Mother, stand up for yourself! He won't have any respect for you if you're always trying to please him. Get tough!"

But I never spoke up. Instead I grew increasingly irritated, and tried hard not to be like her. As to Father, I often feigned indifference to him, assuming what I believed to be an air of independence. Rather than having the desired effect, he merely decided I was unresponsive and lavished more affection on Anne and Sylvia, who were older.

Sylvia, the eldest, was the prettiest, and that alone would have won his admiration. She was also a flirt and charmed him. Anne, the most loving and sweetest, was the most like Mother, a quality that brought out a protective side of Father that he rarely demonstrated toward his wife.

Since I could not make myself prettier than Sylvia, or sweeter than Anne, I decided the only way to get his attention was to impress him with my brain. I engaged him in what I considered were intellectual discussions and asked him philosophical questions, such as,

"How do you know that we all see colors the same way? Why isn't what you see as red, green to me?"

He responded to this query with a scientific explanation of the different wave lengths of light in the spectrum, and how these were received by the retina and sent to the brain.

I would persist, saying, "But maybe I see those wave lengths differently from you."

If I continued in this vein for too long, he would lose patience and call me a stubborn child. I now realize that there was no logical way he could possibly have answered me. My question concerned interpretation of color by the individual brain, and, as far as I know, that's still a mystery.

It was apparent to us, as soon as we were old enough to notice those things, that Father liked the company of young attractive women. He exuded charm whenever one was in his presence, and we later realized that some women patients did more than seek his medical advice. One night, when I was fifteen, Anne, nearly eighteen, had come to my room and closed the door. She sat on the edge of the bed and whispered,

"I think Father is having an affair."

"Why?"

"You know that patient, Laura Carstairs? She's quite pretty with dark hair."

"What about her?"

"I saw her leaving the office last night after eleven," Anne confided.

"How do you know she wasn't seeing him about some medical problem?"

"Because he followed her outside, and I saw him kiss her," Anne replied, making a face.

"He kissed her!" I gasped, "Where was Mother?"

"Probably asleep. The only reason I was up was because I had a paper to finish for English. I went down to the kitchen to get a glass of milk, and I didn't turn the light on. That's how I happened to see them."

"What do you think we should do?" I asked, strangely disturbed.

"Nothing, of course. What could we possibly do? I just hope Mother never finds out."

"Do you think he's in love with her?" I asked, my eyes widening.

Anne smiled, "You really are naive, Connie. Lots of men have extramarital affairs. It doesn't mean they are in love."

"Well, I don't like the idea. It doesn't seem right. Mother should have an affair, too, if he's having one."

"She won't," Anne replied, and I privately agreed. Mother was too timid.

After that night, I remember making a point of studying Mrs. Carstairs whenever I saw her, trying to analyze why Father found her attractive, and hoping to learn something from her. The one attribute I couldn't miss was her self confidence. Unlike Mother, Laura Carstairs knew she had sex appeal. She walked with her head high, and her hips swiveling. She was also about fifteen years younger.

I tried very hard to do well in school and ended up being valedictorian of the class. Father told me he was proud of me, and

I was exhilarated by that for a short time, but his air of aloofness persisted, and I never found the affection and warmth I was seeking. Nonetheless I continued my academic pursuits, hoping to impress him even if I couldn't win his undying love. Father died of a heart attack at the age of seventy, I was thirty-eight at the time and had just been appointed an assistant professor at Bailey. I don't think he ever knew. The failure to bond with my father was painful. I never understood why I couldn't find the way to his heart, and as a result I believe there is a wall of armor around my own.

While I was lying there reminiscing, it struck me that I hadn't spoken to Mother in over a week. After Father died she had sold the old house (I never thought she considered it hers) and moved to a co-op garden apartment. I think she missed Father, but to me she seemed happier. I made a note to call her later in the day. My thoughts then turned to Peter. Was he back yet? I didn't want to call in case he had returned late at night. I assumed I would see him later at work.

The snow had stopped falling when I left the apartment. An accumulation of about two inches lay on the ground, the snow ploughs were at work, and most of the streets were already cleared. A few early risers were busy scraping their areas of sidewalk, making the familiar grating noise of shovel against cement. Everything looked clean and white, but it wouldn't last very long, given the number of cars, buses, and taxis that clog the city. It was around eight when I arrived at the lab and went immediately to the animal room to examine the mice in the cages of the two I had killed and sectioned the day before. The remaining eight animals were alive, but seemed less active than the controls. One, in particular, was very lethargic. Controls are animals alike in every respect to the experimental ones, but they have not been subjected to any experimentation, in this case none was injected with any of the viral segments. On close examination, the controls appeared to have sleeker, whiter coats than their experimental counterparts. I was eager now to examine the tissue sections, but would have to wait another day or two for the fixative to be effective. Obviously something was amiss with the experimental group, but whatever it was, was not apparent.

Saki came into work at nine, and we went over the next steps in the experiment, isolation of another section of the viral genome. This was a complex procedure which entailed removal of all but one domain of the viral DNA in the preparation of vaccine to be administered to the next batch of mice, and which he had mastered very well. Nevertheless, I continued to supervise him closely. We worked together for several hours. He was quieter than usual. "You seem preoccupied today, Saki. Is anything wrong?"

He looked up at me. "Oh, nothing really. I was just thinking of Rachel. Today's her birthday and I didn't have time to call her yet." Rachel was his girlfriend in Israel.

"Why don't you call her now? You can use the phone in my office if you want privacy." The two other lab workers were in and out of the lab all day.

Saki smiled and said, "Thanks, Connie. There's a problem. We had a fight the last time I spoke to her. She wants me to come home for a week or two, and I said I couldn't leave now. She's upset because her mother is ill. She's the oldest and has the responsibility of the younger children, in addition to studying for her Master's degree. It's tough, I know, but I can't afford to fly back and forth now, and besides, you need me here."

I looked at him with concern, wondering what I could do to help. I put my hand on his arm. "It's true, you are needed here, Saki.

But if it's important for you to see her, I think I could manage for a short time without you. When was the last time you spoke to her?"

"Two days ago," Saki replied, "She almost hung up on me. She was crying."

"You must be very upset," I said, gently, placing my hand on his shoulder. "Why don't you call now? She might be feeling better."

Saki looked at his watch, "She won't be back from the university yet. I'll call after lunch. Thanks, Connie." He ducked his head, and I saw that he felt embarrassed discussing his personal life.

I smiled and withdrew my hand. "Good luck. Let me know how you make out."

I left him and went into my office, intending to spend some more time on the grant proposal. However, when I sat down at the desk, I noticed that the red light on my answering machine was blinking. I pressed the 'play' button and heard Julie's voice,

"Connie, Peter called me early this morning to say he wasn't coming in until tomorrow. He asked me to let you know. Sorry, I don't have your home phone number. I'll be in the lab later."

I sat back in the chair, frowning. What was going on? Why didn't he call *me*? I could feel my heart pounding. He certainly knew my phone number. None of this made any sense. Maybe Julie knew more than she indicated in the message. I dialed her extension.

"Julie, it's Connie. Did Peter say why he was staying in Cincinnati?"

"Hi Connie. No, he just said he had to stay another day, and he wanted me to do some stuff for him. He also said to let you know. It was quite early when he called, and I guess he didn't want to disturb you."

"Oh, okay. Thanks for letting me know." As confident as I

tried to sound, this conversation did nothing to assuage my anxiety. I tried telling myself there were logical reasons for Peter's staying on, but I couldn't rid myself of the thought that, after seeing Marcia again, a lingering spark may have been rekindled. Only that would explain why he hadn't called me. I couldn't go back to work, I reached over, picked up the telephone, and called Lynn.

Lynn Stein is a pediatrician at St. George, the hospital affiliated with Bailey. We met when I joined the faculty at Bailey nineteen years ago, where she was a fourth year medical student. Walter knew Lynn's husband, Robert, from college and we began seeing them socially. As it turned out, Robert and Walter had little in common, but Lynn became − and still is − my closest friend.

We agreed to meet for lunch at Foo Chow, our local Chinese restaurant two blocks from the hospital. I arrived first and had just been seated when Lynn came striding in, wearing a dark red cape, and a black beret. At nearly six feet tall, and with her cheeks flushed from the cold, she immediately attracted stares from a number of the other patrons. Oblivious, she slid into the seat opposite me and shrugged out of her cape. Folding it next to her, she leaned forward, her beret perched at an angle atop thick auburn hair, and asked, "What's wrong? You sounded funny on the phone."

I sighed, "Well, I'm probably crazy, but I'm worried about Peter. He went back to Cincinnati and never told me. This morning he called his lab assistant, Julie, and asked her to let me know he was staying an extra day."

"Why did he go back to Cincinnati?"

"Something to do with his son. According to Julie, Marcia wants to put him in a special nursery school. She said he was hyperactive, and she can't handle him. I guess he wanted to see for himself," I replied.

"That sounds logical enough. Why are you worried?" Lynn's eyebrows were raised.

I was starting to feel a bit foolish, but continued. From the time our friendship started, Lynn had been my sounding board, and I valued her advice. "I'm always a little worried when he goes there. Marcia is supposedly very seductive, remember? That's how she hooked him the first time." I said gloomily.

"What makes you think he'd be interested again? 'There's nothing deader than a dead love', besides he's got you now. You really are crazy," she laughed.

"Oh, Lynn, maybe I'm too old for him. I just found out I'm in menopause."

We were interrupted by the waiter, who came to take our orders. When he left, Lynn reached over and patted my hand.

"Well, now it begins to make a little sense. I don't know why some women go into tailspins at the thought of menopause. I'll be glad when it happens to me. No more worries about birth control." Lynn is five years younger than me.

She continued, "Look, Connie, you could pass for a teenager. Besides, I really don't think Peter gives a damn how old you are. There are plenty of younger women around here if he wanted one. Why don't you relax?"

The waiter returned with two bowls of hot and sour soup which he set in front of us. I picked up the ceramic spoon and said, "Thanks. You've made me feel a little better. But I'm still not thrilled to be in menopause."

"How do you know you're in menopause? Are you having hot flashes?" Now she was talking like a doctor, looking for actual facts, and despite my concern, I had to smile. She was a first rate M.D.

"No, no symptoms yet, but apparently my estrogen index is low. The gynecologist told me that yesterday. Oh, and I also found out yesterday that Sarah is pregnant."

Lynn put her spoon down and looked at me. "Ah ha! That's what's behind all this! Come on, Connie, you weren't hoping to get pregnant again, were you?"

"God, no! But it did remind me of my age, and I'm sure Walter is walking around crowing like a rooster."

Lynn pushed her soup bowl aside, "That's fitting, since he has the brain of a chicken." She had never liked Walter, but hadn't admitted it until we were divorced. "Surely you have no regrets about Walter, do you?"

"Absolutely not! But I still can't understand how he could have left me for a bubble-headed girl in her twenties." Recalling the shock and pain I'd felt, I realized that Lynn had touched a sore spot. Regrets? Of course I had them, despite my efforts to move on with my life.

"Look, Connie, you were too smart for him. Walter needed someone who would look up to him. He was never the right man for you, so don't waste energy being mad at him. On the other hand, you seem to be onto a good thing with Peter, if only you could relax and enjoy him. The poor guy is probably having a tough time with his ex-wife, and can't wait to get back to you."

"I hope you're right," I said. "He has to come back anyway because of his work."

The waiter arrived with two covered dishes and bowls of rice which he placed on the table, and poured some tea. I suddenly realized I was famished.

"What's Peter working on? Isn't it something to do with aging?" Lynn uncovered one of the dishes and helped herself to shrimp and snow peas. I followed suit and took a few bites before answering.

"Yes, rather ironic wouldn't you say?"

Lynn waved her hand in dismissal, "No. I think it's fascinating. Is he working on the longevity angle?"

"He's investigating the ends of our chromosomes. All twenty-three pairs of human chromosomes end in the same repeated sequences of molecules called nucleotides."

"Yes, I know," Lynn responded, impatiently. "They're what genes are made of, but how do they affect aging?"

Now it was my turn to become the scientist. "There are only four different nucleotides comprising all our DNA. What's interesting about the ends of the chromosomes is that the sequence of nuceotides is the same in all people and for all the chromosomes, and this sequence is repeated again and again. Those ends are called telomeres, and what interests Peter is that as a person ages the telomeres get shorter and shorter, also shortening the chromosomes. The chromosomes of an old man are substantially shorter than those of a newborn infant. Peter wonders if the change in length is a result of aging or if it is the actual cause."

Lynn leaned forward, her eyes sparkling, "That's really interesting! How's he going to find out, and why are they called 'telomeres'?"

"I asked Peter that same question, and he pointed out that the Greek words 'telos' means 'end' and 'mere' means 'part.' It's the end part of the chromosomes. There are two types of enzymes that affect telomere length, and act on the telomeres every time a cell divides. One is called nuclease, which cuts down the length. The other, telomerase, adds to it. The gene that makes telomerase was identified on chromosome 5 several years ago. Peter is trying to create a mutation of that gene in early mouse embryos, and see how it affects the newborn mice. He wants to see if the telomerase effect on telomeres helps keep animals young by counteracting the nuclease shortening effect, or if there is some other mechanism at work."

Lynn sat back in her chair and pushed her now-empty plate to the side, "It sounds like he might be opening a Pandora's box. Can you imagine what might happen if we can regulate aging?"

"Well, obviously that could become a major ethical consideration, but determining the mechanism of aging is a long way from altering the process. Just as finding a disease-causing gene doesn't cure the disease."

"Yes, but it's a big step in that direction," Lynn persisted.

"I agree," I said, "but we can't curb research because others might misuse what we learn. We'd be back in the Middle Ages." I looked at my watch. "Uh oh, it's after two! I completely forgot, I lecture to the second-year med students at three. I'll have to get out of here in five minutes."

"Yes, I've got patients scheduled, too," Lynn said.

I rapidly finished the pork while she signaled to the waiter for the check. After a few final gulps of tea we paid the bill. When we were out on the street Lynn turned to me and gave me a hug. "I don't care what your ovaries are doing, you still look like a baby," she grinned. With a wave she turned and walked quickly up the street toward the hospital. I stood for a minute and watched her, smiling to myself, before turning to go back to my office. She's right, I thought, I've got to stop being such an ass. I'm as old as I feel, and I don't feel old at all!

# *Chapter 3*

 *Chromosome 3*

Saki was busy talking to one of the other lab workers, but when he saw me opening the door to my office he came over and gave me the news without preamble. "Connie, one of the mice in that second group died."

I had examined this group only that morning. The mice had looked a little seedy, but not on the verge of dying. I wondered what caused this one's demise. "Where did you put it?" I asked.

"It's over there on a dissecting board." He pointed to the counter under the window.

"Thanks, Saki. Look, I'm late for my lecture," I said. "I'll have to examine it later."

The lecture hall was filled with second-year students, more than the usual attendance, possibly in response to the subject of my lecture, 'The role of viruses in gene therapy.' This is an exciting topic for both scientists and laymen. The essence of the lecture was to explain how some viruses can be modified to act as gene delivery vehicles.

When I reached the podium the students were quiet, I started by explaining that the disease-causing DNA of a virus can be removed and replaced with a piece of human DNA containing a normal gene. The shell, or outer part of the virus, contains the 'key' that allows it to enter the host cell. This shell remains intact, and can therefore be used to deliver a normal gene to a person who has a genetic defect. However, the viruses used for gene therapy must be able to insert themselves in the right location. For example, cystic fibrosis is a condition that causes respiratory problems. A respiratory virus must be used to deliver a normal gene into the lung, whereas an intestinal virus, for example, will only deliver a gene to the intestine.

I went on to say that this kind of gene therapy is temporary, and must be repeated when the effect wears off. It differs from gene delivery done in most laboratory animals, in which the experimental gene is inserted directly into the DNA of the developing embryo. This type of germ cell transplant permanently alters the existing gene in the animal as well as in all its future descendants.

The lecture went well, and I left time for questions. Immediately, several hands went up in the audience. I pointed to a young man in the first row.

"Is it possible that viruses will never be completely safe for gene therapy? How can the investigator be certain that some other disease won't occur? Like, you might eliminate Parkinson's disease, but cause something else."

"That's a good question," I said. "We don't know the answer yet. We'll have to observe the long-term effects in laboratory animals before we apply any germ cell transplants to humans." I looked at my watch...the hour was almost up...I had time for one more question and I indicated a young woman in the back of the auditorium.

Her voice didn't carry, I asked her to stand and speak up so she could be heard. She complied, "Can you tell us what you are working on now, and how gene therapy applies to it?"

I explained my work with the Congo virus, and said I was isolating one domain of genes at a time to determine what portion of the hypothalamus was infected and what function it controlled.

"In essence, I am infecting the animals with a watered down version of the virus. So far, I have located the area that regulates body temperature, and found that the mice infected with that segment of virus had fluctuating temperatures. It's important in gene therapy to know what part of the body a virus attacks, so that the normal gene is brought to the right place." Looking at my watch, I concluded, " I'm sorry our time is up now, but if you have more questions, you may visit me in my lab any day this week between five and six."

The students were leaving the auditorium as I gathered my notes and left the stage by the side door.

On returning to the lab, I went immediately to examine the dead mouse Saki had put aside. I repeated the dissection done the day before, putting the sectioned organs in tissue fixative. I was very curious to know what had caused the mouse's death, but I had to wait. When I finished the dissection, I went into my office to jot down some of the findings. One of the things I had noted about all three of the dissected mice was that their coats were yellowish, as were their teeth. I knew this was a characteristic of aging, but all the mice in my experiment were only four months old or less. I wondered if some other disease process was involved, and made a mental note to check the remaining mice daily.

Later, at home, I was fixing some fish for dinner, and thinking about Peter. There was no denying that I missed him. Eating alone is fine once or twice a week, but after that it begins to feel lonely. I wondered what was he doing while I was cooking? Was he having dinner with Marcia?  When was he coming back? Would he call me right away?

I put my dinner on a tray and ate it in front of the television set, watching a PBS special on genetics. Ironically, the program was devoted to the process of aging. The commentator put forth a somewhat limited theory that life forms exist merely to pass on their DNA, and once they have completed that function there is no further need to live, so the process of deterioration begins to speed up. He used salmon as an example, showing a film of the Pacific Sockeye salmon swimming upstream to lay their eggs in the shallow water in which they were born, and there to die.

The message was the same for all species, even though some, like humans, continue to live long past the childbearing years. A grim hypothesis, I thought. The theory was scientifically sound enough, but it didn't take into account other reasons to prolong our lives, like work, friendship, and love. These appear to be attributes peculiar to humans, and may contribute to our relative longevity. Not surprisingly, I found this particular episode of the series irritating. I thought of Walter, and became even more irritated, so I turned on the radio while I tidied up in the kitchen. A short time later, I was in bed working on the Sunday crossword puzzle. I had it nearly completed, but was stuck by a nine letter word or words, starting with 'i' and ending with 'w', meaning "insightful." I was about to give up and go to sleep when the solution came to me; "In the know." I congratulated myself that my brain was still working, and smiling contentedly, I filled in the remaining blanks and turned off the light.

...I am feeding a little girl in a kitchen that seems vaguely familiar ...Is it mine? ...my parents'? I keep spooning food off the baby's face and sticking it back in her mouth. I feel very warm and maternal. When I finish feeding the baby, I carry her up some stairs to a room and put her in a crib. There is no one else around, and I am happy...

I awakened slowly with a sense of sadness and loss, and lay in bed for several minutes, trying to analyze my dream. This is a carry-over from the time right after my breakup with Walter, when I was seeing a psychiatrist. Did the dream relate to my knowing it was no longer possible to have a child? Or was it spurred by Sarah's pregnancy?

I was about to get out of bed when the telephone rang. I glanced at the clock, wondering who was calling me at 7 AM.

"Connie, I'm back! Did you miss me?" I was suddenly wide awake. It was Peter.

"Peter! Sure I missed you. When did you get home?"

"Late last night. Did Julie tell you why I went?"

"She said it had to do with sending Petey to school."

"Yes, Marcia said she wanted to put him in a special nursery school that keeps the children a bit longer than the usual prekindergarten because he seemed hyperactive. I thought she had more selfish reasons, and decided, at the spur of the moment on Friday to go there and observe Petey myself."

"What did you find out?" I asked.

"I decided to put him in the school," he answered, "He's about as hyperactive as a turtle, but I think Marcia will make a better mother if she has more time to herself. She wants to go back to art classes."

"Why didn't she tell you that right away, instead of worrying you with the hyperactive stuff?"

"I think she was afraid I'd say no, or tell her to pay the tuition herself. If she made it seem like the best route for Petey then I'd pay. She's pretty devious."

I smiled. This hardly sounded like rekindled love.

"What time did you get to bed?" I asked.

"Sometime after eleven. I could have used a little more sleep, but I wanted to call you, and kept waking up."

"I'm glad, I'm dying to see you. Can we meet for lunch?"

"Sure, I might be too busy to eat downstairs, though. Want to have sandwiches in my conference room?"

"Sure, I'll even pick them up." Lynn had been right – Peter hadn't been seduced by Marcia.

"You're a doll. See you later," he said and hung up.

I was smiling as I put the phone back in its cradle. I felt great.

It takes Peter thirty minutes to commute from Brooklyn. I arrived first, around eight, and immediately went to the animal room to examine the mice. It was too soon to see any change in the most recent group that Saki had injected the day before, but I wanted to determine if there were any more deaths among the other group. The remaining seven mice were still living, there was no obvious change in their appearance, and I put the two cages back on the shelf.

My work with the Congo virus was nearing completion, and soon I would be able to write an article on it for publication. If the article was accepted by one of the prestigious medical journals, I might receive the increase in grant money that I was applying for. I needed additional money to pay for another lab worker, and to expand my research. This problem is common to all medical researchers, they need money to do their work, and time is taken from that work to write proposals asking for it.

I went into my office to outline a potential new experiment with another virus, and realized I needed a book that was kept in the lab. While I was perusing the line up of books on one of the shelves, the door to the lab suddenly burst open and Peter catapulted into the room, grabbed me about the waist, and lifted me almost to the ceiling.

"What's going on?" I gasped.

"I did it, Connie!" He twirled me around until I was dizzy.

"Stop!" I yelped. He put me down. I grabbed hold of the lab counter to steady myself and said, "You did it? You mean your mutated telomerase gene actually did something?"

"Yes, indeed," Peter threw his arms up in exaltation. "The newborn mice with it are looking old! I couldn't see anything unusual when they were first born, but then I was away for a few days, and wow!" He spoke rapidly and paused for breath before continuing, "I'm really amazed that the process took hold so quickly. It proves that the effect of telomerase is to keep the body from aging. When that gene is mutated, the telomeres are shortened prematurely and old age sets in."

I hugged him. "Oh, Pete, that's great, that's really wonderful!"

"Come look," he said, grabbing me by the arm. He pulled me into the corridor, and propelled me, half running, down the flight of stairs to his lab.

On one of the counters was a cage containing six tiny mice and their mother. The date of birth on the cage showed they were five days old, but instead of normal, active baby mice, these appeared weak and lethargic. Their coats looked dry and yellowish and they moved with difficulty.

"Wow!" I said, looking up at Peter. "There's not much doubt about that!" He was grinning and his dark hair was all tousled. He looked about twenty years old, and I felt a pang of something like envy, sadness, and yearning all mixed up. The qualities I liked most about him, his boyish enthusiasm, which was in full flush now, his ability to have fun, along with the intensity of commitment to his work, and his genuine interest in mine made him incredibly desirable.

"What are you going to do now? Wait 'til they die of old age?"

Peter put his arm around my shoulders and said, "Some, yes, but I'm going to autopsy a couple to see exactly what changes have occurred. I hope I'll find some yellowing of the tissues, which would indicate aging. I can't imagine what else can be causing the change, although I have to rule out some contaminant viruses. There are a couple of relatively new tests I can run. One measures the sugar content of the mouse's body protein, which should increase with age. The other measures the survival time of cells in tissue culture. Cells from an old mouse divide much less rapidly and die out sooner." He tightened his arm around me, and I had a sudden surge of desire, but he was still enthusing over the mice.

"Weight and body temperature are also indications; older mice tend to lose weight and have a lower body temperature. Naturally I'll have to do a chromosome preparation and look at their telomeres, but I don't expect to see much because mice don't show the same shortening phenomenon as humans, it's probably there, but only at a molecular level." He was still breathless with excitement.

I was thinking of something else. "What would happen if you mutated the gene, or genes, for the enzyme that makes the telomeres shorter. Has anyone identified it or them?"

"Yes, a guy named Gorovich at the University of Moscow. He had an article in one of the Russian journals recently stating that he found a telomere-specific nuclease gene, and cloned it. It's located on the long arm of chromosome 7 in mice. It might be possible to knock out that gene, and see what happens to telomeres under the influence of telomerase alone. They might keep growing."

"Why not knock it out in adult mice and see if they get younger?" I asked, "That would really be a *coup*!" The momentary surge of desire I'd had was now replaced by intrigue over this possibility.

"It sure would, but first you'd have to target it to wherever the telomeres exert their effect (the aging center, so to speak), and to do that you'd have to find the right viral vector to carry the mutated gene. That's a big order. Anyway, right now I have to concentrate on this."

"Naturally, I was just leaping ahead." The excitement over Peter's finding was changing to wonder about the relevance of mine. The two mice I had killed, and the one that had died looked prematurely old, and if that was the case, maybe the hypothalamus was 'the aging center' he was talking about. The Congo virus might be the vector for the mutated nuclease gene. It was too soon to know, and I didn't want to say anything until I had more concrete evidence.

"I'm proud of you. This is so incredible!" His arm was still around me, and I turned to kiss him. He pulled me close, and responded with a long kiss, that made me feel the floor was melting under me. The next thing I knew he had picked me up, carried me into his office, and put me on the couch. At that moment all my caution and fear of rejection seemed to have vanished. All I wanted was him.

"I hope Julie or one of the others doesn't decide to come in here," I whispered. They were due in the lab shortly.

"They won't, the door is locked. Now be still," he kissed me and started unbuttoning my blouse. I responded by opening his shirt and running my fingers across his chest.

"Why did we wait so long?" He murmured, as he fondled my breast.

"We needed to. It makes it better." I closed my eyes....


When I returned to my office I was feeling light headed and buoyantly happy, all my fears about Peter had evaporated. The discovery of the telomerase gene and its effect on aging was incredible enough, but my suspicions about the mice in my experiment had me even more excited. I strongly suspected that they might be prematurely old...they seemed to have all the outward signs. Nevertheless, I cautioned myself not to assume anything. The best thing for me to do would be to get on the internet and search the medical journals for any mention of aging connected to the hypothalamus. I looked up at the wall clock. The morning had vanished. I hadn't eaten, but was too keyed up to care. Before leaving Peter's office, we had made a date for dinner that night.

I spent over two hours on *Medline* which lists references to all the subject matter in medical journals by topic. I picked two topics – 'Hypothalamus' and 'Aging' – and went back as far as the system would allow. As I had anticipated, there were many references to each individual subject, but none that linked the two together. The connection, if it existed, was virgin territory. Now I had to contain my excitement and wait until the next day, when I could section the organs and other tissues of the mice I had killed.

Peter made a reservation for dinner at a small French restaurant downtown called La Metairie. We had been there once before and had liked it. It was small, dimly lit, and romantic, with good French country fare. Peter asked for a bottle of St. Emilion right away, and we sat for a while, sipping it before ordering dinner. I wished I'd had time to go home and change my clothes, but Peter wanted us to leave from the lab. I was wearing dark grey pants and a mauve colored turtleneck sweater, not very dressy, but becoming, I thought. He must have agreed because he blew me a kiss across the table.

"You must be on an incredible high right now," I said. "I know I am, I couldn't think about anything else all day." I was having a difficult time trying to keep from telling him what was uppermost in my mind, but I'd vowed to say nothing until I had hard core evidence.

"Yes," Peter took a sip of wine, "It's pretty damn exciting. I'll have to tell Balch about it as soon as I'm certain." Henry Balch was the dean of Bailey Medical School.

"So that he can apply for a patent?"

Peter nodded. "That's the way it is now, unfortunately. Unless you have a patent, someone else can use your finding commercially. Nowadays investigators try to patent genes they've identified without having any idea what the genes do."

"It's too bad everyone is so mercenary. Except you of course."

Peter laughed, "Nothing wrong with wanting to make a few bucks when you're in this business, as long as it isn't your prime motivation. Do you agree with that, Saint Constance?"

"Okay, truce." I grinned. "Tell me more about your visit to Cincinnati. Is everything okay there now? How come you didn't call me?"

"It was a lot better than I expected. Marcia and I didn't even raise our voices to each other. She seemed a lot more relaxed, especially with Petey. As far as I could tell he behaved like a normal happy three year old. She even invited me to stay with her."

"Did you?" I felt a twinge of alarm.

"I did, but only because Mom and Dad were in Florida, and the hotels are so damned expensive. That's the reason I didn't call you. I didn't want her listening in."

My mouth seemed suddenly dry, and I took a long swallow of the wine. I wanted to ask what room he slept in, but was afraid of appearing overanxious and jealous.

"Did you stay there the whole time?"

"Yes, it was only four nights. There didn't seem any point in moving, and I could see more of Petey. I stayed there an extra day so

I could visit the nursery school she enrolled him in." He picked up the menu. "Do you want to order dinner now?"

I had lost my appetite. There was a little voice inside my head saying, stop the nonsense, there's nothing wrong with what he did. He didn't stay there for any reason other than to see his son. But my gut reaction was different. It was saying, did he sleep with her? Is he still attracted to her? Maybe that's why he didn't call.

From the bits and pieces he had told me in the past about Marcia, I gathered she was quite beautiful, and sexy. That seemed to have been the glue that kept them together during their short marriage, and I had no trouble visualizing its resurgence.

I took another gulp of wine and picked up the menu.

I managed to order dinner and eat most of it, meanwhile keeping up a conversation that mainly focused on Peter's discovery and what his next project would be. I wanted to ask him so many other things, and was sure he could see through my attempt to appear relaxed and interested. But he gave no sign of this, I suppose because he was so elated. When we finished eating, I had planned to ask him to stay the night with me, but when the taxi arrived at my building I said, "I'm a little tired tonight Peter. Too much excitement, I guess. Think I'll go right to bed."

He nodded, though he looked puzzled and a little hurt. Then he said, "I'm kind of wiped, too. See you tomorrow."

While I was getting ready for bed I thought some more about what he had told me. Why couldn't I believe he had not slept with Marcia when he stayed at her house. There was nothing wrong with his virility, as I well knew, and he had certainly been attracted to her at one time. His reason for staying there seemed a little contrived. There were certainly plenty of inexpensive places to stay in Cincinnati that were near to her. Why, too, would Marcia allow him to stay there unless she wanted to seduce him. In my estimation, his staying in the house with her would only be confusing to Petey. He was used to them living apart. But then I remembered how passionate he had been with me in his office, and I felt confused. It might just have been the excitement of his discovery, not me after all.

By the time I got into bed, I was too keyed up to sleep, I had forcefully put Peter out of my thoughts, but then my experiment took over. What would the mouse tissues reveal? Were they showing signs of aging or something else? If I had unwittingly found the aging center, it would mesh with Peter's work, and make us even more closely linked to each other. I was quite sanguine about one thing, Peter's interest in his work was the major force in his life, and that gave me the edge, but I would feel more secure knowing he had no other lover.

After considerable tossing and turning, I got up and rummaged in the bathroom medicine cabinet for something to help me sleep. I located some Tylenol PM tablets. God only knew how old they were, since I had no recollection of buying them. I swallowed two, went back to bed, and may have fallen asleep sometime around dawn.

# *Chapter 4*

 *Chromosome 4*

The next morning, I got out of bed at six, feeling tired but impatient to get to work. I'd had a restless night, thinking about Peter and all that had happened the day before. The excitement of his findings, and the fact that they might mesh with mine was still exhilarating. But his wonderful lovemaking was all but erased from my mind by learning that he had stayed with Marcia.

My deep-seated mistrust of men was back in full force. I knew enough to realize this, and tried to be rational by telling myself, maybe it was all very innocent...just as he said, it was more convenient and he saved money, but I wasn't convinced. I shook my head to clear it. If Lynn had been there, she would have set me straight.

It was Friday, and Dave and Josh were coming for dinner tonight. I had to pick up something special for them, but right now I wanted to get to the lab and examine the tissues of the mice I had killed and the one that had died.

By the time I arrived I was feeling better, and eager to examine the mouse tissues and organs that were ready to be made into slides.

This required embedding sections of the organs in paraffin wax to make thin machine slicing possible, and transferring the thin slices to glass slides. Then, I stained the slides to make the cell structure more visible. This preparation took me the better part of three hours. It was nearly eleven o'clock when I finally sat down at the microscope to examine the tissues. After looking carefully at several of the slides, I sat back in my chair and let out a long, slow breath. I was pretty sure I was onto something.

Saki, who had been working at the rear of the lab, heard me exhale and looked up, "See anything interesting, Connie?" He knew which slides I had been examining.

"I'm not certain yet. I think this might mesh with Peter's work and I'd like him to take a look before I come to any conclusions. I'll show them to you when I get back, Saki."

Putting the slides in a box, I went downstairs to Peter's lab. I had decided to play it cool, not tell him what I was thinking, and see what he came up with. The door was open and I saw him talking to Julie. He had his back to me, but Julie saw me and paused, a troubled look on her face. Peter turned and greeted me, warmly, "Hey, there. When did you get in?"

"Around eight," I replied. "I've been working on some slides, and if you can spare a few minutes, I'd like you to look at some of them and tell me what you think. They're from some mice I killed two days ago." I tried to keep my voice calm, but I could hardly wait for Peter's reaction to my findings.

"Sure," he said. Turning to Julie, he patted her hand and said, "I'll talk to you later." She nodded and we went into his office. He took the slides from me, laid them on his desk and slipped one of them under the microscope. After peering through the oculars for a few minutes, and moving the slide around, he looked up and said, "What am I supposed to be seeing? This just looks like muscle."

"It is," I said, "Just tell me if you think it's normal."

"Okay" he said, turning back to the slide. "Well, I see some atrophy of the muscle cells, but not much else. Come on, let me in on it. What's so interesting?"

I passed over another slide. "Take a look at this one. It's the same mouse."

He took the slide and put it under the microscope, increasingly curious to see what had caught my attention.

"This looks like a section of skin, with a loss of hair follicles and some thinning of the epidermis. It's probably from an old mouse."

"Okay. Now what would you say if I told you this mouse was only four months old?" I grinned.

Peter stared at me. "What do you mean?"

I handed him another slide. He put it under the scope and adjusted the focus.

"It's brain tissue," he muttered. "I can't say where."

"The hypothalamus," I prompted. 'Now look at that area in the middle of the slide."

He studied the slide for a while. "Well there's some neuron degeneration and an infiltration of inflammatory cells. Could be an infection."

"It's the Congo River virus," I confirmed, "the one I've been working on. I told you I was knocking out all but one domain of genes at a time. This particular part destroys only the central portion of the hypothalamus, and only one of the mice died. I killed two others to examine their tissues. These slides come from one that I killed three days ago. The other mouse has similar findings."

"It looks as if they've gotten old!" Peter jumped to his feet in excitement.

"That's what I wanted you to verify, I wasn't sure about what changes you're supposed to see in the tissues, and I plan to use the same series of tests you're using to confirm aging."

"Let's see those mice." Peter yelled, grabbing the slide box and pushing me towards the door. "I can't believe this is happening right after my discovery! Did you have any suspicions?"

"Yes, I thought these might be signs of aging because nothing else seemed wrong with them. I wanted to show you the slides first, just to confirm my suspicions."

We hurried out of Peter's office, past a startled Julie, and up the stairs to the animal room. I pulled a cage down from one of the shelves. Three mice were sitting listlessly in the wood shavings that covered the floor of the cage. Their coats appeared dry, their white hair showing a yellowish cast. When they moved, it was with difficulty.

"You say these guys are only four months old?" Peter marveled, peering closely at the mice.

"That's right," I replied.

"Damn! They look ancient, like larger versions of mine. The yellowing of the hair is certainly a strong sign of aging. This is amazing! It must mean that the hypothalamus controls the aging process, and is the site where nuclease and telomerase exert their effect on the telomeres." "That's what I thought too," I agreed. "It also means I may have found the virus to carry a mutated gene to the aging center. What about that?"

Peter hugged me. "God, you are really my dream girl!"

I couldn't stop grinning. "What's the next step, Professor?"

"You tell me! But I think the next step is to run those tests and confirm aging. Then we can try knocking out the nuclease gene as you suggested, by mutating it and using the Congo virus to put it in old mice."

"Do you really think they might get younger?"

"I don't know. I believe Einstein once said 'Time's arrow only goes one way.' But I'd like to see what happens if the telomeres get longer."

"Just think, we may have found the Tarker fountain of youth!" I said, still grinning.

"The Tarker-Gueyer fountain of youth. But don't let's go overboard yet, we have a lot of proving to do."

"I know." I walked over to the microscope and turned off the light. "I'm too excited to do any more work right now. Is it time for lunch yet?"

"Sure, if you think you'll be able to digest food along with everything else that's happening." Peter took me by the hand and gave me a little pull, "Come on, let's go see what's edible in the cafeteria."

Later, when we were eating chicken salad at a table for two in the cafeteria, I decided to throw caution to the winds and ask him about Marcia. I had to know.

"Peter, I have to ask you something... it has nothing to do with telomeres." I paused, wondering how best to phrase my question.

Peter looked up with a puzzled expression, "What is it, Connie?"

I drew a deep breath and continued, "When you stayed with Marcia, did you sleep with her?"

Peter stopped eating and gave me a long searching look, "I'm amazed that you would even think it, after all I've told you about her. You should know me better. The only reason I stayed with her was to be with Petey, and also to save money. I slept on the pull-out bed in the living room." He shook his head, and pushed his hair back with his right hand. "I admit she was a lot easier to take this time, probably because I was agreeing to do what she wanted, but there's no spark left as far as I'm concerned, and I don't think she has any feelings in that direction either."

I felt a lot better. Despite being lovers, a commitment to each other had never been made. He had never said he loved me, and I hadn't told him that I loved him, either. I still really didn't know, but even if I had been sure, I would probably have refrained from telling him. Why? Partly the fear of being rejected, and partly because I wasn't certain that I wanted to be committed to anyone. And there was another concern, one I continually tried to ignore, but that kept resurfacing, that I was too old for him, and that he might want more children.

I reached across the table and grasped his hand. "Okay, I'm sorry, I didn't mean to be nosy. And you're right, I should have known better."

Peter nodded, but remained silent. I took my hand away and he resumed eating, then put down his fork and said, "We have more important things to think about now."

"We do, but I have to quit a little earlier this afternoon, Dave and Josh are coming for dinner. Would you like to come, too?."

Peter frowned, "Too bad, I was hoping we could have dinner again. I think I'll pass on the invitation. You must have catching up to do."

I could tell he was a little miffed, and said, "We made the plans while you were gone."

He nodded, "That's okay, tell them 'hello.' Can we go back to your lab for a while and get some of the tests going on your mice? Then we can start setting up the protocol for the new experiment."

We worked together for a few hours, taking samples for the sugar protein test to confirm aging in my mice, and mapping our plan for the experiment with the mutated nuclease gene. This was the first time we had ever shared a research project, and it seemed natural and easy. I was sorry when I had to stop shortly after six, but Peter said he would continue to work for a while longer. I gave him a quick kiss and ran out the door, with visions of lamb chops in my head.

I managed to find perfect large chops and some fresh asparagus, and decided to splurge on cooked shrimp for appetizers and a key lime pie (one of their favorites) for dessert. Normally, I like to make my own dessert, but nothing was normal about this day. I just had time to put some potatoes in the oven to bake, wash my face and hands, brush my hair, set the table, and make some cocktail sauce for the shrimp when the doorman rang to announce that Dave and Josh were on the way up.

I opened the front door to wait for the elevator. Dave emerged first and greeted me with a brief hug and a kiss on the cheek. I noticed once again how much he resembled his father. The sandy brown hair, now grey on Walter, was worn by Dave in a shaggy, medium-length cut. Father and son had the same dark brown "cow eyes," more deeply set in David, and the same rather long, straight nose and wide mouth. David had broader shoulders and was about an inch taller than Walter's six feet. He was handsome, I thought with a surge of pride.

Behind him was Joshua, the scholar, and I was just as proud of him. Two inches shorter than his brother and of slighter build, he was wearing dark-rimmed glasses over hazel eyes, inherited from me, along with my slightly aquiline nose. I've been told we look a lot alike, and sometimes I can see it too.

"How are you, Metuchka?" Josh always came up with some variation on 'mother.' He gave me a kiss. I hugged him back and took their coats to hang in the closet. Dave headed straight for the kitchen where he immediately opened the refrigerator and extracted a beer.

"Hand me one, too," said Josh, who was peering over his brother's shoulder, "Mmm, I see you've got Kirin."

"Last time you were here you told me you liked that kind, so I try to please. I'm going to have some wine," I opened a bottle of Beaujolais that was on the kitchen counter and poured a glass.

"What's for dinner?" Josh had seated himself on the kitchen stool and was drinking his beer from the bottle. Dave was poking around in the refrigerator looking for something.

"Wow, shrimp!" He pulled out the platter I had arranged with the sauce in the center. "Are these for us?"

"What if they weren't?" I loved these boys! I wished their schedules and mine jibed more often.

"I'd eat them anyway," Dave said, dipping one in the sauce and eating it.

"Now, tell me what you've both been doing," I said when we were seated with Dave and Josh strategically placed on the couch in front of the fast-disappearing shrimp. I dipped one into the cocktail sauce and sat in a chair facing them.

"Nothing earthshaking," Dave responded. " I told you I might get a part in a new  play written by a guy I know."

"Yes, what's the play about?"

"A marine officer who finds out he's H.I.V. positive, he's not gay, and he's a homophobe. I'm trying out for the part of one of the other marine officers. It's the first play this guy has ever written."

"It sounds like a new approach. How's he supposed to have contracted H.I.V.?"

"Not sure. Probably some woman."

"I'd really like to see it, Dave. I hope you get the part. What about you, Josh, anything going on?"

"Same old stuff. I'm also teaching some basic computer programming to freshmen."

" How did you land that job?" I asked, impressed.

"One of the profs asked me if I had some spare time. He said I'd get paid."

"Getting paid is good," I beamed at him. I got up to get another shrimp before they were all devoured, returned to the chair and said, "I'm glad you both decided to come with me to Paris. It should be fun. Where do you think we should go hiking?"

"Oh, there are a zillion places in Switzerland. Dad mentioned Gstaad is beautiful. You went there with him once, he said."

"Yes, we did. You were both too little to come with us. Josh was only six months old. How long ago did you talk to your Dad about this?"

"Last weekend. We had dinner with them Saturday."

"Sarah's pregnant, you know, Muzzer." Josh looked at Dave after he said this, as if seeking his approval.

"Yes, I know. Dave told me. How's she doing? Walter must be very pleased." As I was saying this I realized I didn't want to hear about them. I wished, selfishly, that Dave and Josh never saw their father. Now they were going to have a half-brother or sister, which would bring them closer together as a family and I would be left out in the cold.

"He's strutting around like a peacock," said Josh, "you'd think he never had a child before."

David began looking uncomfortable, so I stood up to end the conversation, "I'd better go start the chops."

They both followed me into the kitchen, Josh carrying the now-empty platter. He was not to be put off, and continued, "I'm going to feel more like an uncle to this kid than a half brother. It's weird. Sarah acts like our sister."

"Well, she's young enough." I put some water in a large skillet for the asparagus, added salt, and placed it on a burner.

David sat on a stool and looked hard at me. "This isn't getting to you, is it Mom?"

"No, darling, why should it? That's all water over the dam, as they say." I felt a surge of affection for David, who, as usual, was able to tune in on my mood, but I had no desire to pursue the subject. "Anyway, I've been so busy at the lab that I haven't had much time to think of other things."

When all was ready, I gave them each a plate with two double chops, and myself one, transferred the potatoes from the oven to the plates, and laid the asparagus on a platter covered with buttered bread crumbs. I asked Josh to light the candles on the table in the dining alcove, Dave brought in the wine, which he and I would share, and Josh had another beer.

"What have you been doing, M? " inquired Josh, as he cut off a large piece of chop and started chewing.

"Well, the past few days have been pretty incredible. If I tell you about them, I must trust you not to talk to anyone. It's based on a discovery of Peter's and he hasn't reported it yet."

"Sure," Josh said, and David nodded. They both looked very solemn.

I described Peter's experiment with the altered telomerase gene, its effect on aging, and my subsequent finding of the virus affecting the presumed aging center in the hypothalamus. I alluded briefly to the new experiment being planned without going into detail.

"Wow!" said Josh, his jaw dropped, "It sounds like you are really on to something. Do you think adding on to those things is going to make the mice younger?"

"Telomeres... we don't know what the effect will be, that's what we want to determine. It'll take a while to find out."

I put some asparagus on my plate and passed the platter to David, who helped himself and slid it across the table to Josh. Josh had stopped eating and was looking excited.

"Wouldn't it be great if we could make ourselves stay young? I'd like to arrest myself right about now."

"How pathetic. You were just beginning to develop," said David dryly.

I smiled, "I don't think you need worry. It's a little premature. Josh will certainly have a few more years to ripen. But seriously, please don't tell anyone about this yet."

"We won't," David replied. "It's pretty heavy stuff. By the way, how's it going with you and Peter?"

Both the boys liked Peter, and, although they hadn't spent much time with him, they seemed to know that we had more than a professional relationship. I don't think they were aware of any particular age discrepancy, and I had never broached the subject, not knowing what they would think if they realized he was almost as close to their ages as he was to mine.

"He's fine," I said, "working hard," and steered the conversation back to them.

While we were eating dessert, David described his new girl, whom Josh had met and pronounced 'cool.' He promised to introduce me to her soon. They left with the remaining portion of the key lime pie divided between them.

I got to bed shortly after ten. For some reason, I was exhausted, and after reading a few pages of a book on astrophysics for the layman, that I had started a week ago, I turned out the light. I went to sleep almost immediately, this time to dream again.

52

....I am sitting on the bank of some river, fishing. My rod suddenly bends over with the weight of what seems to be a large fish. When I finally pull the line in, there is a baby elephant attached to it. Then the little elephant is standing on the shore at the water's edge, but something grabs him by the trunk and drags him into the river. I drop the rod and go to pull the baby free and see what is pulling him. It is a large elephant. The baby is pulled away from me into the water and then the water turns red...

I awakened with a start, my heart pounding. What a horrible dream! What did it mean? I switched on the bedside lamp and sat up, wide awake. All I could associate with the dream was one of Kipling's *Just So Stories*, "How the elephant got his trunk." It didn't make any sense to me. The little elephant in the story had "an insatiable curiosity" that got him into trouble. Could that have something to do with my research project? In the story, a crocodile pulled the baby elephant's trunk until it got long. In my dream it was a large elephant. The mother? What about the blood? Could it have some connection with the birthing process?

I looked at the clock next to my bed. 3:30 AM. It was Saturday and there was no need to get to the lab, unless Peter had decided to start the new experiment right away. I'd call him later, but now I needed to get some sleep. I rolled over and tried to get the image of the bloody water out of my head. I must have succeeded, because when I looked at the clock again it was 7:30.

# *Chapter 5*

 *Chromosome 5*

Unable to sleep any longer, I hauled myself out of bed and headed for the shower. While I was shampooing my hair I heard the phone ring, but decided to let the answering machine take the call. I finished showering, wrapped a towel around me, and proceeded to the machine to see who else was up at 8 AM on a Saturday. It was Lynn, the habitual early riser, asking me to go to an antiques show with her that afternoon.

It was probably a good idea to take some time out from the lab, still, before I called her back, I wanted to check with Peter to see what he had in mind. The phone in his apartment rang twice before he picked up. "It's 8 AM, I hope this call is important," he groaned.

"Good morning," I said brightly, hoping I hadn't awakened him. "It's me, I couldn't wait to find out if you made any progress after I went home yesterday?"

"You, I'll talk to," he replied, warmth entering his voice, "Not much to report, I think we have to wait until the tests come back, and then study sections of mouse chromosome 7 with the nuclease gene. It may be patented."

"I thought they only issued patents for human genes."

"That's true, but what I neglected to tell you the other day was that Gorovich had found the same gene in humans. It has almost the identical sequence. The only difference is that in humans the gene is on chromosome 12."

"Oh. Well that's a bit of a setback, isn't it? You know, I wonder if you shouldn't wait to announce my finding the aging center until we start the next experiment. It's such a logical sequel, a lot of investigators will think of it." I pulled the bath towel up around my neck, where my wet hair had started dripping.

"You're probably right," he agreed, "But I don't want to wait too long, I'm applying for a larger grant. For the time being, let's be mum about both our findings, even around Bailey. If word of this gets out, we'll get a lot more publicity than we're ready for. Hey, I almost forgot to tell you that I'm going to a genome conference in Washington today."

"Today?"

"It completely slipped my mind in all the excitement, I'll be back tomorrow afternoon," he promised. "We'll get together afterwards and I'll fill you in on the whole thing."

I fought the resentment that was beginning to rise to the surface. My silence must have been telling, as he added, "I wish like hell that I didn't have to go, but I'm slated to give one of the talks."

"Not about the *telomerase* gene and its effect?" I said, startled.

"Not really, I'm simply going to say that the *telomerase* effect on telomeres appears to be programmed to lessen as the cell ages, and that there's a strong likelihood that the decrease in the enzyme plays a role in aging."

"Won't there be a lot of questions about that?"

"Probably, but I'll say that I'm waiting to have my latest find published before I reveal anything. Most of them will understand that."

"I hope so," I was still feeling a little miffed, thinking he could have asked me to go with him, as I certainly had more than a passing interest in genetics. Apparently this had never occurred to him.

"I'd much prefer to be staying here and getting started with our project. Maybe you can get some of the preliminaries done while I'm gone, like round up the mice. I miss you already, Connie. See you Monday. "Bye, honey."

He hung up before I could say anything else, and I stood holding the phone, and listening to the dial tone.

Damn him! I thought, as I was drying my hair. Why does he always have to churn me up this way. If he'd thought to tell me yesterday, I might have said I'd like to go too, after all, we are collaborating. Was it just an oversight, or doesn't he think I'm his equal? Then I stopped and shook my head to clear it…of course he does.

After I finished dressing, I called Lynn and arranged to meet her for lunch before the antiques show. She always put me back on track, although lately, I might have been straining her patience.

We met in a coffee shop near the armory that housed the antiques show. The first thing Lynn asked me when we were seated, was whether Peter had returned intact from his trip to Cincinnati.

"You can judge for yourself. He stayed with Marcia the entire time he was there. He told me it was because his parents were in Florida, and because it was less expensive than a hotel. And he could see more of Percy."

She responded, "He didn't sleep in the same room with her, did he?"

"He *said* he didn't."

"Come on, Connie, he didn't have to tell you he'd stayed there if he were screwing her. Why don't you ease up on the poor man? He's obviously nuts about you."

"Okay, okay, maybe I am a bit uptight. He made love to me right after he came back, right there in his office, and that night he told me about staying with Marcia. Yesterday he forgot to tell me he was going to a genetics conference in Washington today, and just informed me before leaving. I'm also a little pissed because he didn't ask if I wanted to go with him."

"Would you have gone?" She asked, looking at me sharply.

"Maybe," I replied. "It's a subject I have a special interest in. And I like being with him," I added honestly.

"Look," Lynn said firmly, "He's an independent guy, and he isn't necessarily thinking in terms of being a couple all the time – especially when it comes to work matters. You and he have so much going, why not sit back and enjoy it, instead of worrying about every nuance. How's his work coming?"

More than anything, I wanted to tell her about the results of his experiment and the serendipitous findings in mine, but decided to hold off until we had definitive answers. I was already regretting having told Dave and Josh, but trusted them not to repeat the news.

"His work is going well. In fact, I think we may be starting a project together. Can't talk about it yet." To avoid saying more, I added, "Hey, maybe you can figure out the weird dream I had last night."

I told her about the baby elephant. She pondered it for a moment, her brow wrinkled in thought. After a few seconds she said,

"That's quite a dream. Could it have something to do with your worry about menopause? Maybe the blood is menstrual blood, and the old elephant killing the young one has something to do with your fear of losing your youth."

"I suppose anything is possible, given my state of mind," I admitted.

"What exactly is your state of mind?" Lynn leaned back in her chair and began eating her salad. I tasted a few bites of mine, then put my fork down to answer her.

"Well, I feel a bit like a yo-yo. I'm very "up" about the work we're doing now – it's very exciting, and I wish I could tell you about it, but we agreed to tell no one until we're more certain of what's going on. And then, I know you don't agree, but I still think maybe I'm too old for Peter, or maybe he's too young for me. That's the 'down'".

"I can't wait to learn more about your work," she urged, "In fact, I may implode with curiosity. As for the age thing, that's ridiculous, as I keep telling you, but since it's on your mind and in your dream, the elephant's trunk is an obvious phallic symbol. Maybe you're afraid your sex life is all over."

"Oh Lynn, for God's sake! You sound like a shrink. How come you didn't go into psychiatry?"

"I'm  just trying to help, my dear. And you asked me to figure it out. I thought you were a proponent of all that."

"I guess I am, but at this point I'm more concerned with what's going on in Peter's head than in mine."

"Do you know anything about his background?" Lynn probed. "How did he happen to choose genetics as a profession?"

"I know that he grew up in Cincinnati, and attended Ohio State. He got his PhD in molecular biology and genetics at Harvard as well as his post doc training, and was doing research and teaching at The University of Cincinnati before coming here."

"That's a good solid background. What about his family?"

"His father is a retired chemist, and his mother came from Nashville, Tennessee. They had three children, the eldest a boy who died at eighteen of muscular dystrophy. He was eight years older than Peter, but Peter remembers him being confined to a wheel chair. His mother was very depressed after his death, and had to have some psychiatric help. Peter doesn't say much about her, only that she improved on an antidepressant."

'That certainly would explain Peter's interest in genetics. What was the other child?"

"A sister, six years older than Peter. He's very close to her. I gather she mothered him  when his mother was caring for their brother, and afterwards, too. I've met her and she's very nice, has a family of three boys, and on top of that she managed to get a PhD in marine biology."

"She sounds impressive. Does she work now?"

"Part time. She does some teaching at Boston University."

"Well, it doesn't require much brain power to figure Peter out. His interest in genetics is obvious, and he is drawn to older women because of his love for his sister, and in particular to you because you're a professional."

I couldn't help smiling. "Congratulations, you picked the wrong specialty. Don't forget he was married to a younger woman who never finished college."

"It just took him a while to figure himself out, and he didn't stay with her. Come on, we've got to get moving if we want to see the antiques." She hailed the waiter and asked for the bill.

The show was being held at the armory on Park Avenue. It didn't take long to wander through the aisles and decide that we probably weren't going to find any bargains. Most of the pieces were either too expensive, or of interest only to collectors. I did manage to find a small, maple bookshelf, perfect for my bedroom. The owner of the store told me the piece was probably just under a hundred years old, and was therefore not a true antique. It was priced at three hundred dollars, and I was about to pay the full price, when Lynn nudged me, and said, "Would you take two hundred and fifty?"

The man thought for a moment, and then said, " I can let you have it for two-seventy five."

Lynn nodded, and I took out a credit card, but he didn't accept cards, and luckily I had a blank check in my wallet. After making out the check, I arranged to pick up the bookshelf on Sunday, the last day of the show, and we moved on. When we were out of earshot I turned to Lynn, "I'm glad you were here. I never think to bargain with anyone. Why don't they just price the pieces at the amount they want to get?"

"I guess because there are enough suckers like you who will pay the higher price. Antiques are almost always bargainable, the price depends on how much the proprietors of the store paid for the item, and how much profit they can reasonably make."

After another half an hour had elapsed, and we had seen all the booths,  I told Lynn I thought I would go back to the lab and do some work. She looked at me askance and said,

"Aren't you the eager beaver! Why don't you come have brunch with us tomorrow, and take a little time off."

I thanked her and said that would be great. The remainder of the weekend loomed empty, with Peter away.

My reason for returning to the lab was twofold; I wanted to see what Peter had done after I went home Friday, and I wanted to requisition mice for the new experiment. But when I arrived at his lab, I was surprised to find the door unlocked, and even more surprised to see Julie there on a Saturday. She was standing with her back to me, at one of the work benches, wearing her white lab coat, and looking very professional, except for her low-heeled red leather pumps. They accentuated her slim legs and ankles, and made her look very feminine. I felt the twinge of envy that she seemed always to engender in me. She turned her head as I entered and immediately glanced away. Had she been crying? Her eyes had looked red. I approached, forcing her to turn around, and could tell I was right; she had been crying.

"What's the matter, Julie?" I put my hand on her shoulder, she appeared very vulnerable, a quality that generally attracts men. Unfortunately it's a quality I don't have. It seems I exude an aura of self-sufficiency, even when I feel vulnerable.

"Oh, it's nothing much, Connie. Sorry, it's just a bad day for me, I guess."

"Come on," I persisted, " Maybe I can help."

She looked at me with a sad little smile. She really was beautiful. "Oh, it's just John, we've broken up."

"I'm so sorry," I said. John Castle was the surgical intern with whom Julie had been living. "What happened?"

"He's accepted a residency at Strong Memorial Hospital in Rochester. He wanted me to go with him and I don't want to stop working here."

"Did he want to get married?"

"No, I think he just wanted to go on the way we were. He doesn't want any real commitments until he finishes his training."

"Well," I said, "that certainly isn't very satisfactory for you. Did you tell him that wouldn't work?"

"Yes, and we decided to split up. I feel really bummed out about it. I came to the lab to try and take my mind off everything, but it isn't working too well."

"When is he leaving?"

"Not until the end of May, but we got into a fight and he moved out."

"Oh, Julie, I'm sorry. Maybe he'll think it over and you'll find a way to work things out. I'm glad you're not leaving the lab anyway. Lots of things are happening here and Peter needs you."

Was I really glad? She was so beautiful I couldn't see how Peter could resist her, especially now that she was unattached. Then I mentally caught myself. Peter was not my father, and would not be easily swayed by a pretty face. I had to believe that.

I asked Julie to give me copies of Peter's notes on our latest experiment and took them back to my office. I wondered if he had let Julie in on what we were going to attempt. She hadn't said anything about it, but she had other things on her mind. His notes described the possibility of an aging center in the hypothalamus that controlled telomere lengthening through the enzyme telomerase, and controlled shortening through the enzyme nuclease. He also had an outline for the new experiment, which entailed mutating the nuclease gene, and using the Congo River virus to transport the mutated gene to the aging center. The purpose of the experiment, he wrote, was to determine whether the telomeres would continue to lengthen under the unrestricted effect of telomerase. He said nothing about how this experiment might effect the aging process.

But my fantasies were already running wild. I was daydreaming about how incredible it would be if it could reverse human aging. Peter had told me that the nuclease gene in humans was almost identical to the one in mice, so it might be possible to replace the human gene with the mutated mouse gene. Instead of injection, it could be delivered orally, in the same manner that the Congo virus had infected people. I mused for a while about my taking it and becoming as young as Peter, my worries about him would evaporate, but that was a little drastic.

What would my father have said about this age reversing procedure? I certainly would have had his undivided attention, since he had such a hang-up about getting old. I imagined myself walking into his office and announcing that I could make him young again. Of course, he would never have believed me, but I would have been able to convince him with the scientific evidence.

Another possibility would be for me to have given the virus to Mother, have her get younger, and watch Father's reaction to that. Poor Mother had been so long-suffering while Father fooled around with younger women. If she had become young and beautiful, too, he would have been sure to take notice.

The first time Father's interest in young women had become painfully apparent to me was when I was thirteen. He had given me a book called *Flatland* for my birthday all about creatures living in two-dimensional space, who were visited by a being from a three-dimensional world. They heard a voice coming from 'above' and were terrified, as they had no concept of 'up' or 'down'; just 'back' and 'forth' or 'left' and 'right'. What fascinated me was the implication that we, too, may be unaware of other dimensions in our seemingly four-dimensional universe. Having just finished reading the book, I wanted to discuss it with him.

As usual on a summer Sunday, there were guests for lunch, and Father was grilling lamb chops outside on a charcoal broiler. One of the guests, a young attractive blonde (the wife of one of the local politicians), was standing beside him. They didn't appear to be having any kind of serious discussion, and I edged closer to him, waiting to speak. When he finally looked over and noticed me he said, "What are you standing around for, Connie? I'm sure your Mother could use some help in the kitchen."

"I just wanted to talk to you about the book you gave me," I answered.

He had looked at the woman and shrugged, "Well, this isn't the best time for that, do you think? That is, unless you want us all to have burnt lamb chops. Talk to me later."

The woman had smiled in my direction, and I could tell she was thinking "run along, little girl." I turned away feeling deflated and angry, as they resumed their conversation. Obviously they could talk to each other without his burning the chops, and I was sure of one thing: if the woman had been old or homely, he would have let me interrupt him. The subject of the book never came up again. I guess he was always too busy to remember to ask me about it.

I returned to Peter's lab and gave the papers to Julie, who smiled at me rather wanly, and said she was just leaving. I walked down the stairs with her, said I hoped things would soon work out, and if she needed to talk some more, I'd be there. She thanked me, and then leaned forward and kissed my cheek before walking off towards the subway station. I watched her go before turning to go back upstairs, and I felt an unexpected surge of warmth and empathy.

The telephone in my office was ringing. I wondered who could be calling me there on a Saturday. Maybe it was Peter saying he missed me. But no such luck, it was an unfamiliar male voice. The caller said, "Hello Connie. It's a voice from the past....Alan Mack."

"Alan! Where are you?" Alan Mack was an old friend of mine from Seattle. He had been a year ahead of me at school, and I went out with him steadily for a while until he left for college and we lost track of each other.

"I just started working at Columbia in the department of genetics," he answered. "I've been there about a month. Yesterday your name came up in connection with the Congo River virus. One of the guys said you were working on it. I was really surprised. I never expected little Connie Gueyer to be engaged in such a cerebral field."

"Same old Alan," I said grinning. Part of our mutual attraction was that we teased each other unmercifully. "How did you end up at Columbia? I heard they're very selective." I retorted. "Seriously, it's great to hear from you. I never knew you were interested in biosciences. I always thought it was physics."

"Well, that sort of segued into molecular biophysics and genetics. Anyway, enough about science. Any chance of us getting together? I'd like to find out what dramatic things have happened to you in the past 25 years."

"My God," I groaned, "That's a quarter of a century! Has it been that long? We'll never recognize each other."

"It's actually a bit longer, I was just giving a round figure. Round figures are pretty common at our age. Do you have one?"

"Only in the right places. When do you want to meet?"

"Some day next week? I'll take you to lunch," he answered.

I hesitated. I didn't know when Peter would return from his meeting, but he had been quite blasé about telling me he was going to a symposium, so I said, "How's Monday?"

"Monday's fine. Do you know a good place to eat? New York is still a foreign country to me."

I thought for a minute. "Do you like Japanese food?" I asked. There was a good restaurant near the subway stop on 72nd and Broadway. It would be easy for him to get there.

"Sushi? Love it," he replied.

I explained where the restaurant was, and we hung up.

What an unexpected call! I was eager to see Alan again and curious to know what path his life had taken. I had heard, via the grapevine in Seattle, that he had married a girl from San Francisco, someone he had met while at Stanford University.

I glanced at my watch. It was just five, and there was nothing pressing for me to do in the lab. I decided the best way to spend the rest of the day would be to go shopping. The stores downtown stayed open late, and were showing spring clothes. Maybe I'd find something new and exciting to wear. I could use that.

I got off the bus at Fifth Avenue and 59th Street and started strolling down the avenue, looking in the windows of Bergdorf Goodman and Henri Bendel. What I wanted to find was a simple suit in some nice color, but almost all the clothes seemed to be beige, black, or grey. I came to a halt in front of Bendel's second window. There, towards the back of the display, was a lovely rose colored dress and jacket. I couldn't tell what the fabric was, it might have been silk, or a light wool. I entered the store and was directed up to the third floor, where a saleswoman approached me. I asked to see the rose dress in the window, and she noted, "Yes, that's one of our nicest outfits. What size are you, about an eight or a ten?"

"Somewhere in between, I think." I replied.

I followed her into a good size dressing room with a large mirror, and tried on the size eight, which fit perfectly. The sales lady was smiling, "Well, you look as though that was made for you, no alterations needed."

"Yes," I said, grinning, "It's very pretty. How much is it?"

"Let me see," she looked at the tag. "It's only four hundred forty-nine, quite reasonable for this designer."

Four hundred fifty was not very reasonable in my view, but I really liked the dress, and decided to splurge. I left the store, box in hand, and feeling very pleased with myself.

As I was waiting on the corner of the block for the light to change, someone grabbed my arm from behind. I turned and found myself face to face with Walter. Sarah, obviously pregnant, was standing next to him. He pulled me to the side to allow the crowd behind him to cross the street.

"Connie! Good to see you. What are you doing down here?"

"Shopping," I answered shortly. "Hello, Sarah, congratulations, Dave and Josh told me you were expecting."

"Yes, thanks, we're out looking for baby clothes."

The "we" was irritating. I could not recall a time when Walter had taken me to buy baby clothes, or any other clothes. He was looking at Sarah with a fatuous expression. Oh, God, I thought. He's so proud of himself, it's sickening.

Turning to me, he said, "I understand you're taking Dave and Josh hiking in Switzerland this summer, Connie. I think it's great."

"Yes, it should be fun," I replied, and started to move away. I couldn't take any more of his condescension. "Good luck with the shopping," I added, trying not to appear too unfriendly.

I crossed Fifth Avenue, and after a few blocks, looked behind me. They weren't there. My heart was fluttering and my teeth were clenched. My enthusiasm for shopping was gone, and so were my uplifted spirits.

But there was St. Patrick's cathedral, a block away, its ornate gothic architecture in stark contrast to the rectangular skyscrapers around it. I entered, and sat in one of the rear pews. The silence and the dim light of the vast interior were calming. I glanced up at the great vaulted ceiling and the beautiful stained glass windows, and then around me, at the immense space, the row upon row of pews, the pulpits and altar. This was truly an island of peace in a frenetic world.

It took a few minutes and some deep breathing for me to regain my composure. I am not a religious person, but neither am I an atheist. Some force or power, I believe, is responsible for the beauty of the universe and the extraordinary symmetries of nature.

But I did not enter the cathedral to pray, only to think and try to understand. Why was I so angry? Was I jealous of Sarah? Certainly not because she was married to Walter, of that I was sure. Was it because she was pregnant? Because she was young? That was more likely, and it explained my anxiety about Peter with Marcia, or Peter with Julie. Despite Lynn's insistence that he had no interest in my age, and wanted me as I was, I remained insecure.

I must have stayed in the pew for half an hour or more, because when I emerged the street lights were on and the sky to the west had a pink glow. The air had become bitingly cold, and I hailed a taxi to take me home.

# *Chapter 6*

*Chromosome 6*

Peter called Sunday evening to tell me he was home. The phone rang after nine, while I was watching the film version of *Carousel*, which I had never seen. When Peter called, I told him I'd call back after it ended, but he said he was going to bed early and he'd see me in the morning or at lunch. "I can't meet you for lunch," I said. "I made a date with an old friend from Seattle."

"Oh, who's that?" He asked.

"His name is Alan Mack, and he's in the genetics department at Columbia. I'll stop by your lab and tell you about him." I felt a tinge of satisfaction.

"Okay, go back to your show." I could tell from his tone he was a little put out. Good.

The next morning I went straight to Peter's lab, and found him at his desk. He stood up and greeted me with a hug. "You're looking very chipper this morning, Connie. Are you spruced up for your lunch date?" I was wearing a dark green suit, not the usual sweater and pants.

I smiled impishly, "No, it's all for you. Don't tell me you're jealous."

"Should I be?"

I made a face at him, "Go ahead, if you want, it'll be good for you." I sat down on the couch, and changed the subject. "How was the symposium?"

"Pretty good. I managed to give my talk without alluding to our findings. All I said was that I had some interesting results with my latest experiment using mutated telomerase in mice, but that the paper was still unpublished so I didn't want to divulge the results yet. No problem."

He paused, "You say this guy is in genetics at Columbia. How come I never heard of him?"

"He's only been there a few months. I have no idea what he's like now, I haven't seen him since he left school."

"Interesting." He narrowed his eyes and flared his nostrils at me, "He's probably fat and ugly. Have a good time."

I laughed, "Thanks a lot. I'll see you later." I got up to leave and blew him a kiss, feeling pleased with myself. I had him worried.

I arrived at the Broadway sushi restaurant ahead of Alan, and sat in a booth waiting for him, and wondering if I'd recognize him after so many years. He'd been a good-looking teenager, but he could have changed drastically. He might have a problem recognizing me too, although I didn't think I had changed that much. I was facing the door so I could examine everyone who came in. Most of them were in pairs, and several singles went straight to the sushi bar. Then a tall man came in alone and seemed to be looking around. He looked vaguely like the boy I remembered. I was about to beckon to him when another man entered behind him. I knew at once it was Alan and waved. As he approached the table grinning, I could see he had aged some, but he had the same dark brown hair and athletic build. I could easily have recognized him in a crowd. Seeing him again made me remember how much I had liked him, more than he ever knew, and I had been crushed when he went off to college and seemingly forgot about me.

I stood up to greet him, extending my hand, he grasped it firmly and said, "Yep, you don't look too different. Not much like an important professor of virology."

"Is that supposed to be a compliment or an insult?" I said smiling, and sat down again.

"Just an observation," he replied, sitting opposite me in the booth. "Actually, you look great. It doesn't seem like thirty years have elapsed."

"Thirty-two to be exact. Last time I saw you I was a junior in high school." I examined him more closely. "You're getting grey." His hair was streaked with white at the temples. It was becoming, I thought. "It looks good," I added. "Now tell me all about you. I heard you married someone you met at college."

I thought his eyes shifted a little. He leaned back in the seat, "Yes, her name was Elaine Marshall. We met as undergraduates at Stanford, where she was a sociology major. We got married when I was in my second year of graduate school."

"What were you studying? How did you end up in genetics?" I asked.

"I had no idea of going into genetics then. I actually wanted to teach physics, but I got really hooked by all the new developments in molecular biophysics instead, and as I mentioned that led me into genetics. I thought it was going to define the future of medicine. What about you? Are you married?" He glanced at my left hand, "I don't see a ring."

"Divorced," I said, "Five years ago." He nodded, but made no comment. I noticed a waiter standing near us, "Maybe we ought to order lunch. Do you want the sushi?"

"Definitely, you order it for two. Would you like some saki?"

"No, I have to go back to work. Otherwise, I'd love it. You have some."

"No thanks, same reason. We'll have to come back here some evening." His blue eyes were dancing. I felt like a teenager being asked for a date and all at once realized he was still very attractive.

I smiled, "There's an even better place downtown." I said, without committing myself. I turned to the waiter and ordered assorted pieces of sushi and sashimi, while Alan watched approvingly.

When the waiter left, I asked, "Does Elaine like sushi too?"

"Not much," he said, "But she's back in California with our two daughters. They're in college there."

He didn't elaborate, so I didn't ask, but it seemed an odd arrangement. While we waited to be served, I told him I had two sons, and a little about my work with the Congo virus. I also mentioned that I was seeing a geneticist at Bailey. When I gave his name, Peter Tarker, Alan exclaimed, "Tarker! Sure, I know who he is. He's pretty well known in the field. What's he doing now?"

The sushi arrived and, while we ate, I explained a little of Peter's work without mentioning his newest find and my connection to it through the Congo virus. I said I'd like him to meet Peter, and we agreed to make another date soon. He refused to allow me to pay for my lunch, so as we stood up to leave, I said, "Thanks, but the next one is going to be on me."

He grinned, "That sounds like a good deal. We'll go to a more expensive place."

I wrinkled my nose and replied, "It's nice to see you haven't changed. Wily as ever."

He was still grinning and leaned down to kiss my cheek, "Goodbye, Connie. See you soon."

On the way back to work, I wondered about Alan's marital setup. If his two daughters were in college, why didn't his wife come to New York with him? He looked very well, I'd have to tell Peter about that, but I wouldn't tell him how very attractive I still found him. No point in stirring the pot to that extent.

When I got back to Bailey, I stopped at Peter's lab before going upstairs to mine. He was in his office with Julie and they were talking quietly to each other. Julie saw me come in and said, "Hello, Connie." She was still looking a bit drawn.

Peter turned his head and said, "Well, how was your lunch?"

"Fine," I answered, "Alan knows all about you, and said you were already becoming famous in the field of genetics. Very impressive! By the way, he isn't fat *and* ugly, just enormously fat." I grinned.

"Is he really?" Peter responded, his lip curled in a half smile.

"He'd like to meet you sometime, so you can see for yourself."

"Sure, bring him by, if he can squeeze through the door. I wanted to talk to you about starting the next experiment. Do you have a few minutes now?"

I nodded, and turned to Julie, "How are things going, Julie?"

She gave me her sad smile and said, "Better, Connie, I'm keeping busy." She walked out of the office.

I gave her a thumbs up sign and came in, closing the door behind me.

I took the chair opposite Peter's desk and said, "It's too bad about Julie. It sounds as if this guy Castle expects a lot of her, without giving much."

"You've never met him, have you? He's really a nice guy but he has a lot to cope with right now, getting settled into a new job."

Peter shrugged. "It's probably not the best time for him to make other commitments."

"Well, that depends what his priorities are." I grinned and said, "You know – it's a male vs. female thing."

"Oh no! Let's not get started down *that* worn out path." Peter threw up his hands and backed away in mock rebuff.

"Well," I said, "We have a lot to do, fire away. How shall we set up the experiment?" I really didn't want to get too involved with Julie's problems, especially with Peter. I was still somewhat nervous about Julie's relationship with him, despite the voice of reason saying I was dead wrong.

Peter and I had other things to accomplish, all under the cloak of secrecy about the nature of the experiment. We knew we were playing with potential scientific dynamite, and until we were ready to announce the results, we didn't want anyone asking questions or putting together their own answers.

It took us several weeks, until the end of March, before we were ready to begin the new experiment. We had awaited – and finally received – copies of the nuclease gene from a center in France that acts as a library of identified genes. Then, we had mutated the gene to render it ineffective. After we had cloned it, we inserted it into the Congo River viral shell which would deliver the mutated gene to the mice. Because the virus is transmitted orally, we introduced the viral potion by oral syringe. The normal nuclease gene would be knocked out and replaced by the non-functional mutant gene. The mice we used were all close to two years old, the equivalent of eighty-year-old humans.

As we had expected, the infant mice from Peter's previous experiment and the two month old mice from mine showed similar signs of aging. All had elevated sugar protein tests, yellowing of the tissues, and shortening of the telomeres (measured by molecular sequencing of the chromosome ends). These findings in my mice also confirmed that the location of the aging center was in the hypothalamus, since the Congo River virus had attacked that area.

During this period Peter and I were together every day, working sometimes into the night, to painstakingly map out the protocol we were to follow. By the end of the day both of us were pretty exhausted. Week days and weekends were indistinguishable, and we talked of little other than the work we were doing.

I had many questions about the ethical considerations of tinkering with the aging process, but Peter refused to get involved in this before the fact. He felt that predicting the outcome of an experiment would somehow color our evaluation of the results. I didn't agree, but since there was no one else with whom to share my thoughts, I kept them to myself. In quiet moments away from the lab, I thought often of the uproar that would ensue if we did actually find a way to reverse aging.

Despite our increased closeness, we made love infrequently. Maybe it was because we were mentally and physically so tired every night, or maybe it had to do with our focus on the experiment. I didn't know about Peter, but I was so keyed up that I didn't miss sex. Then, too, my decreased libido might be due to menopause, and I thought about starting the hormones. I decided to wait until my schedule was less intense.

When we did make love, it sometimes seemed a little strained, and lacking in passion. Maybe it was me, but I felt Peter's ardor might be cooling too. I would sometimes catch him giving me a questioning look. Once, when I asked him what he was thinking about, he looked away and answered, "Nothing special."

This might have given me cause for concern, but because we were working so well together, and preparing for the start of the experiment, I didn't pursue the issue.

Other concerns immediately arose. The day before we were to begin injecting the mice, I was in my office making some notes. The door was slightly ajar, and Saki suddenly opened it and asked, "What are these for?" He was holding one of the cages of mice to be injected.

This was hardly unusual. In fact, Saki took care of all the animals in my lab, and would naturally have noticed any new ones. I cursed myself for not having prepared a plausible explanation, but rather than deceive him, I decided to offer a half-truth.

"They're for a genetics experiment I'm doing with Peter, Saki. I'm afraid I can't tell you anymore for now. We've agreed not to discuss it with anyone until we know the outcome, and it may very well turn out to be nothing at all. If that sounds mysterious, it's just because we don't want to deal with a lot of questions until there is something positive to say. I promise you'll be the first person to know when the time comes, but until then I have to ask you to be very discreet."

Saki stared at me intently through his dark-framed glasses. Then his puzzled expression gave way to a look of deep thought, as if scanning all the possibilities in his brain. Finally he nodded his head slowly. "Okay, Connie. How long do you think it will take?"

"We're going to start the experiment tomorrow, I don't think we'll know much for a few weeks anyway. Meanwhile, could you take care of feeding these mice along with the others? If you don't know the purpose of the experiment, you won't anticipate the results. It will keep us from making that mistake too, if you are the one who sees them everyday. I can't stop you from speculating, I'm sure you will, but please, only to yourself. And, Saki, thanks for not asking a lot of questions."

"It'll be hard not to," he said, "but I'll try." I could not have asked for more; he had great integrity.

As soon as he left I considered and reconsidered the advisability of keeping him in the dark. I trusted him completely, and I knew that he might be a little hurt by having the secrecy extend to him. After all, he was in charge of the day-to-day mouse care, and it seemed unfair not to let him in on what was being done to them.

In truth, the reason I had given was not entirely correct. I was almost certain he would not make any premature judgements. Weighing the pros and cons, I finally decided to discuss the situation with Peter, and walked down to his lab. The door to his office was open. Peter was at his desk talking to Julie, who was seated in a chair across from him. They stopped their conversation the minute they saw me. Immediately I wondered what they'd been discussing. Julie forced a smile, and I smiled back a bit stiffly. To all appearances they had been having a cozy *tete a tete*, which I was now interrupting.

"Are you feeling any better?" I asked Julie, unnecessarily, because she appeared very composed.

"Yes, thanks, Connie. Peter's helped me put a lot of things in perspective. He also told me something about the exciting experiment you two are starting. I'm really looking forward to working with you on it!"

I flashed a questioning look at Peter, who quickly responded, "I told Julie we had a new hypothesis to do with the function of telomeres, and we were going to test it in mice. I also stressed that it must be kept confidential."

I was stunned! Here, I had thought I'd been bending our agreement by my talk with Saki. My face must have registered my annoyance because Peter said, "Did you want to speak to me, Connie?"

"Yes," I replied, "I'll just be a moment."

Julie rose from her chair, and said, "Thanks again, Peter." She went out, closing the office door behind her, and I waited for Peter to speak.

He shifted uncomfortably in his chair, and said, "Now, please don't be upset, Connie. I wanted to cheer her up, so I told her we would need to have her around for a new experiment. She was a big help to me with the telomerase gene, and I guess she was thinking that her assistance wouldn't be needed any longer. That, on top of her problems with John, was making her depressed. I didn't say anything about your virus or the nuclease gene."

"When did you tell her?"

I guess my irritation was showing, because he continued, somewhat defensively, "Come on, Connie, give me a break. I told her a few days ago… next to nothing, just that you and I were collaborating on a new investigation of the function of telomeres, and that we would need her help in the lab."

I had a feeling he wasn't being completely candid, and I still resented her involvement. "I guess that doesn't give away anything," I said, grudgingly. "But what do you plan to have her do? The mice are in my lab, and I've already asked Saki to take care of them. I also refused to tell him the nature of the experiment. Now I'll tell him it's got to do with telomeres. I wish we'd agreed on what we were going to say to others – and when – earlier."

Peter stood up, walked over to me, and put his hand on my shoulder. With his other hand he tilted my chin up so that I was looking directly into his eyes.

"Hey, I'm sorry, I should have considered your relationship with Saki. It slipped my mind because I wanted to help Julie. But there should be enough work to keep both of them busy. The mice have to be monitored on a daily basis: they have to be weighed, their temperatures checked, and have weekly bloods for sugar protein content. We have a lot of mice to look after when you include the controls. Saki could probably do all that alone, but it wouldn't give him much time to do his other work." He stopped and looked at me closely. "Is anything else bothering you? You seem to be a bit preoccupied?"

He was right. I had been feeling irritable, but I hadn't realized I was so transparent. Damn this menopause thing! I sat down in the chair Julie had vacated and said, "Sorry, Peter. I guess I've been a little stressed out by waiting to start this project. Aren't you impatient to get it going?"

"Damn right, I am! But we can both wait until tomorrow. Go speak to Saki, and I'll take you out to dinner. We deserve a night out, don't we?."

He stood over me, pulled me to my feet, and gave me a hug, "Try to relax, Connie, I'll see you later."

I hugged him back, feeling much happier. "Righto," I said and gave him a quick kiss on the cheek.

I was glad to see that Saki was still in the lab, and asked him to come into my office for a moment. Pretty much repeating what Peter had told Julie. I briefly outlined what Peter and I were planning, without revealing the link between my experiment with the Congo virus and Peter's telomere work.

I could see, by Saki's expression, that he knew he was still not getting the whole story, but he graciously accepted what I told him and agreed to carefully monitor the mice. I knew it was only a matter of time before he came to his own conclusions, and as he was leaving, I added, "Saki, I know how observant you are. If you see a change in some of the mice, write it in the day to day notes, and don't tell me or Peter about it. We want to be able to view them with fresh eyes after a certain period of time, probably several weeks."

Saki gave me a little half smile, that crinkled up his eyes. "Don't worry, Connie, I'll try to keep my mind a blank slate, and I won't speak to anyone." He closed the office door behind him.

I sat at the desk, thinking how lucky I was to have him working in my lab. I knew he would go far in his research, and I often urged him to stay in America. But he was adamant about returning to Jerusalem.


Peter and I had dinner at Mario's a nearby restaurant frequented by the MDs and professors at Bailey for their home-cooked lunches, and a haunt of local residents at night. Mario's specializes in northern Italian cuisine, and has particularly good pasta. It's small, with about twelve or fourteen tables covered with red-checked tablecloths. The walls have been stripped down to expose red brick, and in the rear is a niche with wine racks holding numerous bottles.

We were given a table near the back where we had privacy and could speak about what was uppermost in both our minds. We ordered pasta and a bottle of Chianti, and while sipping the wine, I related to Peter what I had told Saki, along with my impression that he was aware I was holding something back. Peter nodded his head and looked thoughtful,

"I imagine Julie has her suspicions, too. I've been thinking that could be an advantage, if they are going to be doing the day-to-day checking. All they need to know is that we're doing another telomere experiment, that way they won't be looking for any particular changes.

It's better for us not to see the mice on a daily basis too. It'll keep us from imagining changes that don't exist."

"Hah! I beat you to the punch," I grinned." I already told Saki exactly that. How long do you think we should wait before checking on the mice again?"

"I think about three weeks. Meanwhile, we should be up front with Julie and Saki, and tell them why we're waiting so long."

"I don't know about you," I admitted, "but I'll be climbing the walls. Three weeks is a long time, and I'm not sure I understand why we have to wait."

"You know, if there are changes to be observed they'll take place gradually. I've been doing my experiments this way for a long time. The findings are much more obvious, and you don't lose anything by waiting. Besides, it's a test of will power," he chuckled, squeezing my hand.

" Okay, okay. I'll try, but it won't be easy."

Peter picked up his wine glass and clicked mine, "Here's to will power."

Our waiter, Bernardo, arrived with my ravioli, Peter's cannelloni, and two mixed green salads. We turned to the business of eating, chatted a little with the waiter and stayed away from work topics. Maybe it was because we were both keyed up and eager for the start of the project, but by what appeared to be mutual consent, Peter went back to his own apartment after we finished dinner.

The following morning we met in my lab at seven. Peter and I wanted to get the experiment underway before either Julie or Saki arrived, so we could put code letters on the cages Then, when we were ready to examine the mice at the end of three weeks, we could identify them. We had a total of 40 two-year-old mice, half male and half female; ten of which received the Congo virus holding the mutant gene for telomerase. This would knock out the normal nuclease gene and replace it with its mutated version. Another group of ten mice received the viral shell carrying the normal nuclease gene; the next ten mice received the empty viral shell; and the last ten were not given anything. The last three groups were the controls. Then, we divided each group into cages of two mice of the same sex, for a total of twenty cages. Each cage had a code letter affixed to the underside, to allow the results of testing to be recorded without showing which animals were experimental and which were controls. Peter had written a schedule for Saki and Julie to follow, which consisted of daily weights and temperatures, observation of health and appearance, and weekly tests for sugar protein. I locked the key to the code in my desk drawer. Now all we had to do was wait.

*Chapter 7*

*Chromosome 7* ————————————————————————

They were the longest three weeks I had ever experienced. No matter what I was doing, my thoughts returned to what Saki and Julie were observing. Whatever they found they kept to themselves, and I could only assume there was nothing extraordinary. Peter and I each had our separate projects; I had finished analyzing the Congo River virus, and was writing up the findings for publication. Peter had a list of potential candidates for gene identification, and on two of them, had already begun the preliminary work of locating and screening families carrying a mutated gene resulting in a degenerative neurological disorder.

Despite my being occupied throughout the day, in the evenings I worried about my relationship with Peter. He stayed at my apartment more than his own, and during that period of time we made love only occasionally, and still without any of our former passion. I attributed much of this to the tension of waiting, but I sensed that something else might be wrong.

On one occasion he had followed me out to the kitchen while I put the dinner dishes in the dishwasher. I turned my head and caught him gazing at me with a pensive expression. "What's wrong?" I asked.

"Nothing," he answered, shifting his eyes away. "Why?"

"You were looking at me with a funny expression on your face."

"Was I? I wasn't conscious of it. Maybe you're jittery. We're both under a lot of pressure right now."

"Was I acting jittery?" I wasn't aware of it.

"A little," he responded, "You just seem kind of remote."

"Well, you're probably right. I'm reading you the same way. It's probably the waiting." But I felt there was more to it than that. I wondered if, as co-workers, we had been together too long, and he was losing interest in me.

To my dismay, I also began to notice small signs of aging. My breasts seemed more pendulous, my thighs seemed less firm, and the veins in my hands were more prominent.

One day, while having lunch with Lynn, I asked if she thought I looked older now than I did a year ago. Unable to hide her impatience with me, she heaved a deep sigh.

"Are you still harping on that? I thought we'd covered the issue thoroughly. I suppose if I'd kept track of every wrinkle in your skin, or every grey hair on your head, I might be able to say there were a few more of them. Is that what you want to hear? I've told you six zillion times you look very young, but you're beginning to make *me* turn old and grey, just from listening to all this repetitious nonsense."

I couldn't help laughing, She made all my neurotic worries seem absurd. And yet, when I was away from her for a while they usually recurred.

Then I had another setback. Josh called to inform me that Sarah had had a baby girl on April sixth, and they had named the baby, Catherine. That was the name Walter and I had decided to name Josh, had he been a girl. Catherine had always been one of my favorite names.

Two days before Peter and I were due to reexamine the mice, Saki notified me that one of them had died. My heart sank. Was it one of the experimental animals or one of the controls? We had agreed not to decode the cages until the day of examination. I knew the odds were in favor of its being a control, since there were three times as many of them. It would not be unusual for any two year old mouse to die.

I told Saki to autopsy the mouse and preserve its organs. If it turned out to be one of the experimental animals, we would investigate further. Saki, outside of informing me about the dead mouse, refrained from giving me any clues about how the rest were doing. He was unusually quiet, and I assumed he was offended by the continuing veil of secrecy. I wished I could tell him exactly what we were doing, it was unfair to have him spend so much time on an unexplained experiment.

I wanted to discuss this with Peter and went to his office. He was sitting at his desk, staring at his computer, deep in thought, and seemed oblivious to the rapidly changing geometric figures on his screen saver.

"Peter we need to talk," I said quietly. "I think we're asking a lot of both Saki and Julie to keep them working in the dark."

"Let's wait until we know something, at least," he suggested. "There may be nothing to tell."

"Has Julie been asking you any questions?" I asked

"No," he replied, "In fact she isn't feeling too well. I don't know what's wrong with her, so I sent her home. She said she had an upset stomach."

"Do you think it has anything to do with John?" I offered, secretly hoping they had reconciled.

"No," Peter shook his head, a sober expression on his face. "They still aren't speaking to each other, but I don't think that's the problem. She seems to have accepted that, and she was glad to be busy working. I think she may just have one of those enteric viruses that are going around."

"Well, I'll certainly feel less guilty when I can tell Saki what we're doing. He seems a little resentful. Maybe he feels as though I'm treating him like an outsider. I think I'd feel the same way under the circumstances."

"Well, he'll have to be patient, Connie. Look, we're going to check the mice ourselves in two days. I really think it's better to wait."

"Okay," I said, grudgingly. "You seemed preoccupied with something, Peter. Is anything wrong?"

Peter gave me a searching look. "Funny you should ask me that. I've just been thinking the same thing about you."

"Oh, I'm alright," I said, laughing uncomfortably, " I guess I'm a little hyper about the experiment. Is it getting to you, too?"

"Yeah, to a degree. But maybe not to the same extent as you."

"What do you mean by that?" I shot back. "Why should I have more of an interest than you in the outcome?" Was he implying that I could relate more to the subject of age reversal than he?

"I only meant that you seem to be under more pressure than I am to get the results," he explained.

"Well, I guess I'm just less sophisticated than you when it comes to potential scientific breakthroughs. I haven't made any recent big discoveries." I knew I was being sarcastic, but I was annoyed with him. I'd gone along with his insistence on secrecy, despite my misgivings, and I felt as if I had no control over what was going on. And once again Peter hadn't explained why he was preoccupied. He had just tossed the ball back in my court. Was he now feeling as if our physical relationship was on the wane, just when our professional tie was so close? Was he wanting to find out if I had the same reaction?

He shook his head, "Oh, come on, Connie! Cut it out. You know you're as much of a pro in your area as I am in mine. Look, why don't we compromise. We'll accelerate our schedule and look at the mice tomorrow. One day won't make that much difference."

"Great!" I agreed, pushing my insecurities to the side, "Let's make it early," and added, "Sorry if I was irritable."

I spent a pretty restless night thinking about what Peter and I were going to find in the morning. I gave up trying to sleep at five AM, and got out of bed. My attempts to drag out my usual morning routine, to avoid getting to the lab before eight AM, as we'd agreed, failed. My body wasn't cooperating. I had trouble swallowing an English muffin as well as the coffee, which tasted bland. Finally, after taking what I thought was a long shower, but in fact lasted only five minutes, I was dressed and was ready to go before seven.

I was in the lab at quarter to eight and went immediately into my office and removed the code book from the desk drawer. As it turned out Peter was late, and I paced back and forth and finally moved to the window. I was looking anxiously down at the street, wondering where he was, when the door flew open and he rushed in.

"Sorry, the subway was delayed. Did you wait for me to look at them?"

"Of course," I said, wondering how he could have asked that. Would he have looked if he'd arrived first? And how come he didn't give me a hug? I brushed those thoughts aside and followed him into the animal room, code book in hand. He immediately started lifting the cages down from the shelf, and I realized he was just as eager as I to see the mice, and I helped him set the cages on the laboratory counter in front of the window. Peter, who was examining the mice in the first cage said, "Look at these. They definitely look old. See how slowly they move? And look at their coats - they have a yellowish cast to them, so do the teeth." He held the cage up to look at the code on the underside."A-1," he read.

I nodded and referred to the record book that Saki and Julie had been keeping,

"They've either lost a little weight or stayed about the same. Temperatures are still low or slightly subnormal. The sugar proteins are unchanged and only recorded for two weeks. I suppose this week's are still in the biochem lab." I opened the code book and found the cage number, "According to the code, these are controls with just the viral shell."

In the next two cages, the mice had the same appearance as the first, and the findings were similar. They were also controls, one with the viral shell alone and one with the normal nuclease gene inside it. The mouse that had died had come from the latter cage. So far, nothing to get excited about. I pulled the next cage forward and opened it.

"My God, look at these!" I yelped. The two mice inside were scurrying around, one of them put his front feet on the side of the cage, wrinkling his nose and sniffing, as though wanting to get out. Their coats were pure white and sleek.

"Wow!" Peter exclaimed, "what a difference!" He picked one up and pulled back the upper lip. "The teeth are white too. They even look heavier. What does the record say?"

I referred to the record book, "They've gained at least two grams, their temperatures are all up at least a degree from the initial readings, and two sugar proteins are down!"

I looked at the code book. "They're in the experimental group," I said triumphantly. We exchanged an exuberant look.

Then Peter cautioned, "Don't let's get carried away yet, we have to see the others."

I was busily examining the remaining cages and pulled four more forward. "Well, look at these little guys, they look like the others, Peter."

Peter looked at the mice in the four cages and nodded, "They do look pretty active and sleek. Are they also the ones with the mutated gene?"

I was examining the records, "Yes, they're the same code, and they've all gained weight and have lowered sugar proteins!"

"We still have to wait for the last sugar protein report. I also want to look at the telomere lengths before and after," Peter said, but his eyes were sparkling.

"I know, but just between us, can't we be excited? Don't be so damned phlegmatic!" I grabbed both his arms and shook him.

Peter freed his arms and put them around me, "I'm not phlegmatic, I'm the most *un*phlegmatic person you've ever known. I'm just a cautious scientist, and that's what you should be." He rubbed his cheek against mine and then kissed me, hard. This was the Peter I had been longing for. I kissed him back, murmuring happily, "Mmm, you feel good."

He hugged me tight for a moment, then let go of me and said, "Whoa! We have a lot to do before we can be absolutely certain." He moved away, somewhat awkwardly, I felt, and turned back towards the cages.

"I know we do. But we need time for us, too," I said, annoyed.

He continued undeterred, "There's a lot of work ahead of us, Connie. We have to do some autopsies to see what the tissues look like. We also have to wait for the last sugar protein result. The mice's appearance alone is not really enough proof."

I knew he was right, but I didn't need his explanation, and I marveled at his ability to keep science and sex in separate compartments. Or maybe it wasn't so hard for him because...because. Oh, damn, here I was being suspicious again. I returned to the business at hand.

"I'm going to tell Saki about our results now, although I'm sure he made his own observations, and by now has probably figured out exactly what was happening," I announced.

"I guess it's okay, as long as you're sure he'll keep it quiet. We really should repeat the experiment before we make a general announcement. It's going to have an enormous impact."

"Well, Saki is one of us. But of course we ought to tell the dean before the media gets hold of it. Saki won't say anything. How about Julie?"

"I'll tell her. She's still not feeling too great. I wish I knew what was wrong."

"She's only been sick for two days," I pointed out, as we were returning to my office. We nearly collided with Saki, who was just arriving.

"Good morning, Saki," I smiled. Saki needed to feel welcome – and it was time I did something about it. "Come into my office for a minute, I want to talk to you." I nodded to Peter and said, "See you later."

Once in my office, I motioned for Saki to sit down and closed the door .

"I'm finally going to tell you about the experiment you've been helping us with for the past few weeks," I began. "I know you've probably been drawing conclusions of your own. Do you have any general observations to make?"

Saki nodded, "I've noticed a change in the mice in five cages. They seem healthier than they were originally, unlike the others. Have you been treating them with something?"

"Not exactly," I said. Then I described the experiment, based on Peter's work with telomeres and mine with the Congo virus. When I finished, Saki looked as if he had been narrowly missed by a falling meteor. His eyes were wide and his pupils dilated.

"That is *unbelievable*," he said in a hoarse whisper, "It isn't possible! How could they get younger?"

His disbelief was exactly what I needed to hear, I continued on a cautionary note. "We believe the mice did reverse the aging process, but we have to be very sure before we say anything. We have some confirmatory tests to run, and we're going to repeat the experiment before we make any public announcements. It all has to be kept quiet until then."

"Don't worry, I won't say a word, promised Saki. Then, "Did you tell Julie? I know she's been wondering too."

"Peter will," I said, "She's home ill right now, so wait until you're sure she's been told before you say anything to her."

Saki got up and left the office, still looking dazed. His reaction was a prelude to what we could expect when word got out to others. My lab and Peter's would be like subway stations at rush hour unless we could somehow keep them off limits. I'd have to talk to Peter about that. I sat at my desk for a while, thinking, and wondering what kind of genie we were about to let loose on the world.

# *Chapter 8*

 *Chromosome 8*

We had the lab report on the last sugar protein on April fourteenth, which, together with the tissue slides of the mice Peter had autopsied, confirmed that the experimental animals had indeed grown younger. We still had no way of judging how much younger they were, but sequencing of their telomeres revealed a small but definite increase in the lengths.

We then began repeating the experiment using a new group of mice and controls in order to confirm the results. At the same time, Peter and I started writing a paper for the journal, *Nature Genetics*, listing us as co-investigators, and Saki and Julie as assistants. We observed that, several weeks after our initial finding of increased telomere length, the length had not changed. In other words, the rejuvenation effect appeared to be stable!

Our paper was sent out on April twenty-fifth, and once again Peter and I began our nail-biting wait. We had no doubt the paper would be accepted by the journal. The big problem was going to be the incredulous reactions of the readers. After the article was accepted, and before publication, we would speak to the dean of the medical school, and turn the matter of public announcement over to him.

Once the media knew of the experiment, there was sure to be an immediate extrapolation from mice to humans, and we were already prepared to stress how dangerous and premature this idea would be. We did not want to be constantly interrupted in our work in order to deal with such questions, and hoped that the dean would find some way of insuring our privacy, such as making our labs off limits.

Peter and I were both under a lot of stress, anticipating the upheaval to come, and when together, spoke almost exclusively about how we were going to deal with the upcoming publicity. I had difficulty concentrating on anything else, and the mild late-April weather didn't help. I walked through the park every morning on my way to work, and was developing a serious case of spring fever. The daffodils were in bloom, and the branches of the weeping willows by the lake were long and green.

About a week after the article was submitted, on a day that was particularly warm and sunny, I arrived in my office, and immediately opened the window as far as possible in order to lean out. Even though there was no greenery in sight, I could smell grass in the air. I thought of wafting over the city like a leaf, and settling in some secluded spot in the country. After a few moments of deep breathing, I turned to face the accumulation of papers on my desk. I was feeling dreamy and romantic, and it was impossible for me to cope with them now. I wanted to see Peter. I dialed his office and got the answering machine. Damn! Where was he?

As I was pondering this, the phone rang. I picked it up hoping it was Peter. It was Alan, and I had not spoken to him since our lunch.

"Hello, Connie. I hope I'm not getting you at a bad time."

"Of course not," I said, feeling guilty that I hadn't called him. "Alan, I'm so sorry I didn't get back to you sooner. It's been crazy around here. We were doing a new experiment."

"It's just as well," he replied, "I had to go back to California for a few days, and I'm calling to tell you I'll have to go back again." His voice was somber.

"Is everything alright?" I asked.

"Well, it's nothing I didn't expect. Elaine and I are going to get a divorce."

"Oh, Alan, I'm so sorry." I wasn't too surprised either, after learning of their separate living arrangements, and for some reason, I wasn't really sorry. I liked Alan, and wanted him to be happy. And having Alan single and available might make Peter more attentive. "When are you coming back?" I asked.

"Just as soon as we can decide on the terms of the divorce. I'm glad the kids are old enough to fend for themselves. I wanted you to know because – well, I still would like to see you and, of course, meet your friend Peter. May I call you when I get back in town?"

I liked the idea of seeing Alan – with or without Peter. "Of course. Peter said he'd like to meet you, and then we both got busy with the new project. Call me when you return and we'll make a date. I hope all the legal things go easily for you. Divorce is no fun."

"You're right, but I'll survive. I knew you were seeing Tarker, but I didn't realize you were *working* with him. That must be interesting. I'd like to hear about it when I get back."

I wondered whether he'd hear about it from the media first. The likelihood of the results of our experiment being publicized was almost a certainty. If Alan was away long enough, he'd learn of it before I could say anything. I wished I could give him a hint, but I kept silent. We said goodbye, I wished him luck, and put the phone back in its cradle.

Poor Alan, I thought, what a shame that his marriage, like so many others, would end in divorce. But I was somewhat disappointed with myself. It wasn't fair to use Alan as a snare for Peter. He deserved a lot better.

When I heard Saki moving some equipment in the lab, I decided I'd better make an attempt to do something constructive. There was a lot to be done, including further analysis of the Congo viral genome to identify other hypothalamic functions. I retrieved the Congo notes from the file cabinet and spent the rest of the morning shuffling between the lab, my computer, and short conversations with Saki.

Around noon I called Peter's office again. He was there, but sounded harassed. He said he had some problems to iron out with Julie, and I should call him later in the afternoon. When I put down the phone it rang almost instantly. It was Lynn, wondering if I could meet her for lunch in the hospital cafeteria. I agreed as long as it was quick, because I wanted to finish what I had been doing. Lynn was the only person, other than Saki and Julie, to know the outcome of our experiment. With Peter's consent, I had told her about it on her return from a brief vacation two days previously, and she was as fascinated and incredulous as Saki had been. She agreed not to tell anyone, even her husband, Robert, if she could speak to me every time she felt like revealing all.

The cafeteria was crowded and we had to wait in line to get our sandwiches. When we were finally seated at a table for two, it was close to twelve-thirty. Lynn instantly pushed her tray to one side and said in a hushed voice, "Have you heard anything yet?"

She was referring to the response from the journal. As soon as publication was guaranteed, I had promised that she would be free to speak. Keeping anything from Robert was painful for her, and it might have been kinder of me not to have told her, but she had been my confidante for so long that, selfishly, I wanted to be able to talk openly with her.

"Not yet," I replied, swallowing a bite of turkey sandwich. "It takes a while. I'm really sorry, Lynn. I should never have put you in this position. Would you pass me the salt, this turkey tastes like cardboard."

" I'm glad you told me," she answered, pushing the salt across the formica table top, "But I have a feeling Robert knows I'm holding something back. I just hope my facial expressions retain their normal blandness around other people."

"If your facial expression was ever bland, it would be totally *ab*normal, what are you talking about?" I started to laugh.

"I don't know, I just feel I'm walking around with bug-eyes. How do you stay so calm? You're about to set the world on its ear," she said, her eyes sparkling. She took a large bite of her egg-salad sandwich, and leaning across the table, retrieved the salt. Her sandwich was apparently as tasteless as mine. Typical hospital fare.

"I'm not the least bit calm," I admitted. "Actually, I'm trying to keep my cool about the experiment, and so is Peter. And we've become a little distant with each other, maybe because of tension. I know I'm holding back from him. It could be that the idea of menopause is making me a little weird, and I should start taking the hormones."

"Do you mean you haven't started hormones yet? Why on earth not?"

"I just didn't think I needed them. It's an admission of age that I didn't want to make."

"Oh, for God's sake, Connie. That's really juvenile. The whole purpose of those hormones is to *keep* your body from growing old."

I leaned forward and took hold of Lynn's hand. Of course she was right. "I know. I'm nuts. Thanks for pointing it out. I'll try to start behaving like a rational person."

Lynn grinned and squeezed my hand, "I wouldn't recognize you. You'd better pull yourself together before your news hits the street. Then you'll really be under the microscope." She let go of my hand to pull her tray in front of her.

"I'm not looking forward to that," I said. But even as I said it, I wondered if that was really how I felt.

After lunch I returned to the lab and continued working. It took most of the afternoon to set up the next experimental design. I had started an investigation of another nerve specific virus, a close relative of the herpes zoster virus which, in humans, causes chicken pox as well as shingles. However, this virus appeared to be confined to cattle on several adjacent ranches in Texas. The affected cattle had developed neurologic symptoms of staggering gait, and in some, coma and death. I wanted to try and modify the virus in order to create a vaccine, which I would test on guinea pigs, another animal susceptible to it.

The virus had been received in an inactive frozen condition, and when thawed was to be transferred to tissue culture cells where it would grow and multiply. To innoculate the tissue culture cells with the virus, I first placed a small vial of virus under a brightly lit, ventilated hood along with several flat glass-covered dishes containing the growth medium, a single layer of monkey kidney cells. I was wearing my long white lab coat and rubber gloves so as not to contaminate the virus or the growth medium. When I finished with this task, I returned the infected tissue culture to the incubator and switched on an ultraviolet light to sterilize the work area. This was the same procedure I had followed with the Congo River virus.

At around five o'clock, I needed a breather and went down the flight of stairs to Peter's lab to see what he was up to. The door was open, but the lab was empty, and I continued toward his office at the rear left of the lab. When I reached his door, I stopped dead in my tracks. Peter was standing in front of his desk, his back to me. His arms were around Julie, her face pressed into his shoulder. For what seemed an eternity, but was probably only five seconds, I stood there. Then I turned and silently left the lab.

Somehow I managed to return to my office and close the door. My heart was like a trip-hammer, and I was breathing like an untrained marathon runner. I thought I might throw up. Sitting at my desk with my head in my hands, I let out a spontaneous groan. I should have known this, it explained everything. He had probably been attracted to Julie for a long time, but didn't pursue her because of her relationship with John Castle. Now that their relationship had ended, this was the result. I felt so sick and betrayed, I didn't want to see anyone - even Lynn who had supported Peter when I felt insecure about him.

I don't know how long I remained sitting at the desk, taking deep ragged breaths and trying to deal with the pain. When I looked at my watch, it was after six. Nearly everyone would have gone home, but I didn't want to move, my heart still knocking around in my chest, my hands clammy and cold, my mouth dry.

Why did I have to fall in love with him? He was just playing with me because my research coincided with his. He probably did sleep with Marcia when he was in Ohio. It obviously didn't matter to him who he had sex with while he was mooning about Julie. God, I felt awful. I had to get a hold on myself, maybe take something to calm down. Then I remembered that I had some Ativan, a tranquilizer, in my desk, which was probably outdated. I had needed it when I was getting divorced from Walter. Now, in an ironic twist, I was needing it again for a similar reason. I located the pills in the back of my desk drawer and swallowed one, then decided one would not be enough and took another.

My hand was trembling, and I couldn't get the image of Peter holding Julie in his arms out of my head. She was so young and beautiful, how could I ever compete with that, and besides she worked right along side of him. I'd have a fighting chance if I were thirty instead of being nearly fifty and menopausal. I closed my eyes and sat back in the chair. Here I am, I thought, having just found a miraculous way to reverse the aging process, and I was unable to apply it to myself. Or was I?

I was feeling a little calmer as the Ativan began taking effect. My life had just started a huge downward spiral, but maybe there was one way I might be able to stop it. I could experiment on myself.

After all, it was my discovery of the aging center that had made age reversal possible. As it had turned out in the mice, the process appeared to be limited because their telomeres had stopped growing. I would just be gaining a little extra youth. I sat back in my chair, feeling increasingly drowsy.

A short time ago, I had been prepared to slip a noose around my neck, anything to end the misery. Now I could do something that might benefit mankind, and at the same time possibly help myself. I got out of the chair, fighting sleep, and made it to the refrigerator in the lab. The flask containing the mutated gene in the viral vector was on the bottom shelf carefully labeled. I removed the sterile cotton from the mouth of the flask, poured five c.c.s into a calibrated glass, and transferred that to a paper cup. After returning the flask to the refrigerator I went back to my desk. I was struggling to stay awake and having difficulty weighing the pros and cons of what I was about to do.

# Chapter 9

🜉🜉 *Chromosome 9* ————————————————————————

The pillow seemed very hard, and my hand fumbled to rearrange it, but there was no pillow. My cheek was pressed against a hard surface, and I was sitting in a chair...no bed...this wasn't my room. Where was I? The hard surface was the desk in my office! I sat up abruptly. Why was I here? I looked around me. The lights were on, and there was a greyish light coming through the window. The clock on the wall over the door indicated it was six-thirty. Six-thirty? It must be morning because of the light outside. That must mean that I had spent the entire night sitting at my desk. There was an envelope lying on the desk, with the word 'Ativan' on it. I picked it up, and my memory came back in a rush. I'd taken the Ativan to calm down, but it must have knocked me out completely. I remembered thinking one tablet was not enough and taking two.

My head was pounding. I closed my eyes and sat back in the chair. I could still see Julie in Peter's arms, and I wanted to die. What a fool I'd been. How could I have thought he loved me when there was about half a generation between us. Sure, he liked me, particularly when our research projects meshed so well, and he wasn't averse to having sex with me when he couldn't have Julie, but as soon as she was available, he had begun to phase me out. I was on my own now, and I felt used and angry.

I sat up, opened my eyes, and at once saw something else on the desk…an empty cup. Why did that seem so ominous to me? I tried to clear my head. I vaguely remembered going to the lab refrigerator and taking out some of the viral concoction we had given to the experimental mice. What had happened? I had no memory of removing it. I could recall being devastated by what I had seen, and thinking 'if I were younger…' After that, my memory was blank. I stood up and went to the refrigerator to try and retrace my steps.

The flask containing the virus with the mutated gene was sitting on the bottom shelf as usual and showed no signs of disturbance. But I still had a nagging feeling that I had removed it. I turned to look at the sink for a clue and saw the calibrated measuring flask. Then in a wispy dream-like sequence, I saw myself pouring some of the viral preparation into the measurer and then into a cup…the empty cup on my desk. Could I have swallowed it? Given my state of mind last night, I could have done anything. Now I was frightened. I went quickly back to my desk, thinking I might have spilled it in my groggy state, and looked around for a tell-tale spot, but there was none, either in the office or out in the lab. I was beginning to tremble. My hands were icy and my palms sweaty. In my overly tranquilized state, had I actually consigned myself to the rank of a laboratory animal?

I leaned back against the wall to try and gain some control, and took a few deep breaths, yoga-style. The entire sequence of events was coming back to me. I had knowingly and willingly made myself into a guinea pig. I had wanted to be younger, and all it took to push me over the edge was my despair over Peter. Now I was committed to the unknown with a potentially dangerous virus, with no way of ascertaining what the long-term effects were going to be in the mice, let alone humans. My only hope was that those effects would be minimal, or that the mutation would have no effect at all in human chromosomes.

I felt a little calmer, enough to realize that what I had done was totally unprofessional and stupid. True, scientists have experimented on themselves in the past, usually when they are convinced of the validity of their work, and to demonstrate its usefulness to mankind. I had no such excuse. What I did, I did for one person – myself. There was nothing noble about it. Yet, one thing was certain: I would keep my lapse a secret. If my foolish action became known, my status as a research scientist would be called into question, and it would be very hard to get grant money. I had to cover my tracks.

I needed a cup of coffee to clear my head, but first I went into the lavatory to wash my face and hands. I washed the calibrated flask as well, and had just replaced it on the laboratory shelf when the telephone started ringing in my office. It was far too early in the morning for someone to be calling me – it had to be Peter. I let it ring a few more times before picking up.

"Connie, what the hell are you doing there at this hour? I tried to reach you at home last night, I was worried when there was no answer. Where were you?" I took a deep breath and tried to stay calm.

"I had some stuff I wanted to do here, and I woke up very early," I answered, tersely. "I was out late last night." Damn him, I didn't have to explain anything to him.

He paused, "Oh, I see... well, I wanted to talk to you about something. Is it okay if I come by in about half an hour?" He sounded a little depressed, and I hoped he was.

"I guess so. What's it about?"

"I'll tell you when I see you. Are you alright? You sound sort of strange."

"I'm alright."I said, hanging up. I had nothing else to say.


A short time later, Peter walked into my office and sat on my beat-up couch. I was at my desk, trying to equate mouse age to human age. I looked up briefly, and with a nod acknowledged him. I didn't know what to say, and avoided his eyes.

"You look a little beat, Connie. Are you okay?" Peter was looking at me intently with a somewhat puzzled expression. "I've been worried about you. You've been acting so remote lately."

"Yes, I'm okay," I said, shortly. I had good reason to be remote. "What did you want to talk about?"

"It's about Julie. I need some advice."

"Yes, what about her?" I said wearily. I didn't want to listen to his explanations. I wanted to tell him to leave and get his advice elsewhere, but I stayed silently in my chair. Here it comes, I thought.

Peter leaned forward, hands on his knees, "Julie's pregnant."

For a moment I felt I would vomit. I whirled my chair around to face the window, my hand over my mouth and swallowed violently, then turned slowly back to face him, "Well, isn't that wonderful. Are you going to ask me if you should make an honest woman of her?"

"What the hell are you talking about?"

"It's your baby, isn't it?"

"Are you insane? Whatever gave you that idea?" Peter looked at me as if I had just sprouted horns. "How could it possibly be mine?"

"The usual way, I suppose," I replied bitterly, but now there was a wonderful, tiny feeling of doubt.

"You damned fool," Peter muttered. "The last thing I would do is get mixed up with Julie. She works in my lab, she's not my type, and besides I've been waiting around for you to come to your senses, although it looks now as though you've really gone over the edge. Don't you realize that I love you?"

My eyes filled with tears, and I felt an enormous smile forming on my face. "You love *me*! How come you never told me?" I stammered, still disbelieving the words I'd been waiting to hear.

"Of course, I love you, you idiot, but I thought you were cooling off on me. Ever since I came back from Cincinnati you've been acting a little cold. Did it have something to do with my staying with Marcia?"

"Well," I confessed, "Yes, that was part of it. But mainly it was seeing you with your arms around Julie."

"My God, so that's what it was all about! I didn't know you saw me. I was only hugging Julie because she was so miserable. She's pregnant with John's baby, and she's in a mess about what to do."

"I had no idea," I told him. "I'm so sorry. I feel like an idiot."

He stood up and beckoned to me. "Come over here."

I got up and walked tremulously around the desk and into his arms. We kissed for a long time, I felt myself falling and at the same time floating somewhere up near the ceiling. When he finally loosened his hold, I let out a deep sigh and murmured, "Oh Peter, I do love you."

I pulled his head down and gave him another kiss, and he ran his hand lightly up my back to the nape of my neck.

"What are you doing tonight?" he asked in a husky voice.

We didn't wait for the night. After Peter went to his lab to do some work, I returned to my task of trying to convert mouse time to human time. If it took three weeks for the mice to show discernable change, how long would it be for me, if there was going to be an effect? I could still feel the effects of the Ativan, but my mental state had gone from minus one to plus ten. Why didn't I realize long ago that Peter loved me? I'd been so damn busy worrying about my age and menopause that I couldn't see he needed some reassurance, too. Well. I'd make up for that. Lynn had been right after all.

But first, I drew some blood from a vein in my arm. I had to make a chromosome preparation to have a record of my telomere status, in case a change were to take place. All the while I was silently praying that I would never have to look at it. At about three in the afternoon, I called Peter and asked, "Are you terribly busy?"

"Terribly, but let's get out of here." And we did.

Several hours later, lying in my bed, Peter turned to me and said, "Mmmm, that was so great it made me hungry. Do you have anything to eat around here, or should we go out?"

"I could make us an omelet and some salad. There isn't much else, but let's stay here. We won't have to get dressed."

I got up and puttered around in the kitchen, taking out the eggs, and discovering some chives and sharp cheddar cheese. Peter prepared a green salad while I made the omelets. We opened two bottles of beer, put everything on a tray and carried it back to bed. After eating we pushed the tray aside and reached for each other again. I awakened once in the night, and finding his arm thrown across my back, smiled and went back to sleep.

In the morning, while he was still sleeping, I quietly slipped out of bed and went into the kitchen to make coffee. I was thinking about all that had happened. There was no point castigating myself now. The die was cast, and I would just have to wait. My only hope was that the viral preparation would be ineffective. In all likelihood, it would be I told myself. Although mice and humans have a great deal in common, there are significant differences as well, and the human hypothalamus might not have the same type of receptors for the virus. True, the mice had all become younger, and there was nothing wrong with that. But I had no idea what the long-term effects might be. Cancer was a possibility because the effect of increased telomerase on individual cell types had been shown to produce runaway cells, or cancer. But when all cells in the body are subjected to increased telomerase, regulated through the aging center, they all grow younger, as long as no glitches appear to make one type grow faster.

I'm sure I'll be alright, I told myself. Suddenly I felt Peter's arms circling my waist, and turned to kiss him.

"What were you so preoccupied about?" he asked.

"I was just thinking about us, and how long it took to find out we love each other." At least, that was part of the truth.

"We certainly weren't on the same wavelength, were we? By the way, what have you got here for breakfast?"

"Muffins, coffee, juice. Do you want anything else?"

He nuzzled my ear and mumbled, "Mmm, honey."

"Is that an endearment, or do you want to eat it?"

"Both." I gazed at him, sitting across the kitchen counter on a stool, his hair tousled. He looked so boyish and so damn appealing. I told myself that many men marry older women, and it works because women live longer on the average. Peter surely knew I was older than he, even though he never asked my exact age, but he didn't ask because he didn't care, I was the one who had made a big issue of our age discrepancy. Even if I had been in my early forties, and only a few years older than he, I don't believe he would have wanted me to become pregnant. That had been one of my chief concerns, but now I didn't think it was an issue.

After breakfast we walked across the park to work, and Peter told me more about Julie and John. She had discovered she was pregnant shortly after they broke up, but had not told him.
"She said she didn't want him to be pressured into coming back. She thinks she still loves him, but she'd rather have an abortion than force him into a marriage he didn't want. She insists she doesn't want to go to Rochester, especially since she's been so excited about our work here. She thinks that if John knew about our experiment, he might understand her reticence."

"That's probably true," I agreed, "but she'll be able to tell him pretty soon. Don't you think she should at least give John a chance to make up his own mind about the baby? He might want to be a father. She sounds a bit confused," I said.

"You're right. I tried to tell her that the other night, but she wasn't buying it. Do you think you could speak to her. She might be more receptive if it came from a woman. Besides, I have a feeling he loves her, too, and they're both as screwed up as we were."

"Oh, God!" I said, "Not that bad, I hope! Sure, I'll be glad to talk to her, but won't she mind that you told me?"

"No, because I asked if I could get your advice, and she said it was okay, she was thinking of telling you anyway." Peter took my hand. "It's a good thing I got to you before she did."

"You're right," I responded, feeling somewhat ashamed, "my advice might have been a little counterproductive."

We walked in silence for a few minutes, admiring the budding trees and green grass. "I wish we could take a week off, and go veg out somewhere in the country," I said softly.

"So do I, honey, but we have to be around now, I'm afraid." Peter said, in his level-headed way. "God only knows what's going to happen when we tell the dean."

"You're right, and I know it. In fact, it'll be even worse when the article comes out, we won't have any time to ourselves. We ought to make some contingency plans, like finding a little hide-away in some remote spot." I was already imagining a little inn in northern Connecticut or Vermont.

Peter squeezed my hand, "Good idea. Why don't you see what you can come up with?"

I never had the chance to come up with anything. The editor of Nature called us right after reading our submission, which, he said, would appear in the next issue of the journal, coming out May 14th, and would undoubtedly spark immediate coverage by the news media. He warned us that certain newspapers, like *The New York Times*, would publish these findings in their Science section before subscribers to the journal received their copies.

Therefore, he suggested we present our findings earlier at a genetics conference to be held at Cold Spring Harbor on May 12th, just about two weeks away. We agreed, and I convinced Peter to make the presentation, since he was the geneticist. I would be there to answer any questions about the role of the Congo virus in the experiment.

That same day we requested a meeting with Dean Balch, saying the matter was urgent and needed immediate attention. We met with him in his office at 4 PM, and advised him of the results of our experiment. He was, as we suspected, elated both by our findings, and by the potential they provided for increased revenue to the college. He immediately notified the office of external affairs to arrange to keep our laboratories off limits to the media.

On the day we were scheduled to appear, I awakened with a giant case of the jitters. Peter admitted he was also feeling anxious, although he revealed nothing in his behavior.

We rented a car, and on the way to Cold Spring Harbor, we tried to anticipate the reaction of the assembled scientists to our bombshell. It was a balmy, clear day, one I would have thoroughly enjoyed had I not been so keyed up. As it was, the warmth only caused me to perspire more profusely than usual, and I worried that sweat stains might appear on my dark cotton blouse. We were greeted at the entrance to the auditorium by one of the senior geneticists from the Cold Spring Harbor laboratory, who escorted us to our seats in the front row. The remaining seats in the room were, by my estimate, about 75 percent occupied. Peter was slated to speak at ten o'clock, half an hour from our arrival. We were preceded by a scientist from the Genome Project at the N.I.H., who gave a report on the status of human genome sequencing. Then it was Peter's turn. I gave his hand a squeeze and whispered, "Good luck." Looking serious, he rose and went to the podium. His reputation – and mine – was on the line.

First, Peter described his earlier experiment, in which he had identified the gene for telomerase by showing premature aging in newborn mice with site-specific gene mutation. He then went on to describe my accidental finding of the aging center in the hypothalamus while I was analyzing the Congo River virus. Then he got to the final experiment with the mutated nuclease gene in the viral vector given to old mice.

When he described the findings, and showed slides of the experimental and control mice, there was complete silence in the auditorium. Then came the sound of an enormous collective intake of breath, followed by pandemonium.

The geneticist who had greeted us got to his feet and called for order. He asked that Peter be allowed to finish his presentation, after which the audience could ask questions. As anticipated, the audience was amazed and disbelieving. Peter was besieged by questions. Some, directed to me, involved the Congo River virus as a gene vector, but most had to do with the potential for human application: Was it possible, and, if so, would it be practical or ethical?

Peter responded by saying it was much too early to make a prediction about possible human applications. Although the likelihood of some existing similarities was strong, it would be difficult and dangerous to test the hypothesis without a great deal more knowledge of the long term outcome in mice. As to the ethical considerations, he would leave that to the government ethics committee.

The questions seemed endless, and we could have stayed there forever trying to answer them, but our host finally ended the session by saying that there were more presentations to follow. We managed to break away from the insistent group that followed us out of the auditorium, and escaped in our car. We were both uncharacteristically silent on the drive back to Manhattan. I had been pondering the unanswerable question: what would this mean to our personal futures, and to that of our fellow human beings? Peter must have been having the same thoughts because he turned to me when we were about halfway home and said, "Well, now that the embryo has life, I wonder what the nature of the creature will be."

So did I, and I hoped it wasn't another $E=MC^2$.

The day *Nature* came out the calls started coming in from all forms of news media, scientists, nonscientists, and cranks. We were inundated and were happy to accept the loan of a secretary from the dean's office to field the calls. The following day, my intercom buzzed, and the secretary told me one of my friends was on the phone. It was Alan, who was still in California.

"Hello, Alan," I said, pleased to hear from him. It had been weeks since we'd spoken. "Sorry, we've been getting so many calls we had to hire a screener. How's everything going with you?"

"I don't wonder you're getting a lot of calls," he responded, ignoring my question. "You and your friend Peter are celebrities. My God, girl! Why didn't you tell me you were about to set the world on fire? You can't imagine the kind of press you're getting out here in California. It's as if you'd found the Holy Grail."

"I think I'd rather have found the Holy Grail; we could just send it on to the Vatican and forget about it. As it is, there are a lot of questions about our methods, our motives, and the ethics of future use. Of course, just about everyone wants to personally benefit from this." I shifted the phone to my other ear, and sat down at the desk, "When are you coming back? I could use some sage advice. Peter and I feel like going off to a desert island, if one still exists somewhere."

"I could recommend a ranch in Montana that's pretty deserted, but don't go yet, I ought to be back in New York soon, if all goes well. Then I'll be happy to give you my sage advice."

"When? Are you divorced yet?" I asked, curious. If he was, Alan sounded remarkably calm.

"Not yet, but we've agreed on the settlement terms, so as soon as the lawyers deliver the appropriate papers to be signed, I'll be off." In fact, he sounded much cheerier than he had the last time we spoke. Thank God I have an understanding department head. He knows what it's like to get a divorce, and let me take off until I got things settled.

"Well, just give me a little advance notice and the three of us can have dinner. I might even prepare one of my gourmet meals,." I said.

"That's some enticement. Dinner at home with the two most notable scientists in today's world. I should bring my video camera."

"If you do, I'll throw you out. I'm up to the kazoo with all of that." But part of me was basking in Alan's laudatory words. I suspected I could become addicted to praise, faint or otherwise.

"Okay, okay,  I'd still like to see your labs sometime. I'll call you soon as I know when I'm coming."

After I hung up, I thought about all the notoriety Peter and I were getting. At first it was exciting, but as time went on, I began to yearn for my pre-experiment anonymity. Peter, who was bearing the brunt of the calls, felt the same way. I went so far as to get an unlisted phone number at home, and then had to notify my family and friends of the change.

Over the ensuing weeks numerous articles were written in newspapers, scientific journals, and various other publications about the implications of a society without senior citizens, and at what age people would choose to arrest the maturing process, were that possible. Since our laboratories had been made off-limits to the media, we had some privacy, although  medical school personnel and students were constantly at our doors. We instructed Saki and Julie not to allow anyone into the labs without our permission.

Peter was interviewed on several television networks, and continued to stress the potential danger of extrapolating the mice findings to humans. Although asked, I steadfastly refused to give interviews to the press or appear on the public networks; we had agreed that Peter would be the spokesperson. My reticence had a lot more to do with wanting to keep a low profile because I, too, might be one of the experimental animals. This clouded my euphoria over my relationship with Peter, even though I kept telling myself that, in all probability, nothing bad was going to happen to me.

*Chapter 10*

*Chromosome 10* ——————————————————————————

    Several days before Peter and I had attended the Cold Spring Harbor meeting, Julie had come into my office. She sat down in the chair facing me, and to my surprise, announced that she and John were planning to get married. Before I could recover from this news, she reached over and took my hand, adding, "You realize, Connie, that if it hadn't been for your friendship, and Peter, urging me to tell John, I probably would have gone ahead and had an abortion. I was so certain he didn't want to be tied down, and I was totally wrong. He was ecstatic about it. We want to have the wedding pretty soon, before I start looking like a battleship, but we want to invite friends and family. So, we're planning it for June tenth, and I'd like you to be my maid of honor. John has asked Peter to be best man."

    I was totally unprepared for this honor, having been under the impression that Julie had many friends her own age and considered me from another generation. At the same time I was pleased and accepted the invitation, adding that I should be called a matron of honor, since I had been married. She laughed and said that it made no difference to her - the last thing she cared about was protocol.

In the beginning of June, a few days before the wedding, I had a normal menstrual period. It was no surprise, because I'd started taking the hormones I'd been prescribed after Lynn's admonition. What puzzled me a little was that my breasts were feeling quite tender, and I wondered if the dose might be too high. I had bought a new dress to wear, a celadon green, lightweight silk, and had shoes dyed to match.

On the day of the wedding, Julie wore a light apricot-colored silk suit instead of the customary white bridal gown. She had already become a little thick around the middle. Her shiny black hair was arranged in a French twist at the back of her head, and she looked beautiful. Remembering my worry about her effect on Peter, I smiled inwardly. Now I could really appreciate how lovely she was.

John, who looked very handsome in a navy blue suit, never took his eyes off her, and the wedding guests seemed equally enchanted. I got my share of compliments as well. I knew a lot of the medical school invitees, and, as they passed through the receiving line after the ceremony, many made comments like:

"You look fabulous, Connie," and "You should always wear that color."

I began to feel like a peacock in full regalia. Peter, who overheard some of these remarks, at one point pinched my back and said,

"I'm going to make you wear a sign that says 'Taken'".

"No problem," I responded, smiling sweetly. "If I can do the same with you."

He grinned and kissed me behind the ear, and whispered that he had never seen me look so ravishing, and couldn't wait to get home. "Home" was either his apartment or mine, depending upon our whim of the moment. We had been spending almost every night together.

Later, when we were "home"'in my bed, he whispered, "What will become of me when you're off in Europe with Dave and Josh?"

"Come with us," I said softly. I meant it, too. Much as I wanted to spend time with my sons, I knew I would miss Peter terribly.

"You know I can't. Someone has to be here to manage all the notoriety. But don't worry, I'll be faithful," he grinned.

I bit him gently on the ear and whispered back, "You better be!"

A few days later I received another call from Alan announcing his return. He wondered if Peter and I were available to have dinner and also show him our labs. After checking with Peter, I called Alan back to tell him we would be happy to show him the labs the next day, June 12th. Unfortunately, Peter had to leave for a meeting that evening. I accepted his invitation to dinner, but as previously arranged, insisted that it would be my treat. After a bit of haranguing, he agreed to let me pay.

Alan showed up in my lab at five o'clock. I had told Saki to send him into my office when he arrived, and when he walked in, I stood up to greet him. He gave me a kiss on the cheek and then stood back and scrutinized me. "You're looking very well, Constance. Fame must agree with you."

"Not really," I answered, "I'll be glad when it all settles down. Have you been on the beach? You look very well too." He did, the suntan was becoming, and he had a playful gleam in his eye. I realized I had very warm feelings toward Alan. Purely friendly, but definitely warm.

"Yes," he replied, "I spent a few days with my daughters. They were a little upset over the impending divorce, but both said they were not surprised."

"That's the hardest part," I said. "Kids can usually see what's going on, but it doesn't make it easier. Will they come visit you in New York?"

"Yes, they both want to come in August, when they have vacations due. I think I'll rent a house somewhere. Any ideas?"

"I'll think about it. Let's go down to see Peter, he's expecting you."

Peter was in his office, writing. He stood and walked over to shake hands with Alan as I was introducing him. Both men seemed to be appraising one another.

"I've heard a lot about you from Connie," Peter said. At the same time Alan was saying, "I've been wanting to meet you even before you hit the headlines." They both broke off grinning.

"Do you want me to moderate?" I asked, pleased that they seemed to like each other. They both chuckled.

"Why don't you," Peter replied.

"Me first," Alan insisted. "I have a million questions.

I heaved a sigh, "Okay, Alan, you're on."

"Let's all sit down," Peter suggested. He returned to the chair behind his desk, while Alan and I sat on the couch.

"I don't know where to begin," Alan said, leaning forward. "I guess at the beginning. When did you decide to investigate telomeres?" he asked Peter.

"Not too long after I decided to study genetics. I wanted to know why the end portions of our chromosomes were the same repeated series of six molecules in all the chromosomes in all vertebrate animals, why they shortened with age, and whether they had anything to do with aging. Simple as that. From there I started investigating the enzymes nuclease and telomerase. One thing led to another. When I came to Bailey and met Connie, everything took off, as you know."

Alan turned to look at me. "Did she tell you I've known her since she was a callow teenager. That was the last time I saw her until a few weeks ago, and until then had no idea of all the ground she's covered. Now it's even more astonishing. You two are big-time celebrities. I understand you have to go to some meeting tonight, Peter. I don't want to keep you from whatever you were doing, but could I just see the famous mice?"

"Sure," Peter said. "I'm sorry about not being able to go to dinner with you, but I agreed to appear on PBS for an interview. I have to represent both of us, since Connie's too bashful."

"She is?" Alan said, raising his eyebrows, "That's not the way I remember her. What's come over you, Connie?"

This was getting a little hot for me. "I was always bashful, Alan. You were so outgoing, you never recognized it." I smiled at him. He was looking at me curiously, so I said, "The original mice are in the animal care facility near my lab. The new ones are there too, they're a repeat of the same experiment, and they're showing the same changes." I stood and went over to Peter, "Good luck! I hope you don't get grilled on ethics again."

I leaned over to kiss him, but he was getting up to say goodbye to Alan. As he was shaking Alan's hand, he said, "That's all people seem to want to know. Whether it will be applicable to humans, and if so, is it ethical? My answer is always the same. It's too soon to predict any outcome in humans, since we don't know the long-term effects."

We said goodbye to Peter, and I gave him a quick kiss under Alan's scrutiny. After showing Alan the mice, we left for dinner at Sushi Say, where we ordered sushi a la carte. It was delicious and expensive, and while eating and sipping hot saki, Alan quizzed me about my role in the now-famous experiment. I explained my investigation of the Congo River virus, and how I had found the aging center in the hypothalamus. Alan listened intently and for once was very serious with me.

"I'm really impressed with this, Connie. You should be very proud of yourself, and so should Peter. God knows where it is going to take you, but that's always a risk when some new technology is discovered. Did Max Planck foresee the advent of computers and microwave ovens? Those are useful applications of quantum physics, but who knows what will turn up in the future. I don't mean to philosophize, I'm certain you and Peter have had enough of this kind of stuff. New doors keep being opened in our civilization, and it's up to us to go through them in the right direction." He sat back in his chair and said, "That's my final pronouncement, for what it's worth. Is it the sage advice you wanted?"

"It'll do, you were always good at giving sage advice." Then, to show I was teasing, I leaned across the table and punched him lightly on the arm. Alan grinned. "Shall we order dessert?" I asked.

Lynn and Robert rented a house on Martha's Vineyard for the month of July and invited us for the long July fourth weekend. Robert, a professor of engineering at Columbia, had no problem getting away in the summer, and Lynn had arranged for a colleague to cover her practice. They convinced us to take four days away from the lab, and I accepted, but with a few pangs of guilt because of my upcoming trip to Europe in August.

Peter had become better acquainted with the Steins after we started spending most of our time together. He liked them both and was eager to go. He said he wanted a rest from all the publicity. I joked that he loved the attention, but knew that he would have preferred being left alone to work in his lab. I had learned more about him in the past few weeks, than in all the previous time I had known him. He was a truly dedicated scientist, and research was paramount in his life. At times I thought it might even have superceded me, were it not for the converging of our projects.

Lynn picked us up at the airport for the twenty-minute drive to their house, a turn-of-the-century, two storey, weathered shingle edifice with a wide veranda. It stood on a small knoll with a distant view of the water, and was surrounded by about two or three acres of field with scattered scrub pines and a few overgrown hydrangea bushes. There was no attempt at landscaping, for which Lynn said she was grateful, because the only outdoor upkeep was a weekly mowing of the coarse Bermuda grass along the dirt driveway and around the house. To one side of the driveway was a hard surface tennis court on which the Steins' two teenaged daughters were playing as we arrived.

"It's full of cracks, but still useable." Lynn explained.

The girls paused long enough to wave before resuming their game.

The interior of the house was comfortably shabby...faded fabrics, wicker furniture, braided cotton throw rugs, window seats, and a big stone fireplace in the living room. Peter and I were put in the guest room off the living room. The rest of the bedrooms were on the second floor.

Lynn left us to unpack, saying Robert had gone to see about renting a fishing boat for tomorrow, and she would be outside watching the tennis. The guest room had twin beds separated by a night table. I closed the door and started to unpack, and the first thing Peter did was pick up the table and move the beds together.

"We'll move it back before we leave," he said.

"Sure," I said, " but I want the table next to me in case I feel like reading."

"Fat chance!" Peter threw me on one of the beds and held me down.

"Not now!" I laughed, struggling to get up. "I love this house, don't you? It's perfect for a vacation."

"Yeah," Peter answered, loosening his grip, "it's great. Do you want to play some tennis later?"

"Maybe we can play doubles when Robert comes back, if it isn't too late."

"What about singles?"

"You know you can beat me at singles, for heavens sake. Why don't you ask Robert."

"I like beating you."

I managed to sit up and threw a rolled up pair of socks at him. "Just for that, you finish unpacking. I'll go see if Lynn wants to walk down to the ocean. Do you want to come?"

"Of course," Peter replied.


When Robert returned, around four that afternoon, having successfully reserved a boat for the next day, we challenged the Steins to a game of doubles. I warned Peter that Lynn was a very strong player, and had been on the Yale women's tennis team.

During warmup he said, "There's nothing wrong with the way *you're* hitting the ball. Have you been taking lessons since our last game?"

"Of course not, why?"

"You just look a lot better, that's why." He grinned, "I think I've got myself a ringer."

I felt pleased, but answered, "Well, don't get too complacent. Lynn and Robert are tough to beat."

The Steins won the first set 7 – 5, and Peter got a determined look on his face. He told me to go up to the net whenever possible, and he would run back, if necessary, to cover the back court. After I served to Lynn, I ran to the net, and Lynn lobbed the ball neatly into my alley. I turned, dashed back to the baseline, and managed to hit a backhand cross court shot to her. She was taken by surprise and returned the ball directly to Peter to put away. Everyone stopped playing to applaud me, and I acknowledged the accolade with a small bow.

When the games were six-all we decided to play a tie breaker. The sun was getting too low in the sky, and shining in our eyes. The Steins won, but Peter was satisfied with the outcome.

"You were terrific," he said. "We nearly beat them. I can't believe you haven't been practicing."

"Scout's honor," I said, smiling.

I was secretly quite amazed at myself. I hadn't played that well since before the break-up with Walter, when I used to have a regular weekend game at the club.

Later, while toweling off after a shower, I wondered some more about my renewed athletic ability. I looked at myself in the mirror. Were my legs and arms firmer than I remembered? Moving closer to the glass, I examined my hair, the white roots were still there, but wait...I pulled out one of the hairs. It was light brown from the rinse for most of its length, then a small amount of white near the scalp, but at the extreme end the root was brown again!

I let out a gasp and sat on the edge of the tub, a burning sensation was running up the back of my neck and my heart was pounding. Was this a sign of getting younger? I wished desperately that

I could get to the lab to examine my telomere length, but I would have to wait. We had four more days of vacation. Oh, my God, I thought, what is going to happen to me?

Peter called from the bedroom, "Are you nearly finished in there, Connie? I want to take a shower too."

"I'll be right out," I answered, forcing myself to relax. I couldn't reveal my anxiety. I hung up the towel, took a few deep breaths, and opened the bathroom door.

Lynn and Robert were sitting outside on the veranda having drinks. I went into the kitchen and poured a glass of sherry from the bottle on the counter, wishing I dared to have a double scotch, or that I could take a tranquilizer. But remembering my last experience with Ativan, I decided to stick with the sherry. After a few minutes of telling myself there was no proof of anything, and that maybe the hormones had caused my hair to darken, I was able to gain some composure and went outside to join the Steins.

Lynn greeted me with, "I can't get over how you played today, Connie. It must be Peter's influence."

"Well, he's pretty competitive, and I didn't want to let him down." Was my improved tennis another sign?

"Don't tell him I said so, but I think he was lucky to have you on his side," Robert said, grinning. "Let's have a rematch tomorrow."

"I thought we were going fishing," Lynn said.

"We are," agreed her husband." But we won't be out all day. I got the boat from ten to three. We'll take a picnic lunch, and we can play later."

Peter, who had just come out on the porch with a drink, sat on the railing with his legs splayed out in front of him.

"What kind of fish are we apt to find?" he asked, looking happy and relaxed. I was glad we'd decided to come.

"Probably blues, and if we're lucky, striped bass," Robert answered. "The captain is an old-timer named Chuck, who knows all the good spots. The owners of this house told me about him."

"Are Pat and Jeanie going, too?" I asked, referring to the Steins' daughters.

"No," Lynn answered, "they're not into fishing. They'd much rather go to the beach and hang out. We should bring our bathing suits, though, because we can swim when we stop for lunch."

"This is really fun," the sherry was having a calming effect, I walked over to Peter and leaned up against him, "Isn't it, Pete?"

Peter put his arm around me and squeezed, "It sure is!" he answered.

The next day was clear and warm, with a gentle offshore breeze. Perfect for fishing, Robert announced. The fiberglass boat, painted white, was about 27 feet long. It had a cabin and a good sized deck in the stern, equipped with two fishing chairs. Captain Chuck was an affable man in his sixties, who guaranteed that we were going to find plenty of fish.

"They're running pretty good now," he told us.

My concern about what was happening to my body had returned full force on awakening that morning. I tried to put my fears away and enjoy the outing, but after catching two bluefish and putting on a show of being pleased, I announced I was going to get into a bathing suit and lie in the sun. I wanted to be alone, try to relax, and get my thoughts together.

When I emerged from the cabin, holding a towel and wearing a one-piece blue tank suit, Robert, who was seated in one of the fishing chairs and happened to be looking my way, let out a low whistle. This prompted Peter to turn around, quickly scan me, and grin with approval. Feeling flustered, I draped the towel around me and moved toward the bow of the boat.

Lynn, who had been standing at the helm, talking to Chuck, turned around to look at me and observed, "Have you lost weight, Connie? You look like a bathing beauty."

"Maybe, I don't know. I haven't weighed myself recently. Now lay off you guys, you're embarrassing me."

I went forward to lie down on the deck. Maybe I should tell them I'm on a new diet, but Peter would know that wasn't true. They'd never guess the real reason, if it turned out to be the case. The sun penetrated to my core, and it wasn't so bad to be the object of a few wolf whistles. Then I smiled. Maybe I should just enjoy the changes that might be taking place in my body and grow young gracefully.

# *Chapter 11*

*Chromosome 11* ————————————————————————

On July 5th Peter and I headed back to New York. Despite my anxiety about getting to the lab, I managed to keep thoughts of telomeres at bay while we had a light supper. Then, tired from the trip and the unaccustomed sun, we went to bed. Peter went right to sleep, but I tossed around for a long time worrying how I was going to get access to the DNA sequencer in Peter's lab without arousing his suspicion. I wanted to see if the length of my telomeres had changed. But first, I had to draw some of my blood and make a chromosome preparation. I had made one the day after I'd swallowed the potion, and I wanted to sequence both specimens to compare them.

It was very unlikely that any change in the length of my telomeres would be visible under the microscope. Nevertheless, that was the first thing I looked for on arrival in the lab. As anticipated, no visible difference was seen between the chromosomes of the earlier and later samples. The only way to see a minor change in telomere length was at the molecular level, using the sequencer. It takes approximately four to five hours for the machine to complete a single run, which was all I needed, but I wanted to be alone in the lab to avoid questions.

That afternoon, I told Peter I wanted to work late, and suggested that he return to his apartment that night. He shrugged and said, "Seeing too much of me?" but there was a twinkle in his eye.

I responded, "No, I'm just giving you a break," and kissed him soundly.

The sequencer 'reads' each individual molecule of DNA, and registers each of the four molecules of nucleic acid in a different colored "blip." Depending on the length of the DNA sample or strand, a graph is produced showing every molecule in order. At the end of the strand, the blips stop and there is a straight line. The samples I wanted sequenced were the ends of three chromosomes from the earlier and present blood samples (I had randomly picked chromosomes 1,8, and 13 from each sample to look for differences in telomere length). I waited until I was certain Peter and the other people in his lab had left, and then set up the gels with the chromosomes, each one in its own lane. Peter had given me a key to his office when we first started working together.

It was about 7:30 PM when I got the sequencing started, and I had two choices. I could go home and return very early in the morning to retrieve the printout before anyone came to work, or I could wait until the run was completed. I decided to wait, because I was never certain when Peter would appear in the morning. He had been known to arrive as early as five, depending on what experiment he was doing, or just because he was awake. I went down to the hospital cafeteria for a snack and some coffee. I was used to retiring early and wanted to avoid falling asleep at my desk again.

That morning, before coming to work, I had examined my face closely in the mirror. A tan is always becoming, and I thought I looked exceptionally well, although not necessarily any younger. The little lines around my eyes were still there. Maybe all this worry was a bunch of baloney, a product of my imagination triggered by a few compliments. It would be a relief if that turned out to be the case. There was no explanation for the dark hair roots, but there might be some hormonal or metabolic reason I didn't know about. The other possibility was just too bizarre and frightening.

These thoughts were interrupting any attempt I made at reading medical journals while I was waiting, and I didn't need to worry about falling asleep, because my adrenaline surge was taking care of that.

While at my desk, waiting for the time to elapse, I realized that I'd been doodling, unconsciously drawing what looked like a double helix of DNA going on and on endlessly. At exactly 11:30, I arose to retrieve the printouts and returned to my desk to examine the results.

The start of the telomere is indicated by the same short sequence of nucleotides or molecules of DNA, which appear over and over until the chromosome ends. At the ends of each chromosome, where the telomere began, I carefully measured the colored 'blips until they ended on the graph, comparing the new and the old specimens.

I could feel my heart knocking against my ribs as the results became clear. Without any doubt my telomeres were longer on the new specimen. I *was* getting younger. There was no longer any uncertainty about what had happened to the contents of the vial. I had swallowed it and was now in unknown territory, with no idea what would happen next.

I sat at my desk for a long time, wondering if I should tell Peter what was happening to me. I would never be able to explain what had occurred, and didn't think he would believe I had no memory of it. The best thing to do was nothing, and hope the change was transitory and that no one would ever know.

As the days progressed, my anxiety was offset by a new physical vitality. I felt wonderful! I stopped taking hormones, and my breasts were no longer tender. It appeared I had begun making enough of my own estrogen and progesterone, and the additional synthetic drugs were simply too much. Peter and I had started running together every morning. After the first few times, I had no trouble keeping up with him, and if he was puzzled by my new energy, he made no comment, probably because he was pleased to have a running companion. We spent a lot of time talking about our experiment and what the next step was going to be. Since I was leaving for Paris in a couple of weeks, we decided to put any further experiments with the altered nuclease gene on hold until I returned about mid-August.

About a week before I was due to leave I got a call from Alan. He apologized for the long delay in getting back to me and said he had been busy at work, as well as searching for a rental house for the summer, which he finally found. Then it was my turn to apologize for not getting back to him about that.

"Where did you find a house?" I asked.

"It's not by the ocean, but it's in a very nice spot on Long Island sound between Norwalk and New Haven. I got it for August. The girls are pleased because it isn't far from some movie theaters. I know you're going away soon, and wanted to see you before you go. Would you and Peter have dinner with me Friday?"

"I think it's okay. Let me check with him, and I'll call you back."

I disconnected and immediately dialed Peter's extension. After posing the question, I could hear him sigh. Then he said, "He's going to think I'm trying to avoid him, but I scheduled some interviews with candidates for Julie's place while she's on maternity leave. I don't know how long she'll be away. I want her to be there too, because she'll be better at evaluating what sort of person would be best. The only time that was good for both of us was after six. Tell him I'll plan our next reunion after you come back. I'm really sorry."

I called Alan back and relayed the message. He responded, "That's too bad, because I wanted to tell him about some of the work we've been doing, but it'll keep. Can you make it?"

I thought for a minute, then said, "I'd love to, providing I get home early."

"I promise you'll be home and in bed by ten. How's that?"

"Sounds sort of boring, but thanks."

"Your fault," he responded, "I was ready to make a night of it."

We arranged to meet in a French restaurant, La Boite en Bois, on the Upper West Side. I didn't know it, but Alan said it was recommended by one of his co-workers. I arrived ahead of him and was pleased to see how small and intimate it was. The brick walls provided the charm of a little French country inn. I had just been seated at a small table towards the rear of the restaurant when I saw Alan enter and waved to him. He came over to sit opposite me and said, "Cute place, isn't it? Doesn't look like they can seat more than twenty to thirty people." Then he did a double take and stared at me, "What have you been doing? You look wonderful, almost the way I remember you as a teenager." His brow furrowed in disbelief. "Is that telomere enhancer catching?"

My hands, which had been resting in my lap, grabbed hold of my knees in an involuntary spasm. Was it that obvious? I had forgotten he would remember me as a young girl and recognize the similarity, especially with the hiatus of thirty years. I laughed uncomfortably, "Thanks for the compliment, but I don't think I'd like to be looking like a teenager again, with all those skin problems and 'bad hair' days. If I look rested, it's probably because things have quieted down some. I was on Martha's Vineyard for a few days."

He was still examining me. "Don't knock yourself as a teenager. You were very pretty, which was one of the reasons I liked you. Well, whatever it is, you look great!"

The waiter was standing over us waiting, and I was thankful for the interruption. Alan ordered a bottle of Cabernet Sauvignon and coq au vin for both of us, oysters for him and tuna tartar for me as appetizers. When the waiter left, I immediately started asking him questions about the house he'd rented, and when that topic was exhausted I wanted to know what he was working on at Columbia. The subject of my appearance didn't come up again, but I could tell Alan was still puzzled. He kept darting glances at me when he thought I wasn't noticing.

After dinner, he took me home in his car, which he had parked in a nearby garage. When we got to my building he suddenly pulled me over and planted a firm kiss on my lips. I sat back, startled, and said, "Whoa!"

"Sorry," he said, "That was unintentional, sort of. It seemed as though we were back in Seattle in another era. I'll behave better next time."

"That's alright," I said, "Thanks for the dinner." I went up to my apartment, feeling disturbed and strangely guilty. Hmm, I thought. That kiss wasn't entirely unwelcome.

Before I left for Paris, I wanted Peter to get to know Dave and Josh a little better, so we all had dinner out the night before my departure. If I was troubled that he was going to wonder about my age when they were born, my concerns were misplaced. Peter treated us all as contemporaries. Josh was still fascinated by the telomere experiment, and once again fantasized about applying it to himself.

Peter listened with amusement and responded, "Neither of you guys should think about altering your genes. Look at your mother! Besides, we haven't any idea what the future has in store for the mice. People are always so anxious to apply medical discoveries to themselves long before there is any evidence of the long term, or short term, effects."

Naturally I found this conversation was very disturbing. Before I could be drawn into it, I excused myself and went to the ladies room, hoping the subject would be changed when I returned. Fortunately, they had switched the topic to skiing.

"We'll check out the Swiss Alps for you, Peter," Dave was saying.

"That's a little out of my league financially, Dave. How about something closer to home, like Sugarloaf?"

"Yes," I put in. "We don't want to become jet-setters."

"Look who's talking!" Peter said, grinning at me. He turned to Dave and Josh. "Take good care of your mother in those mountains, she might be a little brittle."

"Oh. She's a tough old bird, aren't you Mammy?" Josh replied.

This was better. I laughed and nodded.

The symposium on virology was held at the Pasteur Institute in Paris, with me as one of the featured speakers. My topic was the Congo River virus and its effects on the hypothalamus. I spoke about how the virus bound to known sites of hypothalamic functions, such as body temperature control and blood pressure. I didn't emphasize aging, because it was only part of my work on the hypothalamus.

However, because it was also a function that was previously unknown, most of the questions asked after my presentation had to do with that topic. I explained that finding the aging center was serendipitous, and had led to using the Congo River virus as the transport vector for the mutated nuclease gene. I did go on to stress that this was a separate issue.   The moderator agreed that using viruses for gene transport was not the topic of discussion, despite the great interest in "Dr. Gueyer's recent experiment, which has already been amply discussed."

Nevertheless, I had a difficult time escaping from the many "questioners" who surrounded me afterwards, some of whom seemed disposed to lecturing me on the ethics of tampering with natural events. The symposium continued for two more days, and no matter which lecture I attended, I was singled out for questions concerning the nuclease experiment before and after the talk. I was relieved when the conference ended and Dave and Josh arrived.

We met in the hotel lobby, and after I had hugged and kissed them both, David remarked,

"You're looking pretty good, Mom. Are you sure you came here for a virology meeting?"

Oh-oh, I thought, I wonder how this is going to work out. I quickly responded, "Well, maybe it's the vacation from lab work." adding, "We're going to Tour d'Argent tonight, a special treat from your old lady."

"What's tour dargen?" asked Josh.

"Fantastic!" David said simultaneously.

"It's a famous restaurant, especially noted for its duck. A little touristy, but worth it," I explained. "Are you tired? Do you want a nap before we go?"

"No, it's better if we just get into a normal rhythm," David answered. "I'm going to take a shower. Then let's go out and drink an aperitif or something."

I looked at my watch. "It's three now. Suppose we meet down here in half an hour. I made the reservation early for tonight because I thought you'd have jet-lag. We'll have to think of something to do between now and 7:30."

"7:30's early?" Josh marveled

"It is in Paris, Josh," answered David, suavely. He had spent a month in France during his senior year and considered himself an expert.

A short time later, we were sitting outside a small bistro facing the Tuilleries Gardens, sheltered from the sun by an umbrella, and sipping vermouth cassis. I wasn't sure I liked the bitterness, but it was a cool and eminently French aperitif. I was totally relaxed and happy, and if Peter had been there it would have been perfection.   Josh looked around at the broad boulevard and expanse of park, then settled back with a sigh of contentment, "How did the meetings go, Momma?"

"They made quite a big fuss over me. I think I was the featured speaker because of the nuclease gene experiment. I was invited to the Pasteur Institute for lunch and met with some of their geneticists. They asked so many questions, I wished Peter had been there."

Josh sat up, "Did any of them ask about doing the experiment with people?"

"Some of them alluded to it, but we all agreed that there are too many unanswered questions now. We don't know the long-term effect in mice yet."

Once again, this was hitting a little too close to home for me. I glanced at my watch, and signaled to the waiter. Swallowing the last of my drink, I said, "We have a little more time. Why don't we walk over to the Louvre. Tomorrow we can explore Paris a little more.

After a brief tour of the Louve – focusing on the DaVinci paintings, which David especially wanted to see – we went to dinner and all had the special duck. After returning to the hotel, I said, "You both must be bushed. Shall we meet in the lobby at nine?"

"How about nine thirty," Dave said. I agreed and went gratefully to bed.

Two days later we flew to Zurich and boarded the train to Klosters. We had reservations in a small chalet-hotel, just outside the village, recommended by a travel agent acquaintance of David's. It was a typical little alpine inn. My room had a window opening onto a tiny balcony with a view of the Alps in the distance and lush green meadows in the foreground.

We met downstairs to consult with the manager, Herr Bucher, about hiking the next day, and were advised that the trails ranged from easy to very difficult. I decided that after a day or two of hiking the easier trails, Dave and Josh might want to try some of the harder ones. Although they wanted us all to keep climbing together, I was fairly sure that the intermediate climbs would be enough for me.

"We'll do a lot together, and then you two should be free later to take on the advanced trails without being held up."

"Well, we'll see," Dave said.

That evening, as we were finishing dinner in the small wood paneled dining room, a middle-aged English couple seated nearby, smiled at us. The woman asked where we were from and if we'd done much climbing in the past.

"We're Americans from New York. We used to climb every year when the boys became old enough, but I'm afraid I've been a little lax in the last five years," I answered.

The woman looked puzzled, "Are you one family?"

"Yes, I'm their mother."

"My goodness! You certainly don't look a proper age to be their mother," she congratulated me. "What's your secret?"

Josh laughed, "She doesn't want to admit she's taking youth hormones."

The woman stared at me, "Well, if that's true, I'd like to find out where to get them. My name is Elizabeth Conrad, and this is my husband, Nelson."

Nelson Conrad rose to his feet and nodded to us, "Delighted to meet you. I agree with Bess, I hope you will share your secret with us. How long are you planning to stay here?"

"One week," I was feeling very anxious to leave. I was pleased to look young, but concerned over what effect this kind of talk was having on David and Josh.

I said, "I hope you'll excuse me, but we're getting an early start tomorrow. It'll be my first climb in a long time, and I'd better get to bed. I hope we'll see you tomorrow afternoon."

When we left the room, David said, "You cut them kind of short, didn't you, Mom?"

"Do you think so? I really do want to get a good night's rest. I'm sure we'll see them tomorrow and I'll try to be charming."

"It's only nine o'clock. I'm not ready to hit the sack yet, are you, Josh?"

"No way, let's wander around town a little."

"Don't stay out too late," I admonished, "we're having breakfast at six."

The following morning we were provided with a trail map and box lunches, which we put in our backpacks. Then, we set off across the green meadow behind the chalet and started the gentle upward climb into the hills beyond. The air was clear and cool and the grass heavy with dew. As the slope increased, I felt my legs responding with a spring and vigor that was surprising. We climbed steadily up, stopping occasionally to look back at the panorama below, the village seemed part of a toy train layout.

Herr Bucher had marked a spot on the map where we might want to stop for lunch, claiming it was a good half-way point for the first day, but when we arrived at the designated place it was only eleven o'clock.

"Why don't we keep going for a while," David said. "You're climbing very well, Mom."

"It's fine with me," I responded. "You okay, Josh?"

"Sure, I could go on for hours. Let's keep climbing."

We continued up for another hour, the terrain getting rockier and steeper. Looking back at Klosters now was like seeing it from an airplane. I studied the map and exclaimed, "We're on an intermediate trail now!"

"Yeah, if we keep going, we'll get to the top of one of the Alps," Josh declared. He looked ready to press on.

"Not today, Sir Hillary," I stated flatly. "Let's not overdo it. We still have six more days."

We found a flat rock overlooking the valley and sat down to eat the lunch of ham and cheese sandwiches. David produced a thermos of coffee from his pack, and poured some into the cap for us to share.

"You know, Mom, you're in pretty damn good shape. I never expected you to keep up with us so easily. What's going on with you, anyway? It must be Peter's influence." David said, answering his own question.

I nodded. "I spoke to him last night and he sends his love."

"He's really made a change in you," David persisted. "You definitely look and act a lot younger."

"Maybe I wasn't so far off last night," said Josh. "Are you sure you aren't taking a youth hormone, if there is such a thing?"

I forced a smile, "Okay, enough flattery, you must both have kissed the Blarney Stone. I think we should start down now, it's nearly two."

On the way down the mountain, I wondered how to continue explaining my youthful appearance. I had been under the impression that I looked younger than my age before taking the potion, but obviously there was a noticeable change now. If Dave and Josh were aware of it, it must really be visible since they had been seeing me regularly. Subtle changes would not have elicited any comment.

And what about Peter when I returned? Two weeks could make a big difference. How would I explain these changes to him?

I was a little worried after our conversation the previous night, as he had sounded distracted and a little upset. He denied that anything was wrong, saying it was that he missed me and wanted me to come home soon. I sensed there was something he wasn't telling me.

It was nearly six P.M. when we got back to the chalet, and Herr Bucher, the owner, was at the desk when we arrived.

"I was beginning to worry about you," he said. "Did you go for a longer hike?"

"Yes, we went up to this spot," David answered, indicating a point on the map.

"Ach, but that is a long hike for the first day! You are not tired?"

"A little," I replied, "but it was so beautiful we wanted to keep going."

"You misled me. You are all veteran climbers, no?" Herr Bucher was smiling.

"We've done a lot," Josh pointed out, "but we weren't sure how our mother would hold up. She surprised us."

"Ja, she must also be veteran, your mamma. Tomorrow you should try another intermediate trail."

He showed us the route on our map, and after thanking him we left to get ready for dinner.

The fine weather continued for the rest of our stay, and my stamina never flagged. But when Dave and Josh suggested we all try some advanced trail on the last two days, I demurred, mainly because I didn't want to cope with any more comments about my amazing athletic prowess. I told them to go without me, that I'd like a day or two to relax and explore the village. Meanwhile, I had a new worry – my period, which had been regular, was now a week overdue. I thought it might have to do with all the strenuous hiking.

## *Chapter 12*

 *Chromosome 12* ────────────────────

On August twelfth we boarded a SwissAir flight from Zurich to New York. I told Dave and Josh to sit together. I took the other assigned seat, across the aisle so I could catch up on some recent virology articles. The plane was not quite full. A rather heavyset, middle aged woman occupied the window seat, the center seat, fortunately, was empty. To forestall any possible attempts on her part to start a conversation, I removed several journals from my carry-on bag, placed them on the empty seat, and opened one up before take-off. By the time we were airborne and the seat belt lights were off, I had finished one journal and picked up another.

After scanning the index, one report in particular drew my attention. It had to do with the effect of a certain infectious virus on pregnant mice. Apparently, if the mouse was pregnant before the virus was introduced, the animal was resistant to the disease. That started me thinking about the Congo River virus, and wondering what would have happened if any of my mice had been pregnant before being infected. Would that mouse have failed to grow younger? The level of estrogen was high in pregnancy, and could probably account for a lot of unusual reactions.

Suddenly, I drew in my breath, and sat up with a jolt, causing the woman in the adjacent seat, who had been reading a book, to glance curiously in my direction. Was it possible that *I* could be pregnant? My period was late and the timing was exactly right, I had been in the middle of my menstrual cycle just before leaving for Europe, and hadn't used any contraceptive measures with Peter, assuming there was no necessity. Now, I realized that I had been very complacent, and very stupid. The changes taking place in my body would certainly have affected the ovaries, and there were other telling symptoms: slight nausea in the morning and breast tenderness for the past week, all of which I had ignored.

I glanced over at Dave and Josh, who were playing gin and were oblivious to my turmoil. What was I going to do if what I suspected was true? How could I explain to them that their nearly fifty-year-old mother was pregnant? What would Peter say, and did I want to start over with another child? How could I continue with my work and take care of a baby? Should I have an abortion and not tell anyone? I felt as if a swarm of bees had been let loose in my skull. Yet somewhere in that crazy hive was the tantalizing thought that it would be wonderful to have Peter's child.

I rose from my seat and went back to the lavatory to try and regain some composure. While splashing cold water on my face and eyes, and reapplying lipstick, I was once again struck by my youthful appearance. "I look about thirty-five," I muttered, "young enough to be pregnant."

As I stood in front of the glass, staring at my reflection, and wishing there were some outward sign to indicate what was happening, my self-examination was interrupted by someone jiggling the door. I opened it and returned to my seat, just as the stewardess arrived at my row with the drink cart. If pregnant, I should probably not be drinking alcohol, but since this was still uncertain, I decided a glass of white wine would help me relax. The woman next to me was sipping a glass of red wine and put her book aside as she smiled at me. "Are you returning from Europe or visiting the United States?"

Trapped, I thought, as I smiled back at her, "We're coming home from Switzerland. I've just been on a hiking vacation with my two sons."

"Oh, are your sons on the plane too?" she asked.

"Yes, they're sitting right over there," I said, looking across the aisle.

She followed my glance and her eyes widened in astonishment. "*Those* are your sons?"

I nodded, thinking, "Not again".

"You must have been a child bride!"

"I was very young. Where are you from?" I added hoping to change the subject.

But she was not sidetracked, "You don't look over thirty now. My daughter just got married and she's twenty-eight. Young people are waiting much longer to marry these days."

"Yes, it's wiser." I turned my head, and seeing that David and Josh had finished their game, said to them, "Do you know what movie they're showing later?"

"It's 'The Edge', Mom. Have you seen it?" asked Josh.

"Yes, it was pretty good. Maybe I'll watch it again." My seat mate had picked up her book, so I was spared further quizzing and resumed reading my journal. But nothing was registering. There was only one thing on my mind: I had to get a pregnancy test kit as soon as possible.

It was early afternoon when I finally got back to my apartment. The taxi dropped off Dave and Josh, then waited for me while I ran into a pharmacy and bought the kit. The test is positive if a blue line appears in a small window, when the tip of the device is held in the stream of urine. I held my breath as I performed the test, then held the object up to examine it. It was positive.

I left the bathroom and sat on the edge of my bed, gazing at the telephone. I wanted desperately to call Peter, but should I tell him? I felt so ambivalent. I was pretty sure he would like another chance to be a father. I knew he seldom saw his son in Ohio, but he was so dedicated to his work that he might not want anything to interfere with it. I lay back on the bed and closed my eyes, hoping to have some sort of revelation. One thought seemed to be paramount – *I* didn't want an abortion. It had to be his decision. Sitting up, I reached for the telephone and called his office – Julie answered, "Welcome home, Connie. Peter's right here."

"Connie! You're back! I didn't expect you so early. What time did you get in?"

"We were right on time, and there was no traffic for a change. How are you, darling? When am I going to see you." I was tempted to go straight to his office and tell him the news

"I wish I could drop everything and come over now, sweetheart, but I'm in the middle of some tests. Is 6:00 tonight alright?" He sounded a bit weary. I decided to wait.

"I'll try to contain myself. I've missed you."

"Same here. I love you." Peter rang off, missing my "I love you too, Peter."

I put the phone down. I would tell him the news when I saw him and could assess his reaction. Lying back on the bed again, I felt a huge sense of relief. It was much better this way. There would be no more deception. If he wanted the baby, I wanted it, too, and I was certain that there would be some way I could continue my research as well. I ought to get up and unpack. Suddenly drowsy, I closed my eyes.

I awoke disoriented. Sun was streaming on the bed, so it must be morning, I reasoned. My room in Klosters had faced east. Then, I realized I was on my bed at home, looking west at a late afternoon sun. The digital clock on the night table read 5:30! I'd been asleep for over two hours, and Peter would be coming soon.

Fifteen minutes later, showered and dressed, I put a bottle of white wine in the freezer to chill, and sat in my study to sort out mail and listen for the intercom announcing his arrival. On the dot of six it buzzed, and I ran out into the hall. When the elevator door opened I threw myself into Peter's arms. He grabbed onto me so tightly, I could hardly breathe. He lifted me off the floor, and then gave me a long hard kiss.

"God, I've missed you!" he exclaimed. Then, standing back, he appraised me. "You do look marvelous! In fact you look unbelievably *fantastic*. What on earth have you been doing?"

"Maybe it's the mountain air. You look pretty fantastic yourself." I wanted Peter to stop staring at me, as flattering as it was to be gazed at adoringly . Did I look that good?

"You've got to be kidding!" Peter shook his head in disbelief. "I've been pining away and working like a dog."

"Well, you still look fantastic to me." Taking him by the hand, I led him into my living room.

Peter couldn't stop staring at me. "I'm serious, I've never seen you looking better. It can't just be the vacation."

"Of course, it isn't. Most of it is *you*. You make me feel wonderful, and vibrant, and young. I don't think I ever felt this way before. The anticipation of seeing you was like being on some incredible high."

"I know what you mean. But I wish it had the same visible effect on me."

"It did. You just can't see yourself." I put my hands on his cheeks. "Ask anyone. You look like a man in love, I'm happy to say." I rubbed my nose on his. "Would you like a glass of wine?"

"Sure." He was still looking at me with an incredulous expression. It was making me very nervous, and I went into the kitchen and came back with a glass of wine, which I handed him. Now was the time to tell him.

"Aren't you having any?" He seemed puzzled.

"Sit down, Peter, I have something to tell you."

His look changed to concern and he sat on the arm of the couch. "What's the matter?"

"Well, I don't know how you're going to take it, but, well, it seems that I'm pregnant."

"*Pregnant!* Are you sure?" He grasped the back of the couch, his eyes wide with amazement.

"Yes I tested myself, and I have all the usual physical signs." I confirmed.

"I'm stunned," he looked it, too. "How do you feel about it?"

"Well, a lot of that depends on you, darling," I replied tentatively.

"I guess I'm in shock, but I think it's wonderful. Somehow, I never expected it to happen."

"I can't say I was expecting it, either." I walked over to where he was perched. "Do you want to have a baby, Peter? Our baby?"

He stood up, put his arm around me, and led me over to sit with him on the couch.

" Yes, I would love to have a baby, your baby, but how will this affect your research?"

"Well," I admitted. "I can't deny I've been thinking about that. It would be a bit of a problem, but I want to have your baby, Peter. Maybe we could get someone to help out after he or she is born."

Peter now was wearing an expression of pure delight. "I can't believe it! Pregnant! Of course we can get someone to help, and I'm not a total loss around the house either. But are you certain you want to go through with it?"

"Yes. I've only one request."

"What is it?"

"That we get married. It's better for the baby."

"Of course we'll get married, darling," Peter said, kissing me on the side of my head. "I was going to ask you even if you weren't pregnant. Would you still have said 'yes'?"

"Things were going so well this way, I might have hesitated, but not for very long." I kissed him back. "Are you sure you're not going to mind having someone living with you all the time?"

"I'd mind a lot if it were just 'someone', but as long as it's you it'll be alright."

I leaned forward and tweaked his nose, "Is it okay with you if we go out to eat? I just didn't feel like cooking tonight."

"Sure, where?"

"There's a little Greek restaurant two blocks away that serves delicious moussaka."

"Let's go," he grabbed my hand and pulled me to him.

A short while later, we were seated in the back of a dimly lit little restaurant, holding hands across the table and waiting for the moussaka to arrive. I was sipping seltzer with a twist of lemon. Peter had a glass of red wine in front of him. He was still beaming at me with an astonished expression.

"What have you been doing besides working?" I asked

"Not much," he shrugged. "I did go back to see Petey for a few days. I *didn't* stay with Marcia." He grinned. "Mom and Dad were home, I took Petey there with me."

"You could have stayed with her, I trust you now, I grinned back. "How's everything going at the lab?"

His smile faded. "I was waiting for you to get back from your trip to tell you. I'm a little concerned about our mice."

"Why?" My stomach lurched.

"They've been losing weight."

"Losing weight? What do you think it means? Are they sick?"

"No, they're not showing any signs of illness. In fact, they're livelier than ever. I think they may just be continuing to get younger. I've tried to stop the process by..."

He stopped in mid-sentence. My face must have been dead white.

"What is it, Connie? Do you feel sick?"

I was struggling to compose myself, but I felt faint. I must have tightened my grip on Peter's hand for a moment, then I pulled away. "Do you think they'll keep on getting younger? Are they getting any smaller?" Then, because he was looking at me with concern, I added, "It's okay, I've been getting morning sickness, which hits at odd times."

He nodded sympathetically. "That doesn't last too long, does it?

"It's usually gone by the end of the first trimester. You started telling me that you were doing something to stop the process. What is it?" My heart rate had gone up and the thumping seemed loud enough for Peter to hear.

However he didn't seem to notice and continued, "First of all, we don't know if they're getting any smaller, we just started taking measurements. Unfortunately, it never occurred to me to get an initial record of each mouse's length. What I'm experimenting with now is some way to reinfect them with the Congo River virus carrying the normal *nuclease* gene. The problem is they now have an immunity to that virus. Do you know of another we could use?"

I was feeling more and more frightened, "Not offhand, but I'll certainly search the literature tomorrow. You know, Peter, I feel like I'm about to 'whoops.' I don't think I can face moussaka, after all."

"Do you want to order something else?" he asked, concerned. A small frown appeared on his forehead.

"No. I'm really sorry about this, but I think the best thing for me to do is go to bed. It's probably a little jet lag on top of the morning sickness. I can easily go home alone. Why don't you stay and have your dinner?"

"Don't be ridiculous! I'm going to walk you home." He called over the waitress and explained that I was feeling ill. He paid for our drinks, and hand in hand, we left. But my mind was no longer on Peter, or our baby. It was on my chances of survival.

At the door to my apartment he said, "I think I should come up and get you safely in bed?"

"No, please don't, darling. I'll be fine after a little sleep. I can easily get myself into bed. It's just being in the first trimester. I was the same way when I was pregnant with Dave and Josh." Peter still looked worried, but let me kiss him goodnight. The minute the door closed, I collapsed on the couch, my heart pounding in every cell of my body. The mice were losing weight and, according to Peter, getting steadily younger. They might start getting smaller, too, and then? I couldn't bear to contemplate what might eventually happen if he was right. I stared blindly at the bookshelf in front of me.

Why had I never considered the possibility that the mice would continue to grow young? I had stupidly assumed that the process would be self limiting, but what was apparently happening now made perfect sense. There was nothing to block the action of telomerase, and it would just go on adding length to the telomeres. What I didn't want to accept was that if they continued to grow young they would eventually become helpless infants, and even if they were given a surrogate mother, they would get more and more immature until they died. Could that be my fate, too?

I got up from the couch. There was no way I could sleep without some help. I fished around in my travel case, found some sleeping pills, and swallowed one. Then, ignoring the rest of my unpacked luggage, I undressed and got into bed. I lay there a long time, trying to quash the image of me as a young child being tended to by Peter. And Dave and Josh? It was unthinkable. How long would it take before I was their ages?

# *Chapter 13*

 *Chromosome 13* ——————————————————————

My sleep had been deep but not very restful. I awoke shortly before seven and lay quietly for a moment, pleased to be in my own bed. Then, with a sudden jolt of panic, memory returned, and I sat up abruptly, fighting a wave of nausea.  The movement of my head had produced a dull pounding headache, and my mouth felt lined with Kleenex. After several deep breaths, I managed to get to the medicine cabinet in the bathroom, and downed two aspirin tablets. The sky outside the bedroom window was darkly overcast, and I could see a tree on the street below swaying wildly. A major storm seemed imminent, and I had to get to the lab before it became impossible to find a taxi. I needed to see those mice for myself and learn what was in store for me.

Dressing quickly, I brushed past my unpacked bags and hurried out the door. A few drops of rain had begun to fall when I hailed a cab, and we got to Bailey in the middle of a violent summer storm. Thunder, lightning, and high winds were metaphors for my state of mind.

I didn't expect anyone to be in the animal room so early in the morning, and was surprised to find the light on and the door open. Peter was standing at the far end of the room with Saki. Both had their backs to the door and appeared to be examining several cages of mice on the counter in front of them. They didn't see me. Saki was speaking in a low voice, "....a week ago and today they seem to have lost an average of about one centimeter in length."

I stood silently, straining to hear.

"It's happening pretty fast," Peter said.

I had turned to stone. I could not breath. At that moment Saki turned and saw me in the doorway. "Hello, Connie! Welcome home!"

Peter whirled around exclaiming, "I didn't expect you here so early. How do you feel today?"

"Better, thanks," I lied. "I just needed some sleep. Tell me what you were talking about. I only heard the last part, that they're getting shorter." I tried to control the trembling of my legs by tightening the muscles.

"Yes, we were discussing the mice. They're losing length as well as weight." He continued, as if thinking out loud. "They received the altered gene on March 28 and it's now August 20. The normal life span for mice is around two years, which they were when we injected them. If they are now at the stage where they are losing weight and skeletal mass, and continuing to add length to their telomeres, they must be close to infancy...somewhere in the vicinity of six weeks to one month old. That means that every month they regressed three to four months, or about one sixth of their total life span. If we're going to stop this spiral we'll have to come up with something pretty damn fast, or we'll be left with non-viable embryos."

Now there was nothing I could do to stop the trembling. I feverishly tried to calculate the ratio of mouse to human regression. If every month a mouse regresses a sixth of his life span, and if I were getting younger at the same rate, and the average human life span is around seventy-five years, I would be losing around twelve years every month. It *couldn't* be happening to me at that same rate, because I would now be a child. There had to be something wrong with my calculation, but I was too muddled to figure it out.

My face must have registered some of these thoughts, and I became aware that Peter was looking at me with an anxious expression. When our eyes met for an instant, I immediately lowered mine. Undeterred, he walked across the floor to me and said quietly, "Come down to my office for a minute, Connie." I followed him down the stairs, unable to respond. After he had closed his office door, he put his arm around me, and led me to the couch.

"Now I want you to tell me what's going on, Connie" he said firmly after we were both seated. "You're obviously having a problem with something, and it isn't just the baby, is it?"

Suddenly I felt an enormous urge to unburden myself. I realized that, to get through this, I had  to have his help and advice, regardless of the consequences. Besides, I was so frightened, nothing else mattered. Clasping my hands in front of my face, I muttered, "I don't know how to tell you this, Peter."

He dropped his arm from my shoulder and his eyes narrowed., "What? What is it?"

I squirmed sideways on the couch away from him and moved my hands up the side of my head to press against my temples. "Oh God, Peter! This is so hard to explain," I took a deep breath before continuing in a hesitant voice. "Do you remember back in May, when we were having all those misunderstandings, and I saw you with Julie? Well, that really put me in a terrible state. I was very depressed, even fantasizing that you loved her, and not me. I wasn't completely rational, at that time. In fact, I just felt as though the bottom had dropped out of my world. I knew I needed to calm down and remembered I had kept some Ativan in my desk. I took two of them and they must have really knocked me for a loop, because as a result, I did something very stupid."

Peter was sitting immobile, staring at me.

"Go on."

Summoning up all my courage, I continued, "I went to the refrigerator, half-drugged, actually, and removed the flask containing the preparation we made for the experimental animals. I didn't remember doing it when I first came to, but I found an empty paper cup on my desk, and retraced my steps. When I saw the calibrating flask in the sink, it all came back.

"Yes, so...?"

"Well," this was even harder than I expected. "I...I had measured out and swallowed some of the viral preparation." I couldn't look at him.

"You did *what?*" he gasped, His face was white.

"I swallowed it," I repeated miserably, "I prayed it wouldn't have an effect on me, but then I started changing...getting younger."

He stood up and looked down at me, an expression of incredulity on his face. "How could you possibly have done such a thing?'

I was hugging myself and staring blankly at my knees. How was I going to make him understand? "I don't know, I was very angry at you, and miserable over the prospect of life without you. That, plus the effect of the tranquilizer pushed me over the edge. I felt drunk, and I remember thinking if I were younger..." My voice cracked. I couldn't go on.

Peter's eyes were closed and his lips pressed together. I could see the muscles working in his jaw. After what seemed an eternity of silence, I whispered, "Say something."

"How long have you known?" he asked in a monotone.

"Since the weekend of July 4th. I suspected something when we were at the Steins, and I ran some tests when we returned. I'd taken some of my blood when I found the empty vial. This time, my telomeres had gotten longer."

"Why didn't you tell me then?" He demanded, a mixture of hurt and anger in his voice.

"I was too ashamed, I guess. I couldn't believe I had done such a thing. I've gone over it a thousand times in my head. I was a little crazy. I thought I was too old, and that you didn't have any interest in me for that reason. I thought you wanted to have more children, and I wouldn't be able to bear them. I was beginning to have symptoms of menopause, and I just felt everything was over for me. When you told me you loved me the next day, I'd have given the world to know I hadn't done it." I started to cry.

Peter walked over to the window and stood with his back to me. I continued to weep quietly, wishing he would come over and comfort me, but he continued to stand there studying the grey sky and dark buildings of the campus. Finally, he spoke in a deep muffled voice as though forcing the words out.

"You told me that the reason you looked so well was because of me, and I believed you. I thought it was because you were happy and because you were pregnant. Oh my God! If this is really happening to you, there's no way you should have a baby." He clasped the back of his neck with both hands, and I could see his fingers whiten with tension. "How could you possibly think I'd want you to go through with a pregnancy under these circumstances?"

"I wanted to have your baby. I didn't know then about the mice." I sobbed. There was no way to describe the pain I was feeling.

He turned now to face me angrily. "It doesn't make a damn bit of difference whether the mice are getting younger or older. The point is, neither of us has any idea about the long-term effects of the experiment. You, as a scientist, should have been aware of that, even in your drugged state."

He was right, and I knew it. If there had been a gun in my hand at that moment, I'd have held it to my head and pulled the trigger, I was so miserable. I couldn't explain to myself what had happened that night. Try as I might, there was no rationale for my action. With tears running down my face, I pleaded, "Peter, please, I need you to understand. I was in a daze. When the drug wore off, I was devastated, frightened and mortified by what I'd done. I hoped it wouldn't work in humans, and when it did, I thought it would be a temporary change. That's what seemed to be happening to the mice."

"Were you going to keep it a secret forever? Didn't you trust me enough to tell me?"

"I was afraid you'd leave me. I knew I'd done something inexcusable."

He took a deep ragged breath, held his hand over his mouth, and turned away again. His shoulders heaved and I could tell he was now crying too. I got up from the couch and approached him, wanting to put my arms around him. When I touched his back he pulled away sharply. "No, just leave me alone for a minute," he said in a hoarse voice.

I backed away, holding a strangled sob in my throat. After a few moments I said softly, "I need your help, Peter. I'm frightened."

Once more, gazing out the window, he said, "Yes, you must be."

Then, seeming to straighten his shoulders, he took out a handkerchief, blew his nose, and turned around to face me. "I don't know how much time we're going to have. Do you have any idea what your approximate age is now? I'd guess late thirties." He made this statement in a dry, matter-of-fact voice that wrenched at my guts.

"I think that's about right," I answered in a whisper.

"At that rate, there's no possibility of your sustaining a pregnancy for eight more months. You've already lost about ten years in three months. That's a little slower than the mice, but not if you consider their life expectancy. You would probably have a natural abortion in two to three months, so it's better to have it now before you start to look pregnant."

I had returned to the couch and sat slumped over, all my earlier fears replaced by an overwhelming depression. Peter continued speaking in a cold, precise way I had never before heard him use.

"I'm working now on some way to try and reinfect the mice, maybe using another virus. You're more knowledgeable about viruses than I am, and I suggest you look into the method of antibody reversal, although it doesn't appear to work with this virus, because I tried it. But there may be some alternative I don't know about. You may have access to another neurotropic virus that could be used for transport, or you should start looking for one."

I shook my head. It was pure chance that had led me to the aging center in the hypothalamus. I knew of no other virus that would affect that area..

"Even if we succeed in finding a way of restoring the nuclease gene," he continued, "there's no telling how the mice will respond. That will have to be determined before you try anything. There's a possibility that they could suddenly show rapid aging."

"I'd rather have that happen," I mumbled. I felt terribly alone, like an alien on a remote planet. "If I'm doomed either way, I'd rather die old than as an infant. It would be too devastating for Dave and Josh," I glanced at Peter, who was pacing the floor with his right hand pressing the nape of his neck as if to support his head. He seemed not to have heard me. I got up from the couch, head down, shoulders slouched, and walked to the door. He didn't stop me when I opened it and walked out, closing it softly behind me.

I stumbled up the flight of stairs and down the dark, empty hallway leading to my office like a blind woman, touching the wall for guidance. It didn't matter anymore whether I lived or died. I knew Peter was shocked and disgusted with me. The fact that I was drugged was immaterial, I had done it – committed what to him was a mortal sin. I suppose I could have told him that others in the past had used themselves as guinea pigs in the interest of science, but he and I both knew that was not my reason. The true reason he was so angry and cold was that I hadn't told him before today. Maybe he was right. Maybe if I had said something about it right away...but I had just found out he loved me, I couldn't risk it then. And later, when I was sure I must have known how he would have responded, and I didn't want to face it.

Somehow I had arrived in my office and I sat hunched at the desk, forehead pressed to my folded arms. I saw myself getting younger and younger, eventually becoming a child, and then a toddler, barely able to speak or to walk. Being cared for by whom? Surely not my own sons, that was too incongruous. I now had two alternatives – neither appealing: to die now by some rigged-up accident, or to have an abortion and try to reverse what was happening to me.

If I chose to kill myself, I would have to make it appear accidental. Suicide would be devastating to Dave and Josh. Maybe a laboratory accident with a lethal virus, but that would endanger others. An automobile accident? That was too uncertain, unless I drove a car off a cliff and it would clearly be called suicide.

I shook myself out of that train of thought. Killing myself was the coward's way out. I didn't want to end my life on that note. I may have lost Peter's love, but I still had a chance to salvage my self-respect, and maybe gain back some of his. I had to pull myself together and proceed as a scientist. Taking a deep breath, I raised my head. The room seemed lighter. Turning to the window, I saw the rain had stopped and some sunlight was slanting through the clouds. It reminded me of 'Hope' in Pandora's box.

I rose from the chair and paced around the small office, trying to marshal my thoughts. Peter had said the mice were now immune to the Congo River virus, and hence it could not be used to carry the normal nuclease gene. That might not, however, apply to me. The first step would be to test my blood for Congo River virus antibodies. Peter had all the reagents for the test in his lab, but I couldn't go back there. I would have to requisition them from central supply. No, that would take too long, I realized. So I would have to go and get them myself.

It was now close to 8:30 A.M., and people would begin arriving in the various laboratories. I didn't want to talk to anyone, so I opened the door to the hall tentatively and glanced out. Then, seeing no one, I hastened to the elevator, pressed the button, and was poised to enter when the door opened and I collided with Lynn, who was getting off.

"Connie! I was just coming to see you. I called you at home and decided you might be here when your answering machine came on. My first appointment was canceled this morning, so I decided to see if you were here. I've missed you! How was your vacation?"

I stopped breathing and backed up, incapable of dealing with this encounter.

"Uh...Hi, Lynn."

"What's the matter? You look like you've seen a ghost. Did I scare you?" She peered curiously at me.

"Oh...no, no. I was just going to get some stuff I need for the lab."

"Well, come back and talk to me for a few minutes first. I want to hear what you've been up to!"

I couldn't think of a response, so I allowed Lynn to take me by the arm and propel me back down the hallway to my office. When we were both seated, facing each other she said, "So, tell me about it. You know, outside of acting like a frightened rabbit, you look marvelous. The vacation must have been good for you?"

I was trapped, and I knew that I couldn't lie to Lynn, so I took a deep, jagged breath, leaned back in the chair and focused on the wall to my left. "Lynn, you're not going to believe what I'm going to tell you, and if you do, you'll think I'm insane." I paused. " I have a terrible problem."

I couldn't look at her, but her voice was sympathetic. "It can't be that bad, Connie. Tell me about it. And, by the way, I think I know you well enough to testify to your sanity."

I continued to study the wall and said, "You may not know me as well as you think you do. And, as to my sanity..." My hands squeezed together, "You remember in May when we had lunch and I was so uncertain about Peter. I never told you what happened that night."

She listened without interruption, except for a gasp when I told her about swallowing the mutated viral preparation, and another when I said the mice were continuing to get younger. When I finished speaking, I turned toward her. Her face was white and she shook her head mutely. After a long moment of silence, she sighed deeply, "Oh, God, Connie." I could feel my eyes welling with tears again. Finally she spoke, "You said Peter was trying to reverse the process. What's he doing?"

"He was trying to get the normal nuclease gene back into the mice, but they're immune to the viral vector we used, the Congo River virus. He wants me to see if I can come up with a new virus, but I don't know any that affect the hypothalamus. He is totally shocked by what I did, and I don't think he cares that I was drugged." Now I was crying openly. "He's acting so cold and remote, like he doesn't know me or love me anymore."

"Connie, I'm certain he's in shock, just as I am. You have to suspend any assumptions right now. What were you going to get when I ran into you?"

"Some chemicals to check my antibody titer to the Congo River virus. I want to determine if I'm immune to it too."

Lynn got to her feet and came over to my side of the desk. "Come on, I'll go down there with you. You probably could use some help at this point." She held out her hand.

I looked at her and burst into uncontrollable sobs as she bent down and put her arms around me.

*Chapter 14*

$\textbf{a b}$  *Chromosome 14* ────────────────────────────

Once we had assembled the necessary materials, it didn't take very long to test my blood for antibodies to the Congo River virus. To my dismay, I had them, just as the mice did. I, too was immune to reinfection, so that avenue of escape was closed. Although this didn't come as a big surprise to me, it did make me more depressed. However, Lynn was wonderful, a true friend in need. She refused to let me lose hope, and advised me to do a computer search for another virus. I was not very optimistic about finding one, since the Congo virus was new in the annals of medicine, the way AIDS had been in the 1980s. It had, fortunately, been contained, and any new virus with similar characteristics would surely have been publicized by the media. I said as much to Lynn, but she insisted I look anyway. Meanwhile, she was going to speak to Peter and find out if he had any new ideas. I shook my head mutely and went back to my office to search the internet.

After a lengthy perusal of *medline* on the internet, including current journals on virology and infectious diseases, I came up with nothing. I half-expected Lynn to have returned, as I had been searching for several hours, and assumed she had gone back to the hospital. I went into the lab. It was empty. Saki must have left early, or still be working with Peter. I tried unsuccessfully to focus on what to do next. I could not stop my thoughts from returning to the image of what would happen to me as I became younger and younger, slowly losing brain power in a reversal of the normal losses of aging. My demise would be finite and everyone would see it coming. Eventually I would not be able to comprehend what was happening to me, but those who could would find it terrible. I didn't know how long I would have the ability to think as a scientist, but imagined I would be aware of the onset of failing perception. But by then I could easily be in my early teens, and clearly recognizable as a teenager.

I tried to recall how I had been then. Was my brain fully functional? I remembered reading that the physicist, Stephen Hawking, had theorized: If the universe ceased to expand and started to implode on itself because of gravitational pull, time would flow backward. He subsequently changed his mind about this, but at the time his theory meant that on Earth, history would proceed backward to the dawn of civilization, to the birth of the planet, and eventually to the big bang. Time had certainly reversed itself in my body. Was I a minuscule example of what was to come? Had he been right after all? When we played around with telomeres, were we interfering with the laws of physics as well as biology? I shuddered. I was certain of one thing, when I reached the point of intellectual regression, I would end my life, but until then I had to keep working to find a solution.

I shook my head deliberately to clear my thoughts and return to the matter at hand. There wasn't much time. I had to think of something. The door to my office opened quietly and Lynn stuck her head in. Seeing me sitting at the desk, she said, "Good, I'm glad you're here," and walked in closing the door behind her. "I've just had a long conversation with Peter and I think he's come up with something."

"What? How's he acting?"

She sat on the chair opposite the desk. "Well, he's in a state of shock, and he's upset that you didn't trust him enough to tell him much earlier, but he still intends to try to help you. He wasn't surprised to learn you have antibodies to the virus, and he went to see Gordon Simms, the oncologist."

"Whatever for?" For a moment I thought the mice had developed tumors.

"It makes good sense. He explained that the animals were continuing to grow young, and he thought he might be able to stop the process by reinfecting them with the virus to which they were now immune. He wanted to depress their immune systems with chemotherapy."

Why hadn't I thought of that possibility? I wondered. It was like a ray of light in a black tomb. But even as my spirits rose a notch, I thought of Peter, his scientific mind always at work, the emotional part deeply buried and suppressed. I knew that I, too, would have to become more like that if I was to survive. Still, it was good to know he was trying so hard to help.

"Did he say anything to Simms about me?" I asked, with some trepidation.

"No. He just inquired about which drugs to give and their dosages. But he was very clever. He knew Simms wouldn't know the dose for mice, so he asked what to do if he were treating a human, and said he could extrapolate to mice. Simms of course, knew all about the nuclease gene experiment and its result. He was very glad to help in any way, told him all the pitfalls of the large doses of chemo needed to sufficiently weaken the immune response. I know about them because we use them in leukemia patients who have marrow transplants. The main problem, as you know, is susceptibility to any infection." She stopped for a moment and looked at me intently.

"If Peter is going to use chemotherapy on the mice, he has to devise a way to keep them in a sterile environment, and isolated from each other. But the other problem is the bone marrow, since high doses of chemo knock it out. While this is necessary in the treatment of leukemia, when you want to transplant cancer-free marrow, if you only want to weaken the immune system enough to allow for reinfection with the Congo virus, you would not want to destroy the marrow. The problem is, in the mice, it would be difficult to know exactly what the effect of the chemotherapy would be. So it might be advisable to take some marrow before treatment in case it becomes necessary to implant it."

"Well, I wouldn't need that, would I?"

"Probably not, but your blood count would have to be closely monitored. It actually wouldn't be a bad idea to have some of your marrow in reserve, because you are probably going to need big doses of chemo to get sufficient depression of your immune system and enable the Congo River virus to reinfect you ."

"How long would this take?" I said, getting up from the chair, and going to the window to lean against the sill. I was getting restless, hoping that I wouldn't have to wait until Peter was certain of the results in the mice.

"It doesn't take long to depress the marrow, maybe a week. But then you would have to see if they become reinfected and if the normal nuclease gene is having an effect. You would know more about how long that takes than I do."

I did. It was too long for me, but I knew Peter would insist that we wait for the results in the mice before I started the drugs. We had waited three weeks to examine them after they received the mutated gene and by then they were clearly younger. But it wasn't necessary to wait that long to see the beginnings of a change. If they were going to start getting older, there would be subtle alterations, such as decrease in telomere length, increase in sugar proteins, and possibly early weight gain and growth. If there was a trend in that direction I wanted to start the drugs immediately.

I explained this to Lynn. There had been no reason to hurry then, but there was now. I had told her I was pregnant and had to have an abortion, so now it became even more pressing. But Lynn, as usual, was way ahead of me.

"Connie," she said, coming over to where I was standing and putting her arm around me,

"Peter thinks you should have the abortion as soon as possible, particularly if you are going to have chemotherapy. You would probably abort then anyway, and it would only make for more possible complications, including risk of sepsis. I'll take you to a gynecologist I know who isn't connected to this center." She squeezed my shoulders with her arm."I know this is tough, but should I set it up?"

Reluctantly, I nodded, "I was just thinking about it. I know I have to do it. Now that Peter doesn't want the baby anymore." I looked down at my feet, trying not to cry. Were any tears left in me? "Can we do it soon?"

"I'll call right now and see when he can do it, but I also want to tell you that it wasn't an easy decision for Peter either. He really wanted that baby." She picked up the telephone.

The appointment was made with a Dr. Langland, whose office was in Englewood, New Jersey. He apparently knew Lynn, and agreed to see me in his office after hours that day. Lynn said she would drive me there. The route took us across the George Washington Bridge, and up the Palisades parkway, a scenic drive I normally enjoyed. This time, it might just as well have been shrouded in dense fog. I saw nothing. Lynn and I didn't talk much either. I was preoccupied with the impending loss of the baby, Peter's child, and what I felt was my last link to him.

The prospect of large doses of chemo loomed like an evil specter. Lynn had told me that I would have to be kept from all contact with people during the time I was immunosuppressed, and I wasn't sure how this was going to be accomplished except in the hospital. I knew for certain that I would not want that, and I finally broke the silence by asking her if hospitalization was a necessity. She continued to look at the road ahead, and then, after a few moments of hesitation, replied, "It could probably be done in your apartment, but you have to be strict about not letting anyone in to see you, even delivery boys. I think we're a little ahead of ourselves here, Connie. We have to wait to see if the mice have a good response first."

I didn't respond, but I was thinking: if this is my only option, why does that matter?

When I entered Dr. Langland's office building, which he shared with three other gynecologists, there were four women in the waiting room, only one of whom looked pregnant. I wondered how many of them were also there for fetus removal. Two were reading magazines and seemed serene, the obviously pregnant one was busy knitting, the fourth was the one I suspected might be coming for an abortion. She was very young, in her late teens, I guessed, and she played with her fingers while sitting on the edge of her chair. When I had come into the room, she was the only one who glanced at me and quickly looked away.

A nurse appeared at the entrance and called two names, one the young girl's. She jerked her head up, picked her bag off the floor, and darted another look at me. I noticed that she, too, wasn't wearing a wedding ring. Was she also going to see Dr. Langland?

A few minutes later my name was called. It wasn't really my name, but one that Lynn had invented for me. I didn't respond at first, but when the nurse called it again I jumped up. I followed the nurse to an examining room, and was told to disrobe from the waist down and put on a gown. "What am I doing here?" I asked myself, feeling a sense of unreality. This was just a routine gynecological examination and I wasn't pregnant. If I thought about the life that was being snuffed out, I would lose my self control.

When Dr. Langland entered the examining room, he greeted me and asked how Lynn was. It was as if I was dropping by for tea, and calculated to put me at ease. Unfortunately it had no effect. I must have looked nervous, and he said, "Have you ever had an abortion before?" When I said "No," he described the procedure, saying it was somewhat painful, but of short duration, and later I would have cramps for a few hours, which he could control with medication. He questioned me about previous pregnancies, and general health, then told me to get on the table with my feet in the stirrups. Just a routine exam, I said silently. A speculum was inserted, and then the nurse handed the doctor a suction instrument. He said, "This will be over in a minute," and I felt a sudden very sharp pain, followed by an intense cramp, that took my breath away.

"It's all over now, just lie here for a few minutes, until you feel like getting up. You may have some bleeding, and you should use a sanitary napkin, but no tampons. I'll have a prescription for some codeine at the desk when you leave."

So, that was it. All over, no more baby. I was thankful, in a way, that it was painful. I wanted to feel the pain for a life lost so easily. The cramps let up a little and the nurse, who stayed in the room, helped me sit up. I managed to get dressed and pick up the prescription. There was no sign of the young girl, and I hoped she was okay.

Lynn was waiting in the car, my self control vanished when I saw her. I started to cry silently, and Lynn put her hand over mine and squeezed it. She didn't say anything, but I could feel her empathy. After a while I said, "Thanks, I don't know what I would have done without you."

"Don't thank me. I know you'd do the same for me if I needed it. I'm going to drive you home, and I'll stay the night. I called Robert and set it up while you were seeing the doctor."

"You're amazing. No wonder you're such a good pediatrician," I said, wiping my eyes, "you always sense what is needed." I had been dreading going home alone. We stopped on the way to get the codeine for my cramps, which were quite severe, and drove the rest of the way in silence.

The next day I asked Lynn to accompany me while I talked to Peter. I didn't want to face him alone. I wondered what he had said to make Lynn feel he wanted the baby, but I was too depressed to ask. As we entered his office, he gave me a long, searching look which I found hard to interpret. He quickly reverted to the business-like attitude of the previous day. When we were seated he said, "I gather Lynn has told you about my conversation with Simms." I nodded, and he continued, "I've started the mice on chemotherapy, and as soon as they are suitably immunosuppressed we'll challenge them with the Congo River virus. I don't think we'll have any results for several weeks. We'll just have to wait."

I shook my head, "Peter, what's the alternative? It really doesn't matter what happens to the mice. I have to take a chance on this because there is nothing else."

Lynn and Peter started speaking at the same time and Peter won out, "For God's sake Connie, I don't know if this is going to kill them, or have another effect on them. The mice could grow old immediately, for all I know. You've waited this long, you can wait a few weeks more. Don't make the same mistake twice."

That was hitting below the belt, I looked at Lynn, but she was nodding in agreement. "You must wait, Connie. What's the point of putting yourself through a miserable course of chemotherapy if it doesn't work. Maybe there is an alternative. Something might turn up."

I was outvoted, and I needed them. I knew I could count on Lynn to understand my desperation, but all I was getting from Peter was the scientific approach. I could have been another laboratory animal. Yet, he had given me that look – sadness, disappointment, or was it regret? Whatever it was, he would not tell me. I flashed a glance at Lynn, and then said very quietly to Peter, "I've had the abortion."

He looked away, and I couldn't see his expression. When he turned back to face me, there were tears in his eyes, and he said very quietly, "I'm sorry, Connie. I guess we didn't have any other choice."

Lynn, who was sitting beside me on the couch, put her hand over mine and said, "I told Connie that if she does receive chemotherapy, she can stay isolated in her apartment. It's not as safe as staying in isolation in the hospital, but I can't admit her, and word would get around that she's there if she's another doctor's patient. This way I could come in periodically to monitor her blood, and see if she needs anything. Of course, I would see to it that she maintains strict isolation. Only I would be able to see her."

"That sounds alright," Peter responded, "I should have some inkling about the mice at the end of two weeks. It'll probably be only at the telomere level in the beginning. I think we should wait until we see what other effects there are, if any."

There was nothing more for me to say except, "Okay, thanks." I rose from the couch and Lynn followed me out the door. When we were alone in the hall she took my arm. "He's right, you know. Two weeks isn't going to make that much difference."

"Maybe not, but it can't be much longer than that," I answered, looking at my unblemished hands. "I never thought I'd be happy to see liver spots and prominent veins."

During the waiting period, Lynn and Robert did their best to keep me occupied. They took me to the movies, out to dinner, and invited me to spend the weekends with them. Lynn asked me if she could tell Robert what was happening and I consented, knowing it would go no further. My contacts with Peter remained cool and professional. He called me periodically, but only to keep me informed about the status of the mice. I had several telephone conversations with David and Josh, during which I tried to sound normal, and I must have succeeded, because they made no comment to the contrary. There was no way of knowing what Julie and Saki thought about the obvious change in Peter's and my relationship. If they did notice anything, they kept it to themselves.

It was the end of August, and there was a late summer lethargy about the campus with many of the students and faculty on vacation. The hot humid weather and diminished activity added to my depression and made it difficult for me to work at anything, I spent a lot of time on the internet, searching fruitlessly for something I might have overlooked that would provide an alternative to the chemotherapy. After two weeks of this, I was exhausted, and had just finished one of these sessions, when the phone rang. It was Alan. I took a deep breath and tried to sound upbeat. It wasn't easy.

"Hi Alan, are you back? It's not the end of August yet. How did the house work out?"

"The house was fine. It was a four-week rental, and that was long enough. The girls had a great time. We had a visiting membership at a beach club, and they met some boys, so that took care of everything – from their point of view. There wasn't a helluva lot for me to do. I met several unattached women, and took a couple out to dinner. They were nice enough, but nothing special. Anyway, it was relaxing. I played some tennis and a few rounds of lousy golf. How was your trip?"

Oh God, I thought, how can I keep up this banter? I tried. "It was fine. Dave and Josh had a good time. We did a lot of hiking in the mountains."

"Any chance of seeing you?" Alan asked, "It's easier to assess a person face to face."

I considered his question. Alan was a friend – one I knew and trusted. Maybe I should see him. I answered somewhat flirtatiously, "Why do you want to assess me? You already know me."

"I don't know. I just have a feeling you need assessing from time to time. You might need an oil change. So, when do I get to see you?"

An oil change? I needed a complete overhauling. "When do you want to meet?" I parried.

"Tonight? Is that too soon? Will Peter be joining us?"

"No, he can't, but it's okay for me. What time?" While I was saying this, I wondered about my ease in saying Peter was busy. I didn't want to ask him to join us. In fact, I didn't even know if he'd want to.

After a pause Alan said, "I'll pick you up in my car at six. Can you be downstairs? I assume you'll still be at work."

"Yes, I'll be there." I promised. After I hung up, I sat back in my chair. What the hell was I trying to do? Did I think I was going to be able to keep up this charade? I knew I needed a beacon in the present gloom of my life. Alan, like Lynn, had the ability to provide one, even if it was only temporary.

I was standing on the front steps of the Lab building at six, waiting for Alan, when the door behind me opened. I felt a tap on my shoulder, and looked around, surprised. It was Peter. Now I was in a quandary.

"Waiting for someone, Connie?" He asked, keeping his hand on my shoulder.

I had no choice but to answer, "Yes, Alan is taking me to dinner."

Peter removed his hand, "Oh, that's nice," he replied, cooly. "I imagine he'll be able to cheer you up." I detected a note of sadness. Then he added, "I wish I could provide it. I hope you have a nice time. Give him my regards." He kissed me briefly on the cheek and strode away towards the subway.

A few minutes later, Alan drove up. He leaned over to open the door, saying, "Sorry, were you waiting long?"

I got in and said, "No, I just came down." I smiled at Alan. He was such a nice guy.

Alan looked at me intently, "You look younger than ever, I'll be accused of cradle snatching. You must be still on vacation." I was prepared for this now. It was becoming an old refrain. I would have given my right arm to hear someone say I looked tired and haggard.

"It's misleading," I answered, "I've been hard at work. I think I need more than an oil change. You look very well yourself. How's the work going?"

Alan put the car into drive and pulled away from the curb. "Work's okay, nothing new and exciting to report, but I just got back. I'm taking you to a great little Japanese restaurant downtown where we can get a tatami room."

"Very intimate," I murmured approvingly, "How did you find it?"

"Word of mouth. We have a Japanese post doc working at the lab. Hope he's a gourmet."

I didn't have much appetite, but hoped I could fake it. I was beginning to worry that this was not such a good idea. I managed to keep a conversation going, mostly about his daughters, while he drove down the West Side highway and found a garage in Soho two blocks from the restaurant which was named Omen. Did that have a special significance?

The interior was elegant, with scrolls and lacquered objects on the walls. Expensive, I thought. We were shown to a tatami room with bamboo and parchment sliding partitions. We had to remove our shoes in order to enter, but thankfully there was a well for western legs under the low table, and we weren't forced to sit yoga style, a position I can maintain for about one minute. We ordered hot saki for two, and even though it was warm and humid outside, it was pleasantly cool in the room. As we were sipping the saki from tiny ceramic cups, Alan looked at me intently, his eyes slightly narrowed. I began to feel very uncomfortable under this scrutiny and was about to object, when he said, "You were right, you don't need an oil change. You don't need anything done to your chassis, but I detect a problem. You don't seem very happy. Is everything okay with you and Peter?"

So much for my attempted coverup, Alan could see right through it. "I guess I'm not a very good actress. We are having a few problems right now," I said, wishing it was that simple. Alan nodded his head with concern, "I'm sorry" was all he said. I waited thinking he would say more, but he remained silent. After a pause, while I wondered what to say next, I was relieved of the problem by the waitress entering the small room in her white socks and placing covered bowls of soup before us. Alan removed the black and red lacquered cover from his bowl and started to spoon the clear soup into his mouth. I waited for an instant, then did the same.

After several moments of silence, he laid his spoon down and said, "I don't want to pry, but if you want to talk about it I'll listen. If not, we'll talk about other things."

I stopped putting the spoon to my mouth and said, "Thanks, Alan. I don't think I can talk about it right now, it's very complicated." At that moment I would have liked very much to unburden myself, but knew I wouldn't be able to cope with Alan's incredulity.

Alan picked up his bowl and drank the remnants of the soup. When he finished he wiped his mouth with the napkin and said, "Okay, anything new with your telomere experiment?"

Little did he know, this topic was no better. I pushed the soup aside and lied, "No, they still look about the same."

He looked puzzled and said, "Do you mean they're static, they haven't aged or regressed more?"

I had to clarify. "Well, the problem is now that they seem to be losing weight. We have to run some tests to see what's causing that." Now I was desperate to get away from this topic. My face must have registered unease, for his look of concern was suddenly replaced by one of skepticism. At that moment the waitress reentered to take the soup bowls and place platters of sushi and sashimi in front of us. I had no appetite now, I wondered how I ever thought going out with Alan would be therapeutic.

When we were alone he said, "Come on, Connie. Something is troubling you. I'd like to help, but don't feel you have to say anything. I have the idea that your problem with Peter is connected to the mice, and you don't want to discuss either. Right?"

I nodded mutely. He continued, "So, we'll talk about other things, and I won't put you through any more third degree stuff. Cheer up and eat some sushi. It's delicious."

I smiled, feeling relieved and said, "You are a great guy, Alan. Thanks for being so understanding. Someday I hope to be less mysterious." There was something therapeutic about him after all. I picked up my chopsticks and started to eat the sashimi.

Later Alan drove me back to my apartment. We had finished eating all that was served while talking about my trip with David and Josh, and about what they were doing. We even discussed introducing his girls to them. I felt more peaceful than I had since first learning of my predicament. Again, at the entrance to my building Alan pulled me over and gave me a full kiss on the lips. This time I didn't resist, and I put my arms around him. When he pulled away he put his hand on the back of my neck and said, "Don't forget I'm here, Connie. If you need to talk, just give a holler."

In the elevator, I wondered how I could have kissed Alan so readily. I had no feelings of guilt about Peter. What had happened?  I thought it had to do with my self-esteem being at rock bottom. I had fallen in Peter's eyes, I didn't think he would ever truly believe in me again. Alan wanted me and I needed that.

# *Chapter 15*

♟♟ *Chromosome 15* ————————————————————————

Three days after my date with Alan I got a call from Peter asking me to come to his office. Lynn was perched on the couch when I arrived – he must have called her. I sat next to her with a dry mouth and a pounding heart. Peter was standing near his desk, holding some papers. He looked directly at me and said, "It's a mixed bag. Of the five mice rechallenged with the virus carrying the normal gene, one aged at a very rapid rate and died this morning. His sugar protein level was very high, and he showed outward signs of aging as well as telomere shortening. I'm not sure whether he died of old age, or as a result of the chemotherapy. He had no antibodies to the Congo virus after the chemotherapy. The rest of them are alive. Two, that had no antibodies after chemo, are aging at a slower rate apparent in their slight loss of telomere length and rising sugar protein, and the other two had some antibody response to the virus after the chemo. I don't know what's happening to them yet. They appear to be holding their weights, the telomeres are the same, and the proteins have not changed either."

He sat on the edge of the desk and looked at me thoughtfully, "In other words, I can't predict what your response will be, Connie."

I shrugged, "Why does it matter? I'll have to take a chance," I rubbed a spot on my cheek. "This morning I woke up to find this pimple on my face. I know one pimple doesn't mean acne, but I haven't had a pimple since I was a teenager."

This statement was greeted with total silence. Peter and Lynn exchanged a glance. I continued, "I have to do this, Peter. Can you get the immunosuppressants for me? Dr. Simms gave you the protocol, didn't he?"

Peter nodded unhappily, "Well, I can't stop you. There isn't any alternative, but I want you to know anything could happen. I can't understand why the response was so variable. It must be related to the strength of the original antibody level in each animal." He paused for a minute, gazing down at his feet, then raised his head to look at me and continued, "I know I haven't been very supportive of you throughout this crisis, Connie. Frankly, I've been in shock. I wish I had responded differently when you first told me, because I really do care. I realize that it will be hard for you to accept that I still love you. I want to help, and I feel so helpless."

Oddly, his admission had little effect on me. Beneath it, I was certain, lay disillusionment and confusion about his feelings for me. "It's alright, Peter," I said. "You have helped. Even if the chemo doesn't work, it's the only possible solution, and you found it." I turned to Lynn, "What's the next step, doctor?"

Lynn had been observing the interchange thoughtfully, moving her glance from me to Peter, and back. "I need some blood from you, Connie, and I think it would be wise to have some of your marrow too, just in case. After you're back to normal we can start the chemotherapy. You better stock up on things you'll need while you're isolated. I can shop for your food. Do you want me to order the drugs, Peter?"

"Yes," he answered, handing her one of the papers he had been holding. "This is the protocol that Simms gave me. It's based on weight per kilogram."

"I can figure all that out and give her the appropriate dosage." She turned to me. "We can go to my office and I'll do a marrow aspiration and take the blood. You can have it done today and get started immediately." She stood up. Peter was again looking at me with an expression I couldn't interpret.

When I rose to leave with Lynn he said, "Good luck to you, Connie, I'll keep in touch by phone." He took a step toward me, then stopped, seeming to change his mind. I looked away from him, mumbled, "Thanks," and followed Lynn out the door.

We descended in the elevator silently. Lynn seemed deep in thought, and I was depressed and could think of nothing to say. When we were out on the street walking to the hospital, she spoke, "Have you thought about what you are going to tell people when you're out of circulation? What are you going to tell David and Josh?"

"I've thought about that," I answered. "We talk on the phone about once a week, but I don't see them very often. In other words, I could be holed up for a few weeks and they wouldn't suspect anything. As far as everyone else is concerned, I guess I could say I'm sick. The only people who might wonder are Saki and Julie."

"Peter could tell them you were advised to stay at home because you were spotting and threatening to miscarry," Lynn suggested.

"They never knew I was pregnant. That would cause more questions than if I just had the flu or something." I didn't want to use pregnancy as an excuse. I wanted to forget it had ever happened.

"Well, I only mentioned it because it would give you more time, in case you have to be isolated for a prolonged period."

"You mean if my immune system doesn't bounce back," I pressed.

She nodded, "That's always a possibility, especially with large doses, but I don't anticipate any problem. You know, Connie, I think Peter is much more deeply concerned about you than you think he is. What he said to you, just now, was the tip of the iceberg. He loves you very much and is in a lot of pain. He told me the only way he can cope is by working as hard as he can to reverse the process. Did you notice how tired he looked?"

"Yes, I guess so. I don't know what to think. He certainly is avoiding all physical contact with me."

"I think he's afraid he will break down. He also thinks you'll rebuff him because of his initial reaction. He's on a very thin edge right now, as far as his emotions are concerned. It's clear to me that his priority is to find a way to save you, and he doesn't want anything to interfere with that. If he succeeds, I think you'll see a big change in his attitude."

"And what if he doesn't succeed?" I said, "How will he be then?" We had reached the entrance to the hospital, and stood for a minute outside the door.

"In that event you'll probably be the one who has to comfort him. But we aren't going to think about that. I have a feeling we'll find the answer." She said this firmly, and taking my arm pulled me into the building. I wished I could be so positive.

After being alone in my apartment for a week, and taking the daily doses of chemicals to weaken my immune system, I was beginning to think jumping out the window was a good option. I was totally bored and too anxious to do anything to relieve the boredom. My only contact with the outside world was Lynn, who stopped by every day, donned a surgical gown and mask, and took my blood to monitor the state of my white blood cells. She also brought me whatever groceries I needed in order to avoid contact with anyone else. I was having all the common side effects of chemotherapy: nausea, fatigue, and hair loss. The hair loss was going to be hard to explain and Lynn had suggested I get a wig made in my hair style and color to wear later and avoid questions.

I spoke fairly often to Peter, who kept me up to date on the mice. There had been no more deaths among the five remaining mice that had received the chemo, but only one appeared to be showing outward signs of aging and shortening of telomeres. Two seemed to be remaining static, or possibly showing some minor telomere shortening, and one continued to grow younger. I found it hard to talk to Peter about anything except the status of the mice. He sounded depressed and worried, and this did nothing to help my state of mind. He continually asked me how I was feeling, and since I felt pretty rotten, I told him exactly that. Why mince words.

Every day I stood in front of the mirror trying to gauge my approximate age by my appearance, but outside of the one pimple, which had disappeared after two days, there were no other physical manifestations to indicate the onset of adolescence. My body was taut, my breasts, which had gotten smaller and firmer, were the same. But the 'bloom of youth' was no longer there. Instead, my hair was getting thin and patchy and I looked sick and tired.

Lynn had told me that when my lymphocyte count was sufficiently low she would bring over the Congo River virus, containing the normal nuclease gene that Peter had prepared for the mice, and attempt to reinfect me with it. I was to swallow it, just as I had done before. Meanwhile, there was one rather odd change in my habits. I now had the radio on all day, tuned to an AM station that played songs and jazz recordings from the fifties and sixties. When I first became aware of this, I assumed it was a way of distracting my thoughts and making me feel less lonely. I then switched over to a classical music station, but soon discovered it didn't have the same effect. I found the classical music depressing, whereas the old jazz seemed comforting. I mentioned this to Lynn and told her it might be an indication of an increase in teenage mentality. On the other hand, I only developed a taste for classical music after marrying Walter, who had a large collection of CDs and old record albums. Lynn's response to this was, "I really don't think that proves anything. Jazz and old love songs are lighter fare, and if you're listening to the words of a song, you're less apt to be worrying about yourself."

"Maybe," I said. But I had my doubts. That wasn't the only thing I'd noticed either. Because of severe nausea caused by the chemotherapy, I did not have any appetite, but when I rarely did want something to eat, all I could stomach was junk food; cokes, potato chips, candy, and the like. When, a few days later, I asked Lynn to bring me some soft pretzels, popcorn, and more coke, she looked worried, then quickly changed her expression, and said, "That stuff isn't good for you. A lot of people on chemo crave it, but you have to eat nourishing food to keep your strength. You are actually quite lucky that you don't feel much sicker. Most patients on very high doses of chemo are bedridden and need constant nursing care"

I knew that was true, but it didn't make me feel any better. I wondered, too, if wanting junk food might be a sign of growing younger, along with my changing taste in music.

On my eighth day of isolation, Lynn arrived to tell me that my lymphocytes were sufficiently low to allow me to take the next step: to try to reinfect myself with the Congo River virus.

She had brought the viral preparation with her in a small, sterile glass vial inside a metal container. Lynn opened the container and then put on sterile surgical gloves in order to hand me the vial.

"I think it would be easier to swallow this if you put it in water," she said.

"Yes, probably," I answered, walking to the kitchen and returning with a half-filled tumbler of water. The vial held a small amount of slightly cloudy fluid which I emptied into the glass I was holding. Swirling it around a little, I lifted it up toward Lynn and, before drinking, said, "Here's hoping."

My hand was shaking, this was "all or nothing." If it didn't work I was doomed. I looked at Lynn, who seemed to be struggling with her emotions, but she looked down, then took an audible breath and said, "It's *got* to work, Connie. The good news is – you can stop taking the chemo, but you have to stay here until your white count is back to normal."

"How long?" I asked anxiously.

"Maybe another week or ten days."

"I'm going crazy," I admitted. "Look Lynn, I've run out of things to do. I have trouble concentrating on anything. I've even taken to playing endless games of solitaire on the computer."

"Don't you have any work you can be doing?" She was frowning slightly.

"It's hard to think of anything, especially when all my papers are in my office. I had more work to do on the Congo River virus, but that's all in the lab. Besides, I just don't feel motivated. I want to be outside running in the park"

"Well, that's a switch. I used to have to pry you away from your research. You don't suppose that's ..." She stopped abruptly, and put her hand up to her mouth, which was covered by the surgical mask.

"Go on, say it. It could be part of getting younger. I just don't know."

"There's no use speculating about that. You aren't going to know much for a while and it's probably all going to turn around. I think I've stayed here long enough, this mask is getting a little damp." She picked up the metal container and said, "I'll see you tomorrow. Is there anything you need?"

"Can you bring me some more video tapes? I've watched all the ones you gave me."

"Sure, anything special?"

"Well, I have kind of a yen to see some good sci-fi. Maybe Star Wars, or something like that. I'll leave it up to you. Thanks, Lynn," I walked over to the door with her, and blew a kiss as she left.

When the door was closed, I went into my study and turned on the radio. It was tuned to the old popular music station, and I left it there. There was no point forcing myself to be intellectual. I had to hope that eventually my tastes would revert to their previous state.

What was more worrisome was the reference Lynn had made to my former dedication to work. Was I losing that, too? I tried reassuring myself – I couldn't work because I needed to have access to the laboratory, but this was not entirely true. I couldn't work because I wasn't motivated, and I wasn't motivated because I might not have a future, and maybe, too, because my brain was becoming untrained.

I walked over to the window and looked longingly out at the street, and at the glimpse of park beyond. It was a beautiful early September day, the heat of August was gone, people were walking briskly along the sidewalk under my widow. I wanted desperately to join them, I wanted to go out, buy an ice cream cone, and stroll through the park. With effort, I turned away and sat down at my desk.

A copy of my will was lying there, drawn several years before when I had been contemplating a trip to China. I had removed it from my files to make certain it was in order. The words "I, Constance Gueyer, being of sound mind, do hereby declare this to be my last will and testament." stared up at me. My beneficiaries might have trouble believing this statement if they ever learned the cause of my demise. How long would it take before I knew what was going to happen to me? The telephone interrupted my thoughts. It was Josh.

"Hi, Mater, how are you feeling? I called the lab and your assistant said you were home with the flu. Is it bad?"

"Not very," I answered, "I have some fever, so I'm told I have to stay home until that's gone." I hated having to lie to him. "Who told you?" I couldn't resist asking.

"Lynn, she happened to be in the lab getting something for you. She knows all about infectious diseases. Do you feel better?"

"A little, how's everything with you, honey?"

"Okay, I'm just getting a little tired of teaching the same old stuff over and over. I'd rather be doing programming. The head of computer science told me I might be able to get a part-time job with some business firm. I've started reading the classified ads, there are a lot of possibilities. David seems pretty serious about his new girl. Did he say anything to you?"

"Yes," I answered. "I think he'd like me to meet her."

"Well, he sees her almost every night. That's pretty heavy."

"It sounds that way, but I'll have to wait until I get over this. Have you met her?"

"No, not yet. We've both been busy doing our own things. I've just had a few phone conversations with him. She got on the line once and said 'Hi'…sounded nice. Well, I have to go teach a class, just called to see how you were. Do you need anything?"

"No. Thanks, darling, thanks for calling."

After putting the phone down, I sat back in the chair and pondered this new development. David wanted me to meet Sandra. When? How long could I continue having the flu? On an impulse I picked up the phone again and dialed Peter's number at the lab. Julie answered and immediately recognized my voice.

"How are you feeling, Connie. What a pain to get flu this time of year. How do you think you got it?"

That was a good question. Where does one pick up the flu in summer?

"I don't know. I suppose I could have brought it home from Europe, I don't know what the incubation time is."

"Well, I hope you feel better soon. Here's Peter." I heard her say, "It's Connie," as she passed the phone over to Peter.

"Hello, Connie," he said, his voice formal and unreadable. "Hold on a minute, I'm going to take this in my office."

After a pause, I heard him pick up and a disconnect click from Julie. "How are you feeling? Did Lynn bring you the virus?"

"Yes, I've taken it. When do you think I'll know if it's going to work?"

"I don't know how long it took to work on you the first time. You said you began to suspect you were getting younger on the July 4th weekend. That was a couple of months after you took the stuff, but some changes had to be taking place before. We should check your telomere length again in about a month."

"Yes, I suppose so that's the first thing. Well, thanks, Peter. I guess I just have to wait, although a month seems like an eternity."

"I know, you must be going crazy. Connie..." He hesitated, Then he said quietly," I miss you."

I didn't know what to say, so I said nothing. "I love you," he continued, "and I want you to be all right. I keep thinking that somehow I'm responsible for what happened, that I somehow gave you the impression I didn't love you."

"How could you be blamed?" I asked him. Certainly I didn't blame Peter. "Look, I was the one who misinterpreted everything, and swallowed the virus." A big lump was rising in my throat and I was afraid I might begin to cry.

"I know, Connie, Lynn pretty much let me have it. She told me that sedatives can have weird side effects in some people. But what worried me was wondering why you thought your age bothered me. It never crossed my mind to care whether you were older or younger. I just loved you the way you were."

"Peter, I...I don't think I can talk about this now. I'm glad you told me, but I need to wait and see what's going to happen."

"Okay, darling, it can wait. I'll call you tomorrow." He sounded upset when he hung up.

So was I. I wanted to love him the way I had before, but didn't know if that were possible. So much had happened...his initial anger when I told him what I'd done, the abortion, my days of chemotherapy and isolation. Now all I could think about was whether or not I would reverse this terrifying process of age regression. If I didn't, it wouldn't matter what I felt. If I did, I would have more time to examine my feelings.

The following day, when Lynn arrived to take my blood, I told her about my conversation with Peter.

"I'm not surprised," she said. "I've told you all along that he was in shock, but I was certain he still loved you. What about you? How do you feel about him?"

"I just don't know anymore. I loved him so much, and then, when I needed him the most, he became cold and angry. I know he was shocked, and he told me he blamed himself and was angry because of that, but it didn't come across that way to me. Look at the way you responded. You were in shock too, I could tell, but you were there for me the whole time."

Lynn looked down at the floor and slowly shook her head. "Connie, you are my dearest friend, but I'm not in love with you. You had become an integral part of Peter's life. He was suddenly faced with the possibility of losing you. It was like losing his right arm or worse, and it was because of *his* experiment and *his* behavior, even though you misunderstood."

"Yes, I guess I know that, but it was my experiment, too. I just need more time. I want to see what's going to happen to me. Maybe I'm behaving childishly. I feel so restless and muddled, as though I'm yearning for something, and I don't know what it is."

Lynn gave me a piercing glance and said, "Nonsense! You have every reason to be confused. Just don't dwell on it. Maybe in a few days you'll be able to get out of this apartment." She looked at her watch. "I have to go now, I have clinic hours. See you tomorrow." She blew me a kiss through her mask.

After Lynn left, I wandered aimlessly around the living room, pausing in front of a table under the window which held numerous framed photographs of my family, a picture history of my life. I picked up a silver framed snapshot of myself with David and Josh. David was about five and Josh three when it was taken, which made me about thirty-one at the time. I studied the picture, realizing I could easily pass for thirty-one now. I put the photograph down and picked up another of myself and my sisters, Sylvia and Anne, taken when I was about eight. I remembered being made to pose in front of the large maple tree on our lawn in Seattle and not wanting to hold still. Father had reprimanded me a little harshly, which accounted for my rather sullen expression. I set the frame down abruptly. I didn't need to reminisce about my childhood when I might actually have to relive it.

Two days went by with no change in the monotony of my life. I scanned the newspapers, watched as much daytime television as I could stomach, and tried, unsuccessfully, to think of something worthwhile to do. If I was going to regress to childhood and die, I wanted desperately to be remembered for something other than having been a human guinea pig. On the third morning, while staring out the window of my bedroom, faced with a repetition of the day before, I suddenly exclaimed, "Guinea pig!" Why had it never occurred to me before? That was exactly what I was, and I should be taking advantage of it. Peter had been focusing only on trying to save me. He hadn't really organized a well-conceived scientific experiment using the immunosuppressant drugs and the dosage of Congo River virus in titrated amounts.

Peter had given the same doses of suppressants and virus to all the mice. The fact that they all reacted somewhat differently when re-challenged with the virus was not surprising, as there was never any attempt made to find the optimal doses, which would have required the use of many more mice. The dosage of immunosuppressant drugs should have been titrated, or given in varying amounts, as well. It could be a very useful experiment.

I turned from the window quickly, went to my desk, retrieved a yellow legal pad from one of the drawers, and sat down. Using a ruler, I made a grid of squares filling the page, then started jotting notes on the margins; the varying doses of immunosuppressants along the top border, and the viral doses along the side.

It was dark outside when, rubbing my eyes, I finally put the legal pad aside. I had finished mapping out an experiment that could apply to the use of any viral vector: a controlled system of delivering genetic material in titrated doses; using immunosuppressants, if necessary, in an optimal manner. Now, I got wearily to my feet and went to the kitchen, where, for the first time since my incarceration, I realized I was hungry, and actually wanted to eat. My first instinct was to finish a bag of popcorn I had opened a day before, but remembering what Lynn had said about nourishment, I chose nutrition instead, taking a chicken pot pie out of the freezer and put it in the microwave oven to defrost.

Early the next morning, I called Peter and described my new experiment. I was delighted with his enthusiastic response..

"You're right, Connie! We should have done it that way, but we were pressed for time. It's really great that you figured it out, with all your other problems. I only wish it could be helpful to you."

"I know, but it can't. It just occurred to me that we were wasting a lot of potentially valuable information. I needed to feel that we could derive something positive out of my situation."

"Get Lynn to bring me the notes you made and I'll try to set up the experiment right away."

"I wish I could be there to help you. God, how I want to get out of here!"

"It won't be long now, I'm sure. I'll call you and keep you up to date on everything. I still miss you."

"I miss you too," I said, truthfully. I did, but I still had a lot to think about and I couldn't tell him what he wanted to hear. Not yet.

Later that morning I got a call from Alan, the first since our last meeting. "Connie, I called your lab and your assistant told me you were home with a case of the flu. Are you okay? I would have called sooner, but I didn't want to bug you. Have you solved your problems?"

I had been sitting at my desk, putting the pages describing my new experiment together to give to Lynn. I leaned back in the chair, thinking 'not again.' I had to come up with another plausible lie, and I was running out of options. "Oh, I'm better, Alan. I think I'll go back to work in a few days. As for my problems, I'm hoping they'll get ironed out, too." None of this was a blatant falsehood.

"How long have you been out of commission?" Alan persisted. If I told him nearly three weeks he would find that strange, but I had no way of knowing what Saki had told him. So I told another whopper, "I had a touch of pneumonia, so I was advised to stay home a few more days on antibiotics."

"That's too bad," he chided gently. "You should have called me. I'd have come over and given you a tune-up."

"Alan, do you always think of me as a car?"

Alan chuckled, "I'm a frustrated mechanic, I think of people as either cars or trucks. That way I don't have to worry about DNA. I have enough of it in the lab."

I laughed (it felt good) and said, "You're a weird one, my friend. So, what kind of car am I?"

"Well," he said, "I think of you either as an Aston-Martin or a Lamborghini. Quality stuff that must be well cared for."

"I guess if I have to be a car, that's a compliment." I was smiling.

"You'd better believe it," he said, "Now, I'm a Toyota Land Rover, sturdy and dependable. Can we make a date when you leave your garage?"

"Were you thinking of driving somewhere?" This was catching.

"Of course," Alan responded, "Give me a call when you're out."

We said goodbye and I hung up the phone, still smiling. I sat motionless for a while, trying to think what kind of car Peter was, and eventually decided I didn't know enough varieties of cars. At least Alan had made me think about something other than myself for a while.

Lynn arrived a little later than her normal hour, and surprised me by striding into the room without the usual mask and gown. She pirouetted in front of me and chanted, "Tra-la! You've been granted a reprieve. You're free to leave the prison!" Smiling broadly, she handed me a slip of paper from the hospital laboratory.

"I guess my count's back to normal," I said, glancing at the report for confirmation.

"Yes, but I wouldn't tempt fate for a few days. Stay away from crowded buses and subways for a while."

"That's no problem. I want to get out and walk or run everywhere. And, guess what, Lynn, I've been doing some work."

"Fantastic! Tell me about it."

I explained my experiment, showed her the protocol, and asked her to give it to Peter.

"You've told him about it? Was he pleased?"

"Yes. He said it sounded good, and he wants to set up the experiment. Hey! I can deliver it to him myself now. I almost forgot."

Lynn nodded, still smiling. Then, her face sobered. "Has anything else changed?"

"Not that I've noticed. Do I look any different to you?"

She had been eyeing my thin patchy hair, an effect of the chemotherapy. "Not really. I've seen you looking better. Do you have the wig?" Before my confinement, she had gone with me to buy a wig that looked very much like my hair. The only difference was that it made me look perfectly coiffed at all times, hardly my usual style.

"Yes, I just haven't bothered to wear it here. Let me get it and I'll go out with you." I dashed over to the dresser, pulled out the wig and slapped it on my head. I couldn't wait to get out of this place!

When I returned, Lynn grinned and said, "That's much better. You almost look like the old Connie."

'*Old*'! Music to my ears. If only it were true.

Getting outside in the air was a tonic for me. The end of September weather had been, and still was, beautiful, and the leaves in the park had just begun to show their fall colors. As we walked, I told Lynn about my friendship with Alan. I had mentioned him to her after he first called me. When I told her he had kissed me, she looked at me sharply and asked, "What about Peter?"

Lynn had been a fan of Peter's from the time they first met. "Let's sit on a bench for a minute."I suggested.

"Are you tired?" Lynn asked.

"No, but for some reason, I think better sitting down. I am not having a romance with Alan. I never thought of him as a rival of Peter's. Certainly not when he first called me. He doesn't know what's going on with me, but he's perceptive and realizes something is wrong. I've had to lie to him a few times and I think he's aware of it, but he doesn't force me to explain anything. He's been great, and he makes me laugh. Peter seems so gloomy all the time now, not that I blame him."

Lynn still looked upset. "Connie, Peter's in love with you. He's worried about you. I don't know anything about this guy, Alan, he may be a prince, but you already have one and he'd be hard to match." She put her hand over mine. "Maybe I'm biased. Alright, I *am* biased. I'm glad this guy is funny and gives you a lift, God knows, you need it, but keep it platonic until you've had a chance to get the rest of your life in order. That's my unsolicited advice."

I patted her hand with my free one. "Thanks, it's good advice, that is if I ever get to have the rest of my life."

"You will," Lynn said emphatically.

# *Chapter 16*

👥 *Chromosome 16* ───────────────────────────────

Free again! What a relief. I might even have been exhilarated, were it not for the sentence of progressive youth hanging over me. There were moments when I actually forgot why I had been imprisoned, but those episodes were brief. They occurred only when I was outside walking in the park, and were always followed by a sinking sensation when the reality of my plight resurfaced. I worried, too, that these carefree moments might be telltale signs of the insouciance of youth, when one feels invulnerable.

The worst moments were in the early morning before arising. One night, I had a dream in which I was a child running on the lawn outside my parents' house in Seattle, skimming along the surface of the grass like a bird. At the end of the lawn, I turned to see Dave and Josh standing on the porch waving to me, calling me back to them. On awakening I was disoriented, thinking myself back in Seattle. Then I felt a spasm of enormous sadness and loneliness, like an icy fist in my gut, as my recognition of time and place returned. It was at such times that I pondered ways to end my life if I were truly doomed to regress to infancy. How could I make suicide appear to be an accidental death?

The trouble with this line of thinking was that I didn't want to die, I wanted to go on working for as long as my brain allowed. I pondered the possibility of faking my death and disappearing. I envisioned creating the impression of drowning by driving my car to a crowded beach, leaving items that would identify me on a beach towel in the sand, and swimming along the shore to a spot where I would have previously parked a rental car containing clothes and whatever else I might need to create a new identity. I would return the car to the agency, call a taxi to take me to the railroad station, and go off to some distant location to continue my work.

However, one of the many problems with this scenario was that it was out of character for me to have gone alone to a beach. Why would I be there? I could think of no logical reason. My sons and friends would suspect suicide and not accidental drowning, and I didn't want that. Another, more pressing, issue was: What was I going to do if I succeeded in disappearing? Where would I go? How could I continue to work without my lab? What would happen to me when I became a child and could no longer care for myself? There was no satisfactory answer to any of these questions, and killing myself seemed more and more to be the only option. But it had to appear accidental, and there I was stymied.

The day after Lynn told me my blood count was normal, I had gone to Peter's lab to give him the protocol for my new experiment. I was wearing the wig, and was relieved that Saki and Julie made no comment on my appearance. Peter, on the other hand, led me into his office and, closing the door, took hold of my shoulders and held me at arms length.

"You look great! I can't believe you just had a rigorous course of chemo." He pulled me toward him, "If you aren't on precautions anymore, I'm going to kiss you."

As his arms encircled me, I felt a surge of desire rise up even more powerful than I remembered. When he pulled back after a long, exploratory kiss, both of us were breathless. His arms still around me, Peter looked down and rubbed his nose on mine.

"Don't say you didn't miss me and you don't love me. I'll never believe it. Not now." he declared, a big grin spreading over his face.

I pulled back a little, trying to regain my equilibrium. Was I feeling love or just plain lust? And did it really matter?

"Peter, we don't know what's happening yet. I'm so focused on surviving, I can't sort out any other emotions. I may be a child in a couple of months, maybe less."

"I know, darling, I've thought about that a lot, too. Whatever happens to you I'll still love you. And if the worst happens, I'll look after you."

"Oh, no! That would be too awful. I can't expect you to do that. What about Dave and Josh. I couldn't bear it for them, either. I'd be better off dead."

Peter shook his head and tightened his arms around me. "No, don't ever think that. There's always a chance we'll find another way to reverse the process if this one fails."

I let him hold me for a minute or two longer, loving how secure and wanted I felt. It was like receiving an infusion of strength. Then I pulled away gently.

"What about the mice? Is there anything new?" I wanted to know.

He bit his lower lip and slid his eyes away from mine. "I didn't want to tell you, but I guess you'll have to know. Two of them are now very small, and are regressing rapidly to infancy. The one that had been showing signs of aging died this morning. The remaining two may be static or aging at a slower rate. It's hard to tell. Did you bring the protocol for your new experiment?"

"Oh, I almost forgot!" I handed him my briefcase from the chair where I had placed it on entering his office. "It's strange that they're having such different responses. How do you account for it?" Oddly, I wasn't surprised at this outcome.

"I wish I knew. It has something to do with their immune response. Some were more susceptible than others to being reinfected with the Congo River virus. That's why your idea is so pertinent. It allows for adjustment of chemotherapy doses according to the individual response."

I shrugged. "It's too late for me, though."

Peter looked at me with such open sadness, I nearly broke down. "I'm afraid it is," he said softly.

During the ensuing days I developed a routine of self-examination, standing in front of the mirror and searching my face and body for any signs of change. I paid special attention to my breasts, which had become firmer and higher over the past months. Now I wondered if they were going to start getting smaller, or, on the bright side, hopefully begin to sag a little. I found these daily examinations unbearably stressful, and almost willed myself to find evidence of aging. Unfortunately, none was forthcoming. It was almost as if my body was in a static, unchanging state.

One of the first things on my agenda, after receiving the news that I was free to leave confinement, was to call my sons and arrange to have dinner with them. I particularly wanted to meet David's new girl, Sandra. If I wasn't going to be around very long, it would be easier for David if he had a good relationship with someone. I still had Josh to worry about. It would help that he and David were so close, and that he appeared to like Sandra. I made a date to take them for dinner Saturday evening.

On Wednesday I got another call from Alan. I was in my office trying to catch up on the work I had missed, and was again having trouble concentrating. My thoughts kept returning to how futile my work would be if I were to continue getting younger. Hearing Alan's voice did perk me up a little. He said, "I gather you're better. I tried you at home and got your machine, but I didn't leave a message. How is everything?"

"Oh, better," I responded, "I've been back at work for three days now. I'm still feeling a little washed out, though," I admitted. "I thought I would bounce back quickly."

"You don't sound in top condition, Connie," Alan agreed, "Do you need overhauling?"

Back to being a car, I answered, "If you mean an oil change, no. I could use a complete tuneup." I had to laugh, as I realized Alan had cheered me up within two minutes of saying, "Hello."

"I'm just the man for you then," he continued. "Why don't I pick you up in my tow truck tomorrow, if that's convenient?"

I thought for a minute. Would I be able to keep this banter going an entire evening? I wasn't sure, but, more than anything, I needed a diversion. "Sure," I agreed, feeling better already. "I'll be parked outside my building at six-thirty or seven."

"Seven, it is," Alan confirmed. "See you then."

True to his word, Alan arrived at my door promptly at seven. I was still in my apartment, trying to determine whether my wig was on properly, and if it looked natural. Casting a quick look outside, I smiled. Alan was waiting in his car. I dashed down, waved "hello," and jumped into the car. Before starting the engine, he looked me over with a somber expression, and said, "You do look a little peaked. You must have had quite a bad case."

"Yes," I responded. "But I feel much better. Where are we going?"

"Are you in the mood for more sushi?" Alan asked, pulling the car out from the curb.

"Always."

"In that case, I think we'll go to a place in Jersey just over the GW Bridge near Fort Lee. I went there a few weeks ago, and the best thing about it, outside of decent sushi, is that it's reasonably quiet."

"Sounds good to me," I agreed. "I hope we don't get into a lot of traffic on the way to the bridge." Seven could still be part of Manhattan rush hour.

Alan shrugged, "We'll take our chances. It's preferable to standing in line at a restaurant. I made the reservation for eight, so we should easily make that."

As it turned out, the traffic was only moderately heavy and we arrived in front of the restaurant five minutes early.

We hadn't done much talking in the car. Alan was busy driving and trying to stay in the faster lanes. When we were seated at a table and had ordered saki for two, he resumed his scrutiny of me, to my discomfort. After a moment of pregnant silence, he said, "I want to ask you a question that you may prefer not to answer. I promise I won't press you. Have you been on chemotherapy?"

I must have paled. I felt my heart jump, "Why do you ask that?" I said, sharply.

"I can tell you're wearing a wig," he answered. "It's a good one, but it doesn't look like your hair because it's too carefully coiffed and the wind doesn't mess it up. I've seen wigs before. One of Elaine's friends had to have chemo. Once you've seen one and know it's there, it's not too hard to spot them."

It had been windy, especially when I came out of my building. I hadn't thought of that eventuality. Should I let him think I had a malignancy, or some weird scalp ailment? While I was pondering this, Alan resumed, "Just say you don't want to talk about it. I'll shut up."

"No," I said, "I can't keep on with this subterfuge. I'm going to tell you what's going on, mainly because you were so near to guessing the truth, and because we are such old friends. But, Alan, please promise not to repeat any of this. You'll understand why when I tell you."

Alan's eyes had narrowed. He ignored the saki that the waitress placed in front of him. I let her pour some in my cup and took a swallow of it. It was hot on my tongue and heated the path to my stomach. It felt good.

"Go on, I promise," he said, looking into my eyes.

"Okay," I took a deep breath, "Remember when you asked me if the rejuvenation thing in the mice was catching?"

He nodded, looking grim. I continued, "Well, it wasn't exactly "catching," I *took* some of the stuff to make myself younger because I thought Peter was involved with Julie, his chief lab worker. I was very upset, and totally wrong in my assumption. I had taken some Ativan to calm down, but I'd probably taken too much, because I got very woozy just before drinking the stuff."

Alan was silent – he hadn't shifted his gaze or changed his expression. I took another swallow of saki and continued, "When you began thinking I looked well, and like the girl you used to know, you were right. I had started getting younger. Because the process seemed to arrest itself in the mice, I had thought, stupidly, that it was a limited process. When I returned from Switzerland, I found out the mice were continuing to get younger, and they would eventually die as premature newborns. That will probably be my fate, too." I looked down, both embarrassed and somewhat relieved.

My hand was resting on the table, slowly Alan covered it with his. The waitress had come up to ask if we were ready to order, but he sent her away, saying, "Give us a few more minutes, but bring one more saki, please. He'd noticed I had nearly emptied my small flask.

"Go on," he said, squeezing my hand.

"Yes, well, I *was* on chemotherapy. I couldn't use the Congo River virus to carry the normal nuclease gene, because I was immune to it. The same with the mice. Peter decided the only way to replace the mutated gene with the normal one, was to lower the immune system and then try to reinfect with the Congo virus carrying the normal gene."

"Did it work?" Alan asked, quietly, his face grave.

"I don't know yet. The mice were a mixed lot. But I had no other option, so I went ahead with chemo. My friend Lynn, a pediatrician, monitored my progress at home, and brought me the new potion when my immune system was sufficiently weakened. My white count just went back to normal a couple of days ago. Now I have to wait and see."

My voice suddenly broke, and I could feel my eyes filling with tears. I turned my head to the side, trying to gain control. "I'm so ashamed of what I did. I know it shocked Peter, but after his initial shock, he's been very supportive." I wiped my eyes with my free hand.

Alan removed his hand from mine, and said nothing for a moment. Then he put his hand back, and said, "Connie, I suspected something, but nothing quite like this. You were beginning to look exactly like you did in the 1960s. The whole notion that anyone could grow younger seemed so preposterous, I discounted the possibility, even though you and Peter had the proof. Now it's happening to you, and I care about you. I want to help you."

I looked up at him, my eyes swimming in tears. "Thank you," I murmured, "I wish you could."

At that moment the waitress came to the table to take our order. Alan looked at me, then quickly said, "We'll have the special sushi for two and two more saki." She nodded and left.

We sat silently for a moment as I tried to gain control. I assumed Alan was attempting to digest what I had just told him. He was no longer looking at me, but seemed to be studying a spot on the table. After the sakis were replenished, he looked up at me, "Let me ask you something. Are you in love with Peter?"

"I was," I replied. "So much has happened, I don't know any more. I feel as though I'm in limbo."

"Well," Alan persisted, "Do you think he loves you?"

"He says he does, but what's the use," I replied bitterly. "My future is a big question mark."

"I believe that's true of everyone, although not to the same degree. Suppose you were dying of some incurable disease. It wouldn't stop you from loving someone." Alan's tone was firm. "You need someone right now who cares for you and can help you through this..." He broke off as the sushi platter was placed in front of us.

When the waitress left he said, "Come on, eat some. You need to gain a little weight. I'm going to look after you, at least for this evening."

I smiled faintly and picked up a piece of sushi.

I managed to eat about a quarter of the pieces. Alan ate most of the rest. He carefully steered the conversation to other topics, like his problems with his soon-to-be ex-wife. Later, when we were driving back to the city, he told me he was going to walk me up to my apartment. Luck was on his side. He found a parking space about a block away and came up in the elevator with me. When I opened the door to my apartment, I turned to say goodnight, but he came in the door with me, and closed it firmly behind him. He put his arms around me and said, "I think what you need now is some loving. You've been through a helluva time, and you should stop blaming yourself. Whatever happens, you're a wonderful, talented woman. Peter is right to love you."

He kissed me long and hard, and I responded. I could feel myself weakening in his arms and knew he wanted to make love to me. I could have used some loving then; he was right, but I forced myself to pull back. Peter loved me, and until I knew how I felt about him, I had to wait. I looked up at Alan, who was still holding me and said, "I can't do this now, Alan. I've had a big soft spot for you ever since school, and you're so adept at reading my moods, I almost succumbed. But I have an awful lot of unfinished business right now. I'm sure you understand what I mean."

Alan didn't release me. He said softly, "I understand, honey. I'll be waiting." He kissed me lightly, let me go, and went out closing the door quietly behind him. I stood unmoving for a while, thinking how easy it would have been to yield. I was confused and frightened, and he was like a sheltering port in a storm. But what about Peter? I knew I would never recapture the love I'd had before, but would we be able to start all over? I was suddenly very tired, what was the use of thinking about the future? I put out the lights and went to bed.

On Saturday evening I again dined out. This time, I went to a small Italian restaurant downtown, where I was to meet Dave, Josh, and Dave's new girlfriend. I was, of course, wearing the wig, and spent a lot of time making certain it was a little mussed. After Alan's reaction, I worried that it would also be obvious to my sons. I was the first to arrive and was shown to a table in the rear. Josh joined me a few minutes later, wearing a blindingly loud short-sleeved shirt tucked into chino pants.

"Hi, Mammo," he bent over to kiss me on the cheek. "You're looking okay. I expected you to be limp and wan from your bout of flu."

"Oh, I feel much better now. How's everything with you?"

"Okay. Nothing new to report. I'm glad you're going to meet Sandra. I like her a lot."

At that moment I saw Dave approaching the table with a tall, dark-haired girl. He bent over, kissed me, and introduced me to her.

I stood up to greet her, "I've heard a lot about you, Sandra. I've been eager to meet you." She had a very warm smile, and eyes that sparkled. I wasn't sure if they were blue or green. David was beaming with pride.

"I'm really glad to meet you too, Dr. Gueyer. Dave told me you had the flu. I hope you're feeling better. You certainly look well."

This subject was one I was trying to avoid. Before dressing to go to dinner I had spent some time trying to make myself look as matronly as possible. I was wearing a tailored lightweight beige suit, with the skirt at a sedate knee length, and low-heeled dark blue shoes. I thought I looked quite ordinary, and hoped she was just trying to be polite.

"Tell me a little about you," I said, steering to a new topic. "How did you and David meet?"

"Oh, I'm a frustrated actress. That's how Dave and I met. We were trying out for parts in a play, and we found out we had a lot in common. I have done a few walk-ons in off-Broadway productions, but nothing exciting," she said, flushing a little. She's ill at ease, I thought, like I was at her age. Immediately, I had the chilling realization that perhaps I would be there again.

"Dave's a little more selective than I," Sandra continued. "He only tries out for more substantial roles, whereas I'll take anything,"

David interrupted, "She's being modest, Mom. Sandra was understudy for the lead in one of the shows. By the way, Mom, you really look incredibly well. What gives?"

Now I was really in trouble. Before I had time to think of a suitable way out, Sandra, who had been looking at me intently, spoke. "I don't know what you looked like before, Dr. Gueyer, but you could easily pass for Dave's and Josh's sister." Josh looked amused, and Dave winked at me. I didn't know what to say, so I simply smiled modestly. However, as all three of them were awaiting a reaction, I knew I'd have to fabricate some response. Certainly the truth was not an option. At least, none of them had commented on my hair.

"Well, that's a very nice compliment, but I assure you I'm their mother. Let me tell you some stories...." I grinned.

Josh broke in, "Hey, what about the experiment you and Peter did? You made mice younger, do you think something like that happened to you? Could it have been contagious?"

There it was. Of course they knew about the experiment. It had been big news, but I hadn't reckoned on Josh with his ready imagination. I laughed uncomfortably.

"That would really be something, wouldn't it? I don't believe what we did was contagious, or everyone in the lab would have caught it! You'll have to come up with another explanation, if you think one is necessary. Maybe I had a facelift."

"Did you?" Dave and Josh asked simultaneously.

"Maybe," I said coyly, hoping to sidetrack.

"I don't believe it," Dave muttered. "You're not the type."

"What do you mean 'she's not the type,'" Sandra broke in defensively, "There is no 'type.' I know lots of people who have had them, and they're all different."

"I just meant she wouldn't take the time to do it, and I don't think she's that focused on her appearance," David replied.

"All women care something about their appearance. Most men do, too," Sandra said, emphatically, smiling at me, "I think you look wonderful, Dr. Gueyer, and if that's the way you achieved it, more power to you."

"Well, did you or didn't you?" Josh was not easily put off.

I decided to play along with this explanation, even though David was right. I would never have had cosmetic surgery. Preoccupation with my work had always taken precedence over vanity, but what I had done was infinitely more out of character, or so I thought. Telling them the truth was out of the question, especially if I continued getting younger. I had to hedge until I knew what was happening.

"Let's just say, I decided to rejuvenate myself a little. I don't really have to tell you how – that's a woman's prerogative." I was ashamed at falling back on that old saw. "Sandra's right, there is nothing wrong with a person wanting to change his or her appearance for the better, so let's leave it at that."

I could tell they were far from satisfied with this, but because of Sandra, they were not going to continue grilling me. The waiter was hovering nearby to take our orders, and we turned our attention to the menu. I didn't have much appetite, but struggled through some broiled fish and a tossed salad, while we kept a conversation going that focused mainly on Sandra, throughout which Dave and Josh kept glancing at me and flashing quizzical looks at each other. I was thankful Sandra was there.

I returned to my apartment that night shaken, depressed, and sick of lying. I took no comfort from the fact that I had not told a bald-faced lie, but had simply intimated that I might have had cosmetic surgery. My sons were far from stupid. They knew me well enough to realize something was amiss. It made no sense for me to have a face lift, particularly when I had ostensibly been home with the flu, and to have used that as a cover would have seemed very odd. I was sure that after a little reflection, they would wonder about it, especially having noticed my youthful appearance and vigor in Switzerland. No amount of surgery could have made me more vigorous. I was rapidly approaching the proverbial end of my rope, and needed some advice. Lynn...I thought. But it was 11 PM and too late to call her. Peter...but somehow I didn't think he would be able to help.

I went into the bathroom to get ready for bed, and stood before the full length mirror on the back of the door. Everything about me looked youthful; my body was slim and firm, my hands smooth and unblemished, my face free of wrinkles. With an audible sigh I removed the wig, and started my nightly ritual of brushing my hair, which now resembled a buzz haircut, to encourage its growth, when suddenly I froze. Looking more carefully at the short hairs, my heart lurched, and I sat down abruptly on the small bathroom stool.

Was it possible? Please, God! Some hairs seemed to be white at the root end! Breathing rapidly, I stood up, grasped a few of the short strands, and yanked them out. No. These were all brown. I jerked out a few more – and there they were – white roots!

Could this mean I was aging? How old had I been when I first started to see grey? Around thirty, I thought. But there was no sure way of knowing what the white roots meant. Anxiety and stress could be turning my hair white, or perhaps the chemotherapy did it. I didn't want to be premature in my assessment, only to have my hopes dashed. I had to have the only real proof; what, if anything, was happening to my telomeres?

There was nothing to be done about that until morning, but I was too keyed up for sleep. "Maybe, maybe, maybe" kept playing inside my head...*maybe* I had a reprieve. After tossing in bed for half an hour, I got up, swallowed a mild sedative, and managed to fall asleep around 2 AM.

I awakened early with a jolting, joyous memory of my discovery the previous night. I had to get to the lab and use the sequencer, but I didn't want to raise Peter's hopes unnecessarily. Because I needed to ask him if it was free, I called and woke him at home. "Uh, oh hi, Connie, what's up?"

"Sorry to wake you, Peter," I began. "Look, is it alright if I use the sequencer this morning? I'd like to measure my telomeres again."

"Why," he asked quickly. "What do you think is happening?" His voice was edged with excitement.

I remained noncommittal. "Probably nothing, but I'd like to keep a week to week record."

"I think I'll need to use it later in the afternoon, but if you go now, it'll be okay."

"Thanks, I'll head right over," I agreed.

"Do you still have the key?" he asked. "I can meet you there."

"Yes, don't rush." I wanted to get going before he arrived and asked more questions. Within five minutes, I was dressed and out on the street hailing a taxi, all the while playing the same refrain in my head, "Please, God, please."

By the time I had drawn my blood and started some of the preliminary work required to isolate my DNA for sequencing, Peter had arrived. He was out of breath, and explained that he had run up the stairs.

"Why?" I asked.

"Because the elevator was taking too damn long, and I wanted to find out why you were in such a rush."

"I wasn't in a rush," I murmured, lying through my teeth. "I was awake and thinking that I should be checking my telomeres on a regular basis."

"When was the last time you did? It wasn't so long ago, as I recall." Peter frowned.

"I don't remember the exact date, but it was before I started the chemo."

"You'll want to check it against the last time anyway," he said, disappearing into his office. He emerged a few minutes later holding a sheet of paper with the four-colored graph of blips peculiar to a DNA sequence.

"Here's the last one, done September fifteenth. Let me know if there's any change." He planted a quick kiss on my cheek, then went back into his office.

It was now the end of October. Six weeks had elapsed, and I expected to see some change, unless, like two of the mice, I was in a static period. I didn't think so. I finished purifying my DNA in the late morning and, once again picked three random chromosomes to sequence; it didn't matter which because the telomeres are the same repeated six molecules of nucleic acid in all chromosomes. These, I put onto the gel, and then into the sequencer. I knew that the process would take a few hours, which for me was a lifetime. Peter suggested we go out for lunch, but I knew I would be unable to eat, or even carry on a conversation. I said I wasn't hungry and wanted to read some journals in the library. He seemed disappointed, but didn't press me.

Outside, I started towards the library, but suddenly veered away and went into the park. Autumn was my favorite time of year, and this day was perfect. If I walked fast and took in the beauty of the remaining red and yellow foliage, it would help pass the time. I set an itinerary for myself: first the zoo, then the carousel, then around the lake and up to the reservoir. By that time I should have used up the better part of an hour, and, if I wanted to continue, I could visit the Museum of Natural History, or the Met. Keep going, I told myself. Don't think.

When I reached the zoo, I paid the dollar admission and wandered over towards the seal pool. I was watching the seals shoot by like torpedoes in the water, when a tentative voice said, "Connie?" I turned to find Walter's wife, Sarah, moving towards me, guiding an elegantly appointed baby carriage.

Oh no! I thought why do I always have to keep running into her, of all people? There was no getting away now.

"Hello, Sarah, how are you?" I greeted her. "How's the baby?"

"Oh, she's just fine," Sarah replied, beaming down at a sleeping infant covered by an embroidered, expensive-looking pink throw. Sarah seemed dressed to match, in a pink sweater and rose-colored skirt.

"We wanted to see the seals." She explained, looking slightly uncomfortable. My cool demeanor must be getting to her, I thought, pleased.

"And here they are," I noted. "Well, I'm afraid I have to get back. Lots of work, you know." I glanced at my watch, wanting to cut this unfortunate encounter short, before the questions began.

But I was too late. Sarah was now openly staring at me. "You look fabulous, Connie. Have you taken some time off?"

I was certain she thought I'd had cosmetic surgery. Well, let her.

"Yes, I was in Switzerland with Dave and Josh in August. How's Walter?" Not that I gave a damn.

"Oh, he's fine. I wish he could spend a little more time with us. He's such a workaholic." She gave me a look which I interpreted as complicity .

Uh-oh, I thought, he's up to his old tricks. I felt a bit sorry for her, and responded with a slight smile, "Yes, I guess that happens to a lot of women."

Sarah flushed a little, as though she might have implied something negative without meaning to. "Well, I suppose it is normal. The problem is, I get a little bored with the routine, but as Catherine gets older I'm sure she'll be more fun."

"Yes," I said, "Let's hope. Look, I have to get back to work. Nice seeing you, Sarah. Say hello to Walter for me. Goodbye, Catherine." I smiled down at the carriage, and left before she could instruct the baby to say 'bye-bye.'

Walking towards the carousel, I felt a strange sense of satisfaction. Walter may have left me for a younger woman, but he obviously hadn't changed his stripes. I wondered what Sarah was going to tell him about our meeting.

My mood shifted. Hmm, I thought, will Walter start quizzing Dave and Josh about my youthful appearance? That would just intensify my sons' suspicions, and they'd be back to me again. What was I going to do? So much depended on what the sequencer revealed.

Now, there was no keeping my mind off the colored blips coming out of the machine. I forced myself to walk rapidly up through the mall to the lake. Then I stopped. This wasn't working. In fact, my heart was pounding so hard from anxiety that just walking on level ground was making me breathless. I turned and slowly made my way back to Bailey.

# *Chapter 17*

*Chromosome 17* ————————————————————————————————

The sequencer was still running when I returned to the lab, but no one was around, and the door to Peter's office was closed. He might have been in there, but I had no intention of checking. I wanted to be alone until the machine stopped and I hoped that would be soon. I was growing frantic waiting.

If I truly believed in the value of prayer, I'd have gone down on my knees. As it was, I could only say over and over, "Please, please..." I didn't even know to whom or what I was beseeching; maybe there was some primal force that governed everything and could hear me. If there was a mysterious power controlling the universe, would it forgive me, or would it condemn me for interfering with the natural order of things?

I returned to my office to wait out the time, but there was nothing I could do to distract myself. My heart was in full crescendo, and my mouth felt as if I had dried it out with a towel. If my telomeres were getting longer, I was doomed. I wondered how long it would take before I began losing my mental sharpness. I had to have an exit strategy before that started to happen. What? How?

Suddenly it came to me. I had been worrying for so long about finding a way to make my death seem accidental. But all I had to do was tell the truth for a change. If my family and friends knew the truth, they would understand that I was going to die anyway, and that dying by my own hand would be better and more dignified than waiting to slowly lose all my faculties. I was reasonably sure that I would have enough time to leave an account of what had happened. Even if I was fortunate and my telomeres were shorter, there were too many unanswered questions about my change in appearance, particularly for Dave and Josh, and it was obvious that I would have to tell them. Also, I was uncertain how fast or slow my aging process would be which was all the more reason to reveal what had happened.

While these thoughts were distracting me from the anxiety of waiting, there was a knock on the door. A momentary wave of panic engulfed me. Then I answered "Yes?" in a cold voice to indicate I didn't want to be disturbed.

"It's Julie, Connie. The sequencer has stopped. Do you want to get the printout?"

Oh, God! "Thanks, Julie. I'll be right there." I assured her, my voice surprisingly calm.

If I had control of my voice, my legs, when I arose, were not responding. They felt made of rubber. I waited behind the door for several minutes to regain some control and allow Julie to return to her work. Then I walked swiftly out of my lab before Saki, who was busy at the far end, could intercept me.

It didn't take me long to retrieve the printout and remove my specimen from the sequencer. Luckily, Julie paid me no heed, and the door to Peter's office remained closed. I returned to my lab and once again evaded Saki, who looked up and seemed ready to speak. But before he could start, I firmly closed the office door.

The colored blips on the rolled-up chart in my hand would, I knew, determine my future. Although I knew what I had to do, I was paralyzed with fear. My teeth were clenched, and my entire body felt rigid and cold. I glanced down at the record in my hand and realized my fist was crunching up the paper. That would not do, as the graph might get damaged. Quickly stepping over to the desk, I lay the paper down beside the earlier printout, and sat down, pressing my fingers hard into my temples. "Do it, Connie, just do it," I commanded myself.

Then, I reached out and picked up the September sequence printout, taken just prior to starting chemotherapy. Once again, as I had in July, I found the starting point of the telomeres. I clipped the printouts together where the telomere sequences started, so that the new was lying on top. Then, very slowly and carefully, I unrolled the strips together along the surface of the desk until the telomere printout on top became a straight line, indicating the end of the telomere. All I had to do now was lift the top sheet and see whether the telomere printout on the bottom was longer or shorter than the one on top.

I was paralyzed. If I picked it up and saw the straight line had started sooner on the under sheet, it would mean that the new specimen's telomere was longer. It would also mean I was doomed. I closed my eyes, and lifted the top sheet. Very reluctantly I looked down at the earlier printout. The straight line was there, but it seemed to start more to my right. With trembling hands I put a paper clip on the telomere ending, replaced the upper printout over it, and placed another clip at that telomere ending. *The lower one was a fraction longer!* I was getting older!

"Thank God!" I said loudly to my empty office. I jumped to my feet, grabbed the two printouts, and rushed out the door, leaving a gaping Saki staring after me. When I ran into Peter's lab, Julie was standing at the sequencer. She turned around when she heard me. I must have been grinning like an idiot, because she gave me a strange look and then a small, questioning smile.

"Is Peter in his office?" I asked. I knocked on the closed door and burst into the room as he was saying, "Come in."

He was at his desk, looking at me with a startled expression. "What's happening? Is anything the matter?"

"Nothing's the matter." I threw the two printouts on the desk, and sat in the chair across from him. "Take a look at those," I was trying to keep a poker face.

He picked them up, and seeing what they were, flashed me a look, before returning his gaze to the graphs. He followed the same method I had used a few minutes earlier, but instead of paper clips, he drew lines to mark the beginnings and ends of the telomeres, and measured them with a tape.

"This one is several centimeters longer, and – don't tell me – it's your printout from September! The new one is shorter!" His eyes sparkled. "It worked! You're getting older again!" He jumped up, pulled me out of the chair, and crushed me against him. I began laughing uncontrollably as he swirled me around.

"You knew, didn't you? That's why you wanted to use the sequencer." He had stopped whirling, and was looking down at me accusingly, "You should have told me!"

"I couldn't," I replied breathlessly. "If it hadn't worked, it would have been terrible. I didn't want to get your hopes up."

"Connie, you didn't have to go through all that agony alone. But I'm curious, what made you suspect something was happening?"

"It was the same sign I had when I first realized I was getting younger; my hair. Only this time it was the reverse; some of the roots were grey."

"That was all you had to go on?" He asked, wide-eyed, "God, that could have been caused by many things that have nothing to do with aging."

"I know. That's another reason I didn't want to tell you," I admitted.

"What the hell, it doesn't matter now." He pulled me close into a long hard kiss. When I pulled away to breathe, he said, his face alight with relief, "We have to go out and celebrate with a bottle of champagne. I'd much rather take you home right now, but you'll probably want some time to digest all this."

I did, but at that moment, he could have made love to me right there in his office. I had the fleeting thought that my hormones, at least, were still very youthful.

Peter still had his arms around me and asked, "Have you told Lynn?"

"How could I?" I laughed. "I just found out this minute. I'll call her from my office. I'm going back there now to try to pull myself together. I feel I've just been granted a reprieve from a death sentence."

"You have, thank God," Peter agreed, kissing me again. "Where would you like to have dinner?"

"You decide," I said. "I'll meet you wherever you say. I do want to go home and change my clothes, before we meet, okay?"

"You'll look gorgeous to me, whatever you're wearing," grinned Peter. "I'll see you later."

I called Lynn at her office in the hospital and got her secretary, who announced that Dr. Stein was making rounds. I left a message for her to call me, then sat back and tried to digest all that had happened.

I had spoken accurately when I told Peter I'd been granted a reprieve. In fact, that was all it was. Based on the results in the mice, my future was still very uncertain. Out of five mice, only two had shown signs of "normal" aging. I considered there had to be some way of determining why the mice had such varied findings. Yet, the longer I sat at my desk, the more muddled I became. Finally I accepted the obvious. I needed to get out of the office.

I went to the window, and stared out at the street below. My earlier exhilaration had vanished, and I now felt oddly empty. The fear of dying as an infant had been replaced with other concerns: How rapidly would I age? For all I knew, I could be an old woman in a year or two. Or, would I age more slowly than others, and watch my children die before me?

A shiver ran through me. I felt as if I were in a different dimension from the rest of humankind. At least the lucky men and women walking in the street below knew that their youth would disappear in a natural sequence of events.

I turned away from the window. Although it was still early in the day, I had no desire to do anything. What was wrong with me? I had just been granted a stay, and now I was in a blue funk, worrying about yet another problem.

The phone rang. It was Lynn, returning my call.

"Hi Connie, I just got back from rounds. What's up?" she asked cautiously.

"The chemo worked. I'm getting older." I told her this ground-breaking news calmly, unlike the announcement I'd made to Peter.

But obviously that didn't deter Lynn, who let out a shriek, "It did? How wonderful! How do you know?"

"My telomeres are shorter than they were on the September printout."

"What a relief! Now I can breathe again." She paused for a second, then said, "You *have* told Peter, I presume? What did he say?."

"He's ecstatic," I smiled briefly. "In fact, we're going out tonight to celebrate."

"Can we meet tomorrow for breakfast? I want to *see* you." Lynn was adamant.

"I don't look any different yet, of course I'll meet you."

" Tomorrow at eight in the Coffee Shop. Is that too early?"

"No, that's fine," I agreed. I was exhausted. As I put down the phone, all I could think of was a hot bath, and a long nap.

Peter called me later and left a message telling me to meet him at "Two, Two, Two," a fancy West Side restaurant. I arrived a few minutes after seven-thirty, and saw him sitting at a table, a bottle of champagne in a cooler next to him. I was wearing a black silk dress trimmed with black velvet, one of my favorites. I was surprised to see that Peter was wearing a dark grey suit. "Where did you get the suit?" I asked, planting a kiss on his lips as I sat down beside him. " I didn't think you were going back to Brooklyn."

"I didn't. I keep one in my office for special occasions, and this is a super-special one. You look fantastic! Have I ever seen that dress before?" Peter couldn't stop beaming at me, and at the same time beckoning to the wine steward, who came over to uncork the champagne.

When he had tasted and approved the wine, Peter watched as the steward poured it into two thin tulip-shaped glasses. Then, Peter raised his and said, "To you, Connie. May you grow up to be a beautiful old lady."

I touched my glass to his and said, "I'll certainly drink to that." I took a sip. "This is wonderful. What is it?"

"Something the wine steward recommended." He took a sip and added, "It is very good, isn't it?"

I took another swallow of the Champagne and felt the bubbles in my nose and down the back of my throat.

Peter was watching me, amused. "Did you know that the smaller the bubbles are in champagne, the better the quality of the wine?"

"No, I never heard of that. How do they measure the bubble size?"

"Beats me, maybe I'll ask the wine steward later." Peter sat back in his chair, his face became serious. "There's something I haven't had a chance to tell you yet, Connie."

My heart dropped. What was it? Some more bad news about the mice?

My face must have betrayed my anxiety, because he said, "Relax, it's nothing bad. Yesterday I got a call from the dean of Harvard Medical School. He made me a very enticing offer, Connie. It seems they want to develop a new center for genetics and genomics, and he wants me to head it. He knows that you and I have been working together, he asked if you might consider limiting your study of virology to gene transport. It seems they have no opening in general virology, but very little is being done in the field of gene therapy. He's going to call you, but wanted to check with me first."

I was stunned and speechless. Just as one challenge was overcome, a new one had replaced it. I couldn't reply.

"I love you, Connie," Peter said, taking my hand. I don't want to go without you. Would you come with me?"

For a moment I couldn't speak. Two months ago I would have said, "yes," without hesitation. Now I didn't know. I needed time to think. I had been to hell and back and I wasn't the same person I had been then. All this must have shown on my face because Peter was looking at me with concern,

"I guess this isn't the best time to ask you with everything happening so fast."

"I'm sorry, Peter," I choked out. "I think the Harvard offer sounds wonderful for you, but I'm not sure it will work for me. Let me think it over."

Just then, the waiter appeared and our conversation ended while we ordered dinner. We both decided on the "special," breast of duck with chanterelle mushrooms and wild rice.

It occurred to me, as we were placing the order, that the last time Peter and I had been out together was the night he told me our mice were continuing to get younger; it seemed an eternity ago.

Peter didn't refer to the Harvard offer again during dinner, but we spoke instead about the different responses the mice had shown to our attempts to restore aging. Peter said it was easier for him to understand no response, as in the two mice that continued to get younger, than it was to explain why one mouse aged so rapidly. He thought if we ran the experiment I had mapped out while still in isolation, we would have been able to get a better idea. He cheered me up by saying he thought that particular mouse was an anomaly that would, in all probability, not occur again.

After we had finished the duck and the bottle of Champagne, dessert was served. Suddenly I felt a little woozy.

"Maybe I'm too young to be drinking so much," I considered aloud to Peter. He laughed and said, " Come on, I'll take you home. It's past your bedtime."

In the taxi, he put his arm around me and said, "Don't feel you have to decide about Harvard immediately, Connie. They won't be ready for at least six months. The building that will house the center is still under construction."

"But they'll want to know about you very soon, Peter," I pointed out. "You can't keep them waiting too long. And what about Bailey, haven't they given you a counter offer?"

"Balch knows about it. He said they'd love to keep me here, but they can't offer me a genome center. As far as Harvard is concerned, they have to give me some leeway. My decision is very tied into yours, and I don't want you to feel pressured."

I sat up, pulling away from his arm, "That's not right, Peter. You have to do what's best for you, and it's a wonderful offer. If I feel that my decision will affect yours, that *would* be pressure."

"Alright, darling. You've had a long day. Get some rest and I'll see you tomorrow." He kissed me in the cab, and I went up to bed, thankful that Peter understood I wanted to be alone. Within ten minutes, I was in bed and, for once, fell fast asleep.

# Chapter 18

ꝸ ꝸ *Chromosome 18*

I awakened early and lay in bed trying to recollect an elusive dream. The harder I tried, the vaguer and wispier it became. For some reason, I was hoping the dream would clarify something in my subconscious and help me come to a decision about Peter. Maybe if I stopped trying so hard, it would materialize again.

Remembering my eight AM breakfast with Lynn, I started the shower. As I stood under the water, I thought about Peter's offer. Harvard was certainly a prestigious place to be, and perfect from his point of view. From mine, it was less so. I didn't like being forced to investigate only one aspect of virology, and I didn't want to leave Bailey. Unlike Peter, I'd been there a long time. They had treated me well, and I felt an allegiance to the university. I continued pondering my new dilemma as I headed out to the Coffee Shop.

I arrived first and ordered orange juice, a cinnamon bagel, and coffee. Lynn, who came in just as the order was being put on the table, asked for the same, and slid into the seat opposite me. She was beaming, "Well, you don't look any older to me, but I'm relieved I won't be having to change your diapers."

"Don't joke about it," I groaned. "It could easily have happened. Now, I don't know how fast or slow the aging process is going to be. The mice all responded differently, so there isn't any way to predict."

Her expression sobered immediately. "I know. But look on the bright side – you're going in the right direction, at least! The other way would have been a nightmare."

"Don't tell me!" I spoke more quietly. "You know, I was actually planning to kill myself long before the diaper stage."

A flicker of horror flashed across Lynn's face. Then she reached across the table, took my hand and squeezed it. "You know, I suspected that. Do Dave and Josh know what's up?"

"No, but I'll tell them now. They knew something was amiss last time we were together. I was saved by the fact that Dave's girlfriend was there, and they couldn't quiz me in front of her. It'll be a lot easier now that I've stopped retrogressing." I took a bite of the bagel.

Lynn added milk to her coffee and began to stir it. "Is there any way to determine if your aging rate is normal?"

I swallowed the bagel and took a sip of juice. "I've been wondering about that. I have some ideas, but I'll need Peter's help. Oh, and speaking of Peter, he's been offered the directorship of a new genetics center at Harvard. He said they'd also like me to come and work on viruses for gene therapy."

Lynn sat back in her chair and looked down at her coffee with a slight frown. "What did you tell him?"

"I told him I needed time to think about it. I'm not sure," I confessed.

She shifted her gaze to look directly into my eyes, "Do you still love him?"

I hesitated, swallowed some coffee, and then said, "I don't know. Something changed when I found out what was happening to me, and after having the abortion. I saw another side of him then. Peter let me down just when I needed him to be strong. I know you said he was in shock, but he was so cold...and, oh, I don't know." I pushed the plate with the bagel to one side, my appetite gone.

Lynn's eyes had not wavered, and I looked down and put the back of my hand to my mouth. After a pause, she spoke, "Well, you're the only one who can decide whether or not you love him."

"Even if I decide I do love him, I don't think I want to leave Bailey," I said slowly. "I don't want to leave New York, either. My sons are here, you're here, I have a nice apartment. I'm free to do any type of virology I choose. Harvard's a wonderful opportunity for Peter though, and I'm worried that he might turn it down if I don't agree to go with him."

"Did he say that?" Lynn asked.

"He implied it, he said his decision was dependant on mine. I told him that wasn't fair."

Lynn appeared increasingly somber. "I know how much he loves you, Connie. All I can say is, take your time." She looked at her watch, put the remainder of the bagel in her bag, and stood up, "Damn! Late again. I've got to get to the clinic. Call me later, okay?" She blew me a kiss, left some money, and dashed off.

I stayed at the table sipping my tepid coffee and thinking. I was fairly certain I would turn down the offer from Harvard, mainly because I wanted the freedom to investigate any aspect of biologically relevant problems, not just viruses as vectors for genes. But there were also selfish reasons: I didn't like the fact that the invitation came to me through Peter, which implied they only wanted me to get him. And, more important, I wanted to find a way to determine my rate of aging.

That brought me up short. Why was I sitting here idling when I could be in my office working? I got up, paid the cashier and went out into a windy November day. Swirls of brown and yellow leaves from the nearby park blew along the street. I could feel a hint of winter in the air and shivered. I should be welcoming winter as a metaphor for my own aging...as long as I received my normal quota of years.

When I arrived at the lab, I had already made a mental list of the things I had to do. First was to see Dave and Josh and tell them what was going on. I opened the door and saw Saki in the isolation room, where the tissue cultures are kept. I stuck my head in to tell him I would be making some phone calls in the office, and he turned and nodded without speaking. We hadn't spoken since I had run out of the lab the day before. He must have been puzzled by my behavior, but this was not the time for me to explain it to him. Dave and Josh came first.

I knew I would probably find Dave in his apartment because he worked late at night, but when Sandra picked up the phone I was mildly surprised. Had she moved in permanently?

"Good morning, Sandra. It's Connie, Dave's mother."

"Oh, good morning, Dr. Gueyer. Do you want to speak to Dave?"

"Yes, please." Normally I would have made a little small talk and asked her a few questions to be friendly.

Dave came to the phone and said, "Mom?" There was veiled concern in his voice. It was unusual for me to call him before noon.

"I'd like to meet with you and Josh, Dave. I have something to tell you."

'What is it?" He asked, obviously alarmed.

"It's nothing bad, just a little unusual. Could you find Josh for me? He must be in a class now."

David still sounded concerned, "Yes, I'll try and track him down. Is it okay to bring Sandra? Actually, we're sort of engaged."

I hesitated. It was one thing to tell my sons, whom I trusted to keep a confidence, but I didn't know Sandra very well. Also, there was always a possibility that she and David might change their minds about each other.

"I'd rather just have you and Josh this time." I emphasized. "I'm sure she'll understand. Call me after you find Josh, and then we can decide on a good time to meet."

"Okay, I'll go over there now and ask what class he's in."

"Thanks, darling. I'll see you later, and don't worry." I knew this admonition would not be heeded, as Dave was a worrier.

I pushed the disconnect bar on the phone and dialed the next person on my list, Alan. When he answered, I said, "Hi, Alan. It's me. I wanted you to know the chemotherapy did the job, I'm actually getting older."

There was a momentary pause, then he answered in his low voice, "That's wonderful news, Connie! I had a feeling it was going to work. Nothing scientific about it, just a premonition. Is everything else working out for you, too?"

I was sure he was referring to Peter. "I don't know, Alan. I have a lot to think about. Right now I have an appointment to tell my sons the whole story. And I'm worried about how they'll take it."

"The important thing is, you're out of the woods," he reassured me. "Kids are pretty resilient. When are you seeing them?"

"As soon as Dave reaches Josh, he said he'd call."

"Well, I won't tie up your phone now. Call me later. I'd like to see you."

"Okay, I will," I said. I placed the telephone in its cradle, and sat back in the swivel chair, thinking about Alan. He was so undemanding, and at the same time so empathetic. I liked him very much. He always seemed to do exactly the right thing, at least for me. The night he wanted to make love to me I had been very needy and depressed, and it would have been so easy to succumb. I felt he realized that, too, and didn't persist when I backed off. At that moment, I came to the realization that another reason I didn't want to leave New York was because of him.

I sat up suddenly and said, "whoa." This was no time to be thinking about that sort of thing. I still had to sort out my feelings about Peter. And I'd been granted a reprieve and needed to have a plan for the research I wanted to do in whatever time was left to me.

I pulled over a blank pad lying near the telephone, and took a pencil out of the center drawer. Maybe it was the scientist in me, but I've always found it easier to think with pencil and paper in hand.

Then, I started making random squiggles on the pad. After a minute or so I wrote and underlined the words *Possible outcomes*. Under this heading I wrote '*1. Age normally  2. Age more rapidly than normal  3. Age more slowly than normal*. Of these three possibilities, the best was obviously the first. I moved my pencil to the second outcome. Here I wrote *rate*. This was the key point, and it would also apply to point three. Everything would depend on how fast or slow the process was. So far, nothing I had written was all that helpful.

I doodled a little more and then wrote *Courses of action: establish rate*. This was easy enough to write, but how was I going to do it. I wrote *?telomere length*. Measurement of telomeres was critical, but how would I be able to tell whether they were losing length at a faster or slower rate than normal? What was normal, anyway?

I decided to follow a group of individuals over a year to enable me to estimate their rate of aging compared to my own. But how many individuals? It was extremely likely that telomere length varied among individuals of the same age. People carry their years differently, especially as they get older. I sat back in my chair. Maybe this investigation would lead to another possibility, one I didn't think most people would want to explore: Would knowing the rate of telomere shortening indicate the approximate time of death?

Now I was beginning to see a new research possibility: A study of telomere length in dying patients, compared to those of healthy individuals the same age. It would also be interesting to follow patients with chronic diseases, such as cancer, heart disease, or diabetes, and again compare the rate of telomere shortening to that of healthy individuals, particularly those from families with a history of longevity. And what about the rare condition called Progeria, when children grow old at the ages of two or three? I wondered if anyone had investigated the length of their telomeres.

This kind of research would take a few years of sample gathering to be significant, and I didn't even know if I would have the time to complete it. If I did, would it be useful to me, or, for that matter, to anyone else?

I sat back in the chair, laid the pencil on the desk, and started chewing the knuckle of my right index finger, a habit I had from childhood, which I reverted to whenever I was deep in thought. After a few moments of gentle gnawing, I picked up the pencil again and wrote: *Three groups (all contemporaries within 1-2 years); 1. Terminal illness 2. Chronic illness with poor prognosis for longevity 3. Healthy.* The study would only be significant if there was obvious telomere shortening in Group One.

I put the pencil down. If I embarked on this investigation, frequent access to at least one sequencer was imperative. As it was, I only could use the one in Peter's lab when it was idle, which was not too often. Unless, of course, I could interest him in the same project. It was, after all, a genetics experiment. Peter was not going to Harvard for six months, if he did go, so I might have time to get started, and maybe to negotiate with him for one of the sequencers.

I realized I was also prepared to tell him that I couldn't leave Bailey for Harvard. I dialed his number, and, when he answered, said, "Hi Peter, are you free? I'd like to speak to you. In person."

"Sure," he said, "Come on over."

On the way out of the lab, I turned on the intercom to the isolation chamber, where I could see Saki through the glass door, and said, "Saki, I'm expecting a call from one of my sons. If it comes, please call me in Peter's office."

"Okay, Connie," Saki replied, without turning his head. He was obviously peeved with my mysterious behavior, and I planned to enlighten him later. He deserved to know.

Peter was at his desk when I entered his office. He started to rise, but I sat quickly on the chair opposite him. He looked hurt. Maybe he was expecting me to kiss him. I decided to get right to the point.

"I've come to a decision, Peter. I'm sorry, but the offer from Harvard really won't be right for me. There are several reasons. The chief one is having to give up the work I'd like to pursue for a more limited type of viral study. I would also have to leave Bailey, where I've worked all my academic life. And, from a personal point of view, it would be harder for me to see my sons and all my old friends and associates."

Peter was frowning and seemed about to interrupt, but I stopped him. "Let me finish, Peter. Of course, I am going to miss you a lot, but the one thing I feel certain about is that you should *not* give up this offer. It's too good an opportunity to pass up."

He was still frowning as I continued, "Peter, there are too many loose ends for me right now. I have no idea how fast I'm going to age, or how slowly. I've thought about how I could investigate that, and I may have come up with an idea, but it will take a while before there are any results."

"What's your idea?" Now Peter's eyes were sad, his voice low.

I told him, and while listening, he leaned against his right elbow on the desk, propped his chin on his hand, and stared at a spot on the wall. After several moments of silence, he exhaled softly, and said, "I understand your need to know, Connie, but perhaps we can come up with another method. Ascertaining time of death would not really benefit anyone except possibly the insurance companies." He smiled wryly. Then sat back in his chair and looked hard at me before continuing, "I'm naturally disappointed about your decision not to go to Harvard. From a professional point of view, I do understand, but I don't think I want to go without you. I love you. I thought you loved me and that we belong together. Of course, my work is important, but you are more important to me than my career. Don't you know that?"

I put my hand to my forehead and started rubbing it. This was going to be difficult, I had to convince him to go for his sake. "Peter, you are a brilliant geneticist. You've been given the opportunity to go to one of the best universities in the country as head of Genetics. Please listen. Don't throw that chance away because of me. I've been enough of a problem as it is. I need time on my own to make up for what I did, and I don't want to have you on my conscience as well. We had a brief, happy time together which was drastically altered by what I did. Too much has happened for us to pick up the pieces and start all over, the specter of my uncertain future will always be there. I would love to have you stay at Bailey, but in my heart I know it would be wrong for you. You have to go."

Peter remained silent for a long time, looking first into my eyes, and then down at a spot on the floor. He sighed deeply and seemed about to speak when the phone rang. He made no attempt to pick it up, so I rose from the chair and said, "It might be for me."

Immediately, he answered the call and nodded to me. It was Saki saying, "Your son David called, Connie. He's at home and wants you to call him."

"Thanks, Saki, I'll be right back." I put the phone down and turned to Peter, "Sorry, Peter, I have to go call David, I want Josh and him to come here so I can tell them what's been going on with me. Can we finish this conversation later?"

Peter nodded, "I'll be here," he said.I couldn't look at him as I dashed out the door.

Dave had located Josh, and said they would come to my office right away. They arrived about a half hour later. When the door was closed and we were all seated, I said, "Before I begin, I want to say that I haven't been completely up front with you. I think you'll understand after I give you the whole story."

My sons were both looking at me with concern. I continued, "I know you have both remarked about my youthful appearance..." I sighed, then sat back in my chair. "It's a long story, and Josh was right when he suspected the telomere experiment."

With that introduction, I went on to describe the events that led up to my fateful swallowing of the mutated *nuclease* gene, my subsequent realization that I was getting younger, the awful discovery that the process would not stop, that I was going to continue to regress, and finally, the chemotherapy, allowing me to become reinfected with the virus carrying the normal gene and reversing the process.

"And that's it," I said, leaning further back my chair. I had told all, but had not revealed my pregnancy and abortion. I didn't want them to know that. Neither one had uttered a sound throughout my disclosure, and they continued their silence for several moments more. Dave had his mouth slightly open, as if in shock, and Josh was staring at some point above my head. His characteristic loquaciousness finally broke through. "Boy, you took a big chance. I never really believed you had done anything like that, I was just imagining a sci-fi scenario."

At that point Dave closed his mouth and sat forward. "Yeah, it explains all the stuff we noticed about you in Switzerland, like your being able to climb so well, and all the comments about how you looked too young to be our mother. Sandra couldn't get over it. Why didn't you want us to know back then?"

"For a lot of reasons. One, I didn't want anyone to know because I was ashamed of having done something so unscientific and stupid. The fact that I was groggy from the Ativan was no excuse. Two, I was afraid that if word got around, I would be regarded as a human guinea pig, and lose all semblance of a private life. But mainly it was because of you two. I didn't want you to have a mother who seemed to be your age. At first I thought the change was transient, that I would get a little younger in appearance, and then the effect of the mutated gene would wear off and I wouldn't have to tell anyone. In most instances of gene therapy that is the case. The mutation, unless it's put directly into the early stage of a developing embryo, has a temporary effect, and has to keep being replenished to remain effective. When I found out, that for some reason, this was not the case, and I was going to get progressively younger, I knew I couldn't tell you. I had to think of some way to disappear or die before I became a child again. I was doomed to die anyway as an infant, and I didn't want you to live through that nightmare."

"Did you tell anyone?" Josh asked, his voice cracked. I could tell he was struggling not to cry.

"Yes, only after I learned that the mice were progressing towards infancy. Then I told Peter and Lynn. Peter worked out the method of reversing the process with chemotherapy to weaken my immune system enough so I could be reinfected with the virus carrying the normal gene, and Lynn made sure I was in isolation, and followed my blood count. Without them, I never would have made it."

David, still looking solemn, said, "You're okay now, aren't you?"

"Well, I'm getting older again, thank God, but I don't know yet how fast or slow the process will be."

Josh burst in, "Do you mean you might get old all of a sudden?" He looked anguished.

"No, I don't think that will happen, but it might be somewhat different, either slower or faster. But hopefully, it'll be normal." I didn't want to burden them with anything else. "Peter thinks it will be normal."

"Can I tell Sandra any of this?" David asked.

I frowned, "I don't know, Dave. I'd like to keep the whole thing confined to Peter, Lynn, and you two." I didn't mention Alan, as they had never met him. "If it ever gets out, I'd have a lot of unpleasant attention, and it would interfere with my work. I'm just worried that if you two should decide to split, she might say something. I know it's asking a lot of you, to keep anything from her, but for now, I'd rather you did. And, David, I like Sandra very much. I think it's wonderful that you are 'sort of' engaged."

Josh spoke up. "Tell her Mom was worried she had something bad, like cancer, but it turned out to be something else that was okay."

"Yes, that isn't too far removed from what actually happened," I said. "Don't say anything about my appearance. Hopefully that's going to change.

"Isn't it weird that you want to look older, and everyone else in the world wants to look young?" Josh laughed. He had regained some of his buoyancy.

"That's true, but if they were faced with starting off old and growing progressively younger, what do you think they'd want?"

"That would make the young looking people older than the old looking people!" Josh was now back in his element, fantasizing.

"Great." Dave said in disgust, "Can we get back to the point? I guess I'll be able to deal with Sandra for now. Maybe later on I can tell her?" He looked at me.

"Let's see if you and she are still together in a year, and plan on staying that way. You are both very young and a lot can happen. I'll tell her myself when that time comes."

Dave nodded and seemed somewhat mollified. Josh stood up, saying he had to get back to go to his eleven o'clock physics lab. We made a date to go to dinner the following week, and I kissed them both goodbye.

After they had gone, I decided to deal with Saki. He was sitting at one of the counters looking through a microscope. I asked him to please come into my office for a minute. When he was seated on the couch, and I was at my desk, I said, "I realize that you have observed some rather strange behavior on my part, Saki. Did you make any assumptions about what was happening?"

I knew he was very intelligent, and wanted to see if he might have linked my behavior to any of the work we had been doing. He looked down at his feet, and rubbed the back of his neck, as though he felt ill at ease. After a pause of a few seconds he looked up and said, "I don't know how to say this, because you might become angry. I drew some very strange conclusions."

"No, I doubt that anything you say would make me angry, tell me."

He hesitated again, and then drew in a breath, "Sometime in July I started noticing how well you looked, and in August, when you returned from your trip, you looked even better... younger. I attributed it to your vacation, but the day after you returned, and came to Peter's lab, you seemed so unlike yourself; you looked frightened. I was there when you went into Peter's office, and I also saw you when you came out. You were very upset by something, and I don't think you noticed me."

I was watching him intently as he continued, "Right after that, Peter started to look very worried. He became irritable and was fixated on the progress of the mice that were growing younger. It was then that I started wondering if the same thing was happening to you. When Julie told me you had been using the sequencer, I was even more suspicious, because none of the work we were involved in required that."

I interrupted him. "I should have realized, that with your powers of observation, you would figure it all out. Did you also understand why I was home with the 'flu'?"

"I think I did after Peter started giving chemotherapy to the mice, and you disappeared. Am I right in thinking the therapy worked?"

"You are, Saki. You are very perceptive, and I wish you could stay here and work with me for good. I'm sorry I was so secretive. Have you spoken about this to anyone else?"

"No. I didn't, mainly because I wasn't certain. Can you tell me why you did it, Connie?"

Once again I recounted the story, and throughout Saki's expression revealed little of what he must have been thinking.

When I finally finished speaking, he remained quiet for several moments. Then, he shifted his gaze to look at me, rose from the couch and said quietly, "Thank you for explaining, Connie. I'm so happy it's all over."

I was expecting him to ask me some questions, but if he had any, he was keeping them to himself. I wondered if I would ever know how he felt, and at that moment it seemed enormously important to me. What I knew for certain was that, however he felt, the information would remain confidential.

I got up, walked over to him, and kissed him on the cheek. He flushed in confusion and said, "Are you about my age now, Connie?"

"Yes, I guess I am, but not for long, I hope," I responded.

After Saki left, I sat for a while at my desk, wondering if he was disappointed in me. I had revealed myself as a fallible woman, not the careful scientist he could admire. But I sensed something else. If he was seeing me more and more as a contemporary, had he started thinking of me as an eligible female? That would be a complication I didn't need. He was right in presuming I was physically about his age, perhaps younger. It was hardly the best setup for a senior scientist employing a junior one. I had to hope that my years of training and experience would continue to give me the upper hand and that my rate of aging would accelerate.

That was my dilemma. I wanted to grow older, but not too old, too fast. I had to find some alternative way to determine the rate of aging, one that did not require following a lot of people. As Peter had mentioned, and I concurred, determining the time of death of an individual was not something most people would want to know. That was what I had been facing as I got progressively younger. Soon, I would have been able to know the precise time I was going to die as an infant.

In addition, sequencing the telomeres in large numbers of people would be very expensive and time-consuming. I pondered some alternative method to use on myself. We had observed that telomeres played a very important role in aging, but what regulated their length was the ratio of the enzymes, *telomerase* to *nuclease*. Young people presumably had more *telomerase* than older ones. Was there any way to measure that ratio? If that were possible, there would be no need for a sequencer. It would require nothing more than a simple set of biochemical tests.

Yet, my knowledge of these enzymes was somewhat limited. Outside of knowing their actions on the telomeres and the DNA sequence of the genes, I was ignorant about how they achieved their particular functions, and how it might be possible to measure them quantitatively.

I logged onto the internet, and after searching in a number of medical sites, I had the answer: The only way to determine the levels of telomerase and nuclease was to find their levels inside the cells of a particular organ, for my purposes, it was the hypothalamus, where they exert their effect on the aging center. In other words, one must biopsy that area of the brain. A biopsy there was much too risky to contemplate, because so many vital functions were controlled in that location. One more dead end. I put the computer on standby, and rubbed my temples. Maybe I should forget about trying to predict my rate of aging. I was the only one with a burning need to know, it would not benefit anyone else, and it was something most people would be fearful of investigating.

All at once, I remembered Peter. We hadn't finished talking. I called him to ask when we should meet, and he suggested resuming our conversation at Ponte Verde, a nearby Italian restaurant, in thirty minutes.

# *Chapter 19*

When I arrived at the restaurant five minutes late, Peter was already seated in a booth at the rear. He looked tense, fiddling with his water glass and looking around, waiting for me. There were a few other patrons sitting in booths, but the place was far from full. Most of the clientele came from the hospital-medical school complex during the day. Peter stood up as I approached and slid into the opposite banquette.

"Sorry I'm a little late," I said.

He didn't respond, but seemed to be studying my face intently. Then he said, "Let's have a drink," and gestured to a waiter. He ordered a vodka martini for himself, and a glass of Chianti for me, then resumed his scrutiny. I was starting to wonder whether he would ever speak, when he cleared his throat and began.

"I spent a lot of time thinking about what you said before you were called to the phone, Connie. I told you I understood your decision on a professional level, and I can also see why you want to be near your sons. But what worries me is what you said about us, that what we had was beautiful for a while, and that everything changed when we found out that what was happening to the mice was going to apply to you, too." He paused. "But Connie, that was not true of me. I never stopped loving you. I grant you I was shocked, even angry, that you were so impetuous, and that you had so little trust in me, but I still loved you. I haven't changed. I just don't know about *you* anymore, and I think that's the main issue between us."

He waited while the drinks were put on the table, then took a sizeable swallow of his martini, as though he needed it. I took a sip of the wine, and waited to see if he had anything more to say.

He did.

"I've often thought when you had to have the abortion, that was the end of your love for me. I should have allowed you to make that decision for yourself instead of insisting on it. Am I wrong? Was that a turning point for you?"

I thought I saw tears in his eyes. I didn't answer him right away. I felt so many emotions churning inside me: the memory of our love, my stupidity and lack of trust, the awful sadness of the abortion, and my need to be free. That need seemed to eclipse almost everything else. I took another swallow of wine. I felt I had to word my response very carefully, and with total candor.

"Peter," I said, finally, "I will always love you. But you're right, something did change after I realized the awful consequences of what I'd done. I wanted so much to have your baby, and later, I understood that an abortion was inevitable. It didn't make it any less painful, and I had betrayed you in so many ways. I began to see myself as a foolish, vain, and jealous woman. That impression grew as I had time to think, and as it grew, I realized the only way for me to make amends, to allow me to regain some self esteem, was to focus on my work and do what I could for other people."

I drank some more wine before continuing, "That's what's happening to me now. I can't be right for anyone until I begin to feel better about myself."

Peter was twirling the stem of his empty glass, studying it closely. "Do you want another drink?" he finally asked.

"Not yet," I said. "You have one if you want."

"I think I will. Maybe we should order dinner, too."

I nodded, and he signaled the waiter. After perusing the menu, I ordered veal and peppers, and he, lasagna and another martini. My wine was almost gone, so I changed my mind, and asked for another glass. As soon as the waiter left, Peter resumed speaking.

"I guess I'm not surprised by what you said, but you know, if I accept Harvard, I won't be leaving for about six months. That may be enough time for you to find the work you want, and feel better about yourself. I think you're being much too hard on yourself, Connie. You're an excellent scientist. I never would have located the aging center in the brain. You have original ideas, and the ability to implement them. The mistake you made was done in a moment of weakness. That moment was more costly than anyone could have anticipated, but for heaven's sake, don't castigate yourself endlessly. You've paid the price ten times over!"

He paused while our drinks were set on the table, then raised his glass to me, "Here's to your ability to grant yourself forgiveness, and start anew," his lips curled in a faint smile. "And here's to your future happiness. I hope I'm a part of it."

I looked down, my eyes had filled with tears. After a moment, I picked up my glass and raised it to him, "To you, Peter, and to your very promising future. I hope we'll always be friends."

Peter reached across and took my hand as I set the glass down. "I hope we'll be *at least* friends," he said, raising my hand to his lips.

We walked back to my apartment after dinner, skirting the park. The November night was crisp and clear, the lights from the tall buildings surrounding the park all but obliterated the stars, and stood against the sky, as humankind's challenge to nature. Our conversation in the restaurant had become easier after I explained my decision. During dinner, I gave Peter an account of my meeting with Dave and Josh, and also with Saki. We had maintained a companionable silence while walking, and just before getting to the entrance, Peter pulled me up to the side of the building and kissed me. I felt myself responding once again, but was relieved when he said, "I'm going to say goodnight to you here, not because I want to, but because you seem to have a lot to think about. Don't forget, I'm not going anywhere for at least six months, and I'll still be working on telomerase."

"Thanks, Peter, you've made everything a lot easier for me." I kissed him again, briefly, and walked into my apartment building.

A myriad of thoughts were spinning around in my head, while I took off my coat and hung it in the closet. Did I really love Peter? Did I want to continue working with him on telomerase? Would it be better for me to forget all that, and start a new investigation? How much time did I have left?

Then, I had a moment of striking epiphany. There wasn't a thing I could do about my aging. Therefore, I had to live like a normal person, and not try to cram everything into some limited time frame. I had been berating myself and vowing to devote the rest of my life to research in order to atone for my mistake, behaving like a melodramatic teenager (maybe that's what I was). As Peter had pointed out, I had lived through enough hell. Now, I should start to enjoy my life.

I realized I was still standing in front of the open closet. I closed the door, and walked up to the living room window. "Have a little fun,"

I said, looking down at the street where people were walking, mostly in pairs. I'll make some dates, read some good books, go to the movies, live outside myself for a change. I felt suddenly light in spirit. Wanting to share the sensation, I walked to the desk in my study, picked up the phone and dialed Lynn. When she answered, I said, "I've come to a momentous decision."

"What?" She asked.

"I'm going to start having some fun," I answered.

"Whoopee!" she chortled. "What brought that on?"

"A bunch of things. I'm not sure, but it just hit me. Hey, do you want to go to a movie?"

"When?" She asked, a little warily.

"Anytime," I took the phone over to the easy chair and sat down.

"Have you been drinking?" Lynn asked. "You sound strange."

"Only a little wine. I had dinner with Peter. And no, I'm not drunk. I told him I was not going to Harvard, and I convinced him to go without me. And I'm glad. But I've begun to realize I was beginning to sound like a religious martyr. Was I?"

"A little," Lynn said, laughing.

"You don't *have* to agree with me. What about the movies?"

"Can I call you tomorrow? We're watching a show on TV."

"Sure," I said, and went to the desk to put the phone back. Then on a whim, I picked up my address book, looked under M, and dialed Alan's number. While the phone was ringing , I wondered what I was going to say to him, and after three rings, I was about to hang up when he picked up the phone.

"Hello," he sounded distracted.

"Alan, it's Connie. Is this a bad time?"

"Oh, hi, Connie. No, it's okay. I was just brushing my teeth. I'm getting ready to hit the sack. I have a mouthful of toothpaste, hold on a sec."

I glanced at my watch, it was only nine-thirty. When he came back, I said, "Sorry. Is this your usual bedtime?"

"Depends. I got in late night last night. What's going on with you?"

"Nothing much for a change. I decided I need to have a little fun, so I'm asking you out for dinner."

"I accept," he laughed. "When?"

"Are you free any time this week?" I asked.

"Let's see, today's Tuesday. Wednesday, Thursday, Friday, or Saturday? Just kidding. How about tomorrow night?"

"Good," I said, "Do you want to try something besides sushi? How about curry for a change?"

"Sure, Do you know any good places?"

"Yes," I answered. "There's one I've been to that's pretty good called Star of India. It's on Ninth Avenue and Fourteenth Street, and I think there's a parking lot nearby.

Alan offered to make a reservation and pick me up at seven. When I replaced the phone, I wondered why I was being so forward, and what, exactly, I was trying to do. He might think I was inviting him to more than just a dinner. Was I? No, I said to myself. He's just a good friend, like Lynn, and now Peter. I need friends and a bit of variety, that's all, I told myself…but, I wasn't completely convinced. Nevertheless, I knew I would stick to my resolve.

The next morning at seven-thirty, Lynn called back. I agreed to meet her in the coffee shop at the hospital in half an hour. I had already had breakfast at home, so I ordered a cup of coffee while she ate. She listened intently as I described my dinner with Peter and my sudden realization later that he was right, I had atoned enough. At that point she nodded in agreement.

"That was why I called you about going to a movie. After I spoke to you, I called Alan and asked him out to dinner."

At that point, Lynn put down her half eaten bagel and said, "What gives with that guy? Are you starting a new relationship?"

"He's just an old, good friend, Lynn," I said frowning.

"How come I'd never heard of him before a few months ago, if he's such a good old friend?" She was looking at me accusingly. Once again she was championing Peter, and I felt a stab of irritation.

"I'm not tied to Peter, Lynn. Last night I told him I needed to be free, and he understood. My main concern now is to get going on some research of my own, but I also want the freedom to see whomever I choose, and to enjoy life a little. The kind of love I had for Peter, before everything started spiraling down, is gone. Maybe someday it can be rekindled, maybe not, but I need time. I hope I have it."

Lynn was quiet for a moment, she seemed to be searching for words, sighed quietly and then said, "I guess my problem is I love you both. I always felt you were so right for each other, from the day you first introduced me to Peter. I think I understood the awful depth of your problem and how it affected you emotionally. I will tell you, there was only one time when I faulted Peter, and probably unfairly. I thought he should have taken you for the abortion. In retrospect, I forgave him, because he was so much in shock at the time."

I looked directly at her and said very softly, "I guess I didn't." My eyes were getting watery, and I wiped them with my napkin, and murmured, "Sorry."

After a pause, Lynn reached for my hand on the table, and murmured. " That says it all. Go to it, sweetie. You'll be fine."

When I got to the lab I called out "Good morning." to Saki, who was busy at the fume hood examining some cages of mice. "Do you have a minute?" I added, "I want to ask you something."

"Yes, I'll be right there," he answered, pushing the cages to the rear of the hood. He followed me into the office, and when I sat at the desk, he took the chair opposite me.

"I want to get your opinion about a new research project, Saki. I think I've gone as far as I want with the Congo River virus, at least for now. Peter is still working on telomerase and I'm happy to leave that to him. I've been thinking for a long time about trying to find a vaccine that can produce immunity to a variety of different viruses. That's a pretty daunting task, and it may evolve into finding some way of interrupting the life cycle of a certain group of viruses. You've met Nathan Mandelbaum, who has a lab on the sixth floor. He's been investigating the enzyme, reverse transcriptase, which is essential to the group of viruses that insert into RNA. I would like to talk to him about collaborating with me to attack RNA viruses in general. What do you think of the idea?"

Saki, rubbed his chin with his hand. He didn't answer me right away, but seemed to be looking at the surface of my desk, as if evaluating the finish. I knew him pretty well and he always seemed to go into a mini trance when he was deep in thought. He broke the silence finally and said, "That sounds like a very ambitious undertaking, Connie. It would be wonderful if we could succeed."

I was heartened to hear the "we." "Yes," I responded enthusiastically. "It would be a big project, and I need your help, Saki. I don't anticipate that we have to work with any virulent level four viruses, like ebola, and we're not set up for them anyway. If we can find some way of interrupting the life cycle of the less dangerous ones, those findings might apply to the more hazardous ones. Anyway, I'm glad you feel as you do. Your help is invaluable to me. Give the project some thought and tell me if you have any ideas of how we can go about the investigation."

Saki gave me one of his rare dazzling smiles, "I'll certainly think about it , Connie." He stood up to leave.

 I rose too and asked, "Have you any news from home? What about your girlfriend, Rachel? I haven't heard you mention her."

"Nothing much that's new. Rachel is still complaining about my long absence. I have a feeling she may give up and find a new man," he added, somewhat airily.

"How do you feel about that?" I probed.

"I don't know. Maybe it's for the best." He shrugged, "How do you say it? There are other fish in the ocean."

I smiled, "I hope it works out well for both of you."

I sat down at the desk again, silently cheering Saki's new attitude towards Rachel. Maybe he would stay here longer than he previously thought. As things stood now, he had less than a year left on his visa.

I spent the rest of the day taking notes from various sites on the web, and going through the stack of journals, which had accumulated during my "illness" (that was how I thought of it).

I left at five-thirty to go home and change for my date with Alan.

Alan arrived at my apartment five minutes early. I had just finished brushing my wig vigorously to muss it up, mostly to get his reaction. I had on my favorite brown tweed pants suit and a turtle neck tan sweater. I glanced again in the mirror before putting on the wig. My own hair was getting long enough that I could dispense with it soon. I was also encouraged by the occasional grey strands. So far, no noticeable new wrinkles had appeared.

When I got in the car, Alan gave me his usual once-over, and said, "Looks more natural, nice work! In fact, you look as though you'd just been Simonized. What gives?"

"My engine was overhauled and I got a new part. I'm going to have some fun, and be a little carefree for a change." I grinned at him.

Alan grinned back. "Right on! I think I'm getting ready for a new part, too."

"Why do you think I called you? From now on I'm only going to be serious from nine, or I should say eight, to five."

"Or maybe six," Alan added. "I wonder how long that will last? It's a good start anyway. Do you want me to tell a joke? It's after seven."

"NO," I said emphatically. "There are only about two jokes I ever found funny after age thirty. You're funny enough as you are."

"I'm trying to decide if that's a compliment, but better I shouldn't ask." He steered the car onto the southbound lane of the West Side drive.

I sat back in the seat, feeling relaxed and content. These were new emotions for me, at least they felt new. The last time I experienced such feelings seemed a lifetime ago. I let the sensation envelop me as I gazed out at the Hudson River on my right. Alan found the parking garage. The restaurant was small, dimly lit, and nearly full. We were shown to a table for two in the back, and sat down facing each other.

Alan ordered a bottle of Beaujolais, and we sipped it as we studied the menu. I finally decided on a medium hot chicken curry.

Alan said he would have the lamb curry on the hot side. I warned him that could be fiery, but he said he liked it that way. During dinner we discussed a variety of topics, including the new work his team was doing on malaria, in conjunction with The Pasteur Institute. I spoke briefly about my new project, which I said was still in embryonic form, but most of the evening was spent in light hearted bantering and reminiscing about our days in Seattle.

On the drive home Alan asked me how my relationship with Peter was working out. I told him about Peter's offer from Harvard, and my decision to stay in New York.

"I want to leave genetics to the geneticists, and get back to virology," I said.

"Does that mean you two are no longer going to collaborate?" Alan asked, his eyes on the road.

"Not officially, I think we'll still share information, but if he goes to Harvard, and I think he will, that may be harder. At any rate, we're no longer a team."

Alan turned to look at me, "Are you saying that applies to your relationship with him too?"

"Yes." I paused, "I'm a free agent, that's the way I want it to be."

"So, how do you see your relationship with me?" He had resumed looking ahead, and I couldn't see his expression.

"Fun," I said. "And free."

He let that ride for a few minutes, and drove in silence down the West Side drive. When we got near to my apartment he looked at me again and said, "Just how free do you want to be?"

I laughed and said, "I should have known you'd put that spin on it. If I'm 'free' with you, I might not continue to be my version of free. Give me time to figure that one out, okay?"

He chuckled and patted my knee, "Sure, Connie, someday you'll tire of all that freedom."

He pulled the car over to the curb. I leaned over to give him a kiss on the cheek; he quickly turned his head and planted a firm kiss on my mouth. "None of that, I'm not your brother," he said, as he pulled back.

"I never thought you were, thanks for the fun evening and call me soon." I got out and closed the door behind me. As I waved goodbye, Alan drove off, leaving me standing there with a big smile on my face. So this was what freedom felt like! Not bad!

Although I had no idea how long I was going to live, neither did anyone else! I realized that I had become a fatalist. Whatever future was intended for me would spin itself out among the stars, or wherever fates are decided. In the meantime I would work and play as fully as I could, and take one day at a time.

# Epilogue

Our mother, Constance Gueyer, died on February 19th in the year 2001. She was fifty-five. It was her wish that this story be made known to alert people to the potential dangers of trying to outsmart nature. In November of 2000, she was diagnosed with a malignant brain tumor that appeared to have it's origin in the hypothalamus.

Up to that time she had been ageing normally. When she was informed of her diagnosis, she said, she was not surprised; her hypothalamus had been meddled with too much, and she refused any therapy. One of her last requests was to have a song by James Taylor played at her memorial service; particularly for the words, "the secret of life is enjoying the passage of time".

She had remained in contact with Peter Tarker after his move to Harvard, and her friends Lynn Stein and Alan Mack were with us at her bedside when she died. She had been working to find a single vaccine that could effectively disarm many pathogenic viruses. Her work will be continued by the Virology Department of Bailey Medical School, and a fellowship has been established in her name.

David Andrew Evans
Joshua Evans

October 2002

# Acknowledgement

*Thanks to Marlene Bloom for her careful editting.*

*Thanks to Dorothy Warburton for the chromosome pictures.*

*Thanks to Robert J. Demarest for the cover design.*

*Chromosome 22*